WHO KILLED
SIMON PETERS?

Paul Hendy

BANTAM BOOKS

LONDON · TORONTO · SYDNEY · AUCKLAND · JOHANNESBURG

TRANSWORLD PUBLISHERS
61–63 Uxbridge Road, London W5 5SA
A Random House Group Company
www.rbooks.co.uk

WHO KILLED SIMON PETERS?
A BANTAM BOOK: 9780553816266

First publication in Great Britain
Bantam edition published 2009

A CIP catalogue record for this book
is available from the British Library.

Addresses for Random House Group Ltd companies outside the UK
can be found at: www.randomhouse.co.uk
The Random House Group Ltd Reg. No. 954009

The Random House Group Limited supports The Forest Stewardship Council
(FSC), the leading international forest certification organisation. All our titles that
are printed on Greenpeace approved FSC certified paper carry the FSC logo. Our
paper procurement policy can be found at www.rbooks.co.uk/environment

Typeset in 12/13½pt Garamond by
Kestrel Data, Exeter, Devon.
Printed in the UK by
CPI Cox & Wyman, Reading, RG1 8EX.

2 4 6 8 10 9 7 5 3 1

For Freddie

'I wouldn't feel so alone, if they knew my name in every home.'

Robbie Williams

1:

An extract from *The Stage* newspaper, 10 January 2008

OBITUARIES
SIMON PETERS
TV presenter 1972–2008

The king is dead.

Simon Peters (35), game show host, TV personality and multimillionaire media tycoon, died on New Year's Day in what police are describing as 'suspicious circumstances'. Wreckage from Peters' personal helicopter was found in the sea off the coast of Portugal, not far from his luxury villa in Vale del Lobo. Crash investigators say the control linkage to the tail rotor on his Robinson R22 helicopter 'may have been tampered with'. His body is yet to be recovered.

Known to millions as the self-proclaimed 'King of Saturday Night Television', Simon Peters first found fame as the co-host of *Slebs*, ITV1's popular weekly look at Britain's celebrity-obsessed culture. He went on to come fourth in

Celebrity Big Brother and the subsequent publication of his controversial diary, *Diary of a C-List Celeb*, turned Peters into a household name. From there he never looked back, and he quickly established himself as one of the country's biggest and most in-demand stars. He appeared on *Celebrities on Ice!*, *Celebrities in Deep Water!*, *Celebrities on Heat!* and *Celebrity Schmelebrity!* He was also a contestant on Channel 5's surprise cult hit balloon-modelling programme, *Balloon Modelling with the Stars!* He was voted off in the third week, but his impressive 'Man holding a Golf Club while taking a Dog for a Walk' received special commendation from the judges.

Diversity was always a key word in Simon's career. In 2007 he turned his hand to acting and played the central character of a murdered game show host in the now somewhat ironic-seeming film *Who Killed Bobby King?* He also appeared in *Holby City*.

But it is as a television presenter that Peters will be best remembered. The TV show that bought him his ticket to the international hall of show-business immortality was the hugely popular aspirational game show *It Could Be You!* He not only presented the show, but he also devised the format and owned the copyright; he even had a number one hit with the theme tune. The TV rights were sold to more countries than any other programme in the history of British television, and in a very short space of time the show earned Peters a reported personal fortune of over forty million pounds, and finally awarded him the status of being a genuine A-list celebrity.

Simon Peters' career had finally exploded like a firework, dazzling everyone as it burst spectacularly into a thousand glittering stars. Although his life on the A-list only lasted for one short year, the impact he made was immeasurable and many of the magical moments he produced were truly unforgettable. Despite the critics' bewilderment at his phenomenal success and his growing reputation for being difficult to work with, Simon achieved his dream, and at first the public loved him for it. If Diana was the 'People's Princess' then Simon Peters was the 'People's Court Jester'. He was one of them: ordinary, average, run of the mill, the boy next door who just happened to be a TV star. Men wanted to shake his hand and women wanted to mother him (he lost his own mother at the age of thirteen). The normality that held him back in the early part of his career was the key to his later success. He was the inspiration to a generation of wannabes. They knew they were nothing special, but neither was he. If Simon Peters could make it, so could they. And Simon Peters had made it.

Simon Peters had made it big-time.

But now he has gone and a nation mourns, alone in their sorrow, united in their grief. The sun doesn't seem to burn quite as brightly, the sky isn't as blue and the grass not as green, as if someone has taken a large remote control and turned down the colour contrast on the plasma screen of life. Television will never be the same without you, Simon Peters. Neither, I fear, will life itself.

We'll miss you, Simon. Thank you for the good times.

2:

Dominic Mulryan (investigative journalist)

It is now six months since the preceding obituary appeared in The
Stage *newspaper, six months since the world was rocked by the news
of Simon's untimely demise. Thousands of words have been written
about the fatality, hundreds of hours of airtime filled by experienced
and well-respected broadcasters pontificating about his unexpected
and tragic death.*

*When Peters died, there seemed to be a genuine sense of shock and
disbelief, and in the weeks following the disaster, the world of show
business paid tribute to someone who then appeared to be one of their
favourite sons. Desperate for quotes, the press clamoured to speak to
the celebrities, the actors, the presenters, the models, the wannabes,
the has-beens and the never-weres. Their reactions were unequivocally
ones of grief, sorrow and an overwhelming urge to inform the public
what a great friend he was, how much he would be missed and what
a sad loss it was to the entertainment industry. Everybody seemed to
have an anecdote to tell, and the words 'legend', 'icon' and 'genius'
unashamedly peppered their sound bites.*

*Some of the tributes were genuine and heartfelt, but many were
empty and hollow and played to the cameras with all the sincerity*

12

of a daytime game show host. As the accolades poured in, it became more and more difficult to remember that towards the end of his life, Simon Peters had actually started to be considered something of a joke. Industry insiders considered him a lightweight broadcaster with no real journalistic background; a Bluecoat who got lucky. The tabloids would take constant potshots at him, eventually creating a public figure of fun and a character the nation loved to hate.

All this was forgotten the moment his helicopter crashed into the sea.

Now, six months later, Simon Peters' body has never been found and the police are no closer to explaining the mystery surrounding his death. The one fact they have confirmed is that the control linkage on the helicopter had been 'deliberately weakened by hand', implying that a person or persons had intended the helicopter to crash. At the inquest, on 12th April 2008, Simon Peters was declared 'missing presumed drowned' and in accordance with Section 15 of the Portuguese Coroners Act 1988, the coroner reported there was insufficient evidence to return anything other than an open verdict.

Nobody knows for sure exactly what happened on that fateful New Year's Day. Was it an accident? Suicide? Or maybe even murder? Everyone seemed to have a theory; no one had an answer.

Until now.

During the writing of this book, I have managed to gain access to the pages of Simon Peters' previously unpublished diary; the diary he kept right up until the time of his death. Written in his own hand, it records his innermost thoughts and foibles, and he'd obviously intended it to be a follow-up to his previous publication Diary of a C-List Celeb. Something about Simon's inner drive and burning ambition can be drawn from the fact that on the first page of the diary, he'd scribbled the words 'Simon Peters: The A-List Years'. Bear in mind that at this point he was still (by his own admission) just a 'desperate wannabe', a meaningless C-lister who many in the television industry had written off as a no-hoper.

What becomes apparent from reading this diary is that Peters was a complex character, full of contradictions and discrepancies. He was the painfully shy wallflower who could be the life and soul of the party, the self-obsessed egotist who worked tirelessly for charity and the publicity-seeking megalomaniac who abhorred any sort of intrusion into his private life. Perhaps the greatest inconsistency of all is that Simon Peters seemed to be loved by millions but despised by those who knew him best. He was nervous, neurotic and riddled with insecurities, but he made his fortune by 'devising' – and I use that term very loosely – a game show where the key elements were confidence and self-belief.

Using all the information I have gathered, I aim to piece together the jigsaw of Simon's life and unravel the Gordian-like knots of ambiguity surrounding his death. I intend to answer the questions that no one else has been able to (Paxman tried. He failed. Newsnight Special, *14.3.08).*

I intend to succeed.

I intend to find out who killed Simon Peters?

As we begin this journey together, let us not forget that the world we are entering is the world of celebrity: a world of veiled defamation and blurred reality where nothing is as it seems and where no one speaks the truth. On the surface we see glitter and glamour, but scratch a little deeper and a seething cesspit of jealousy and bitterness is revealed.

We will begin our journey exactly two years before Simon's death. The following extracts are taken from what, at the time, was his brand-new diary. Remember that at this point he wasn't the huge star he was to become but instead a mediocre, run-of-the-mill C-lister. A fact underlined by his embarrassing eviction from the Celebrity Big Brother Christmas Special . . .

3:

Extracts from Simon Peters' Diary

2 JAN

Fourth!

I can't believe it; surely I should have won.

Fourth!

Not even in the top three. Even Les Dennis got in the top three and he was a miserable git when he was on it. Surely I'm more popular than he is? Maybe I should have cried more in the Diary Room.

I'm not trying to cast aspersions on Channel 4, but I think they should check their telephone-voting system as something has clearly gone very seriously wrong with it. I'm also slightly disappointed by the reaction of the crowd when I came out of the house; they didn't boo me but they didn't exactly cheer either, and I found the wall of sheer indifference quite disheartening (obviously the warm-up man hadn't done his job properly; I'm going to have a word with the producers about that).

Having said that, I've analysed my eviction and despite

the evidence to the contrary, I believe that I actually won the show: it's been obvious for some time now that when it comes to reality television, TV viewers have a collective streak of cruelty, and they've started voting in quite a sadistic manner. Everyone has grown so accustomed to this kind of show that, these days, they don't necessarily keep the person they like in to the end and instead keep in the nutters and the weirdos because it makes for better television. This means the one who wins is usually the transsexual loony; the one who comes second is the gay one who had some sort of conflict with the transsexual loony, and the one who comes third is the blind lap dancer with false breasts who had a conflict with the gay one and a bizarre simmering sexual tension with the transsexual loony. The person who comes fourth is, more often than not, the normal one who is quite a nice guy and if the public hadn't become so cynically astute and brutally voyeuristic about the whole thing, that person would actually be the winner. If you follow this argument through to its logical conclusion, you'll find that I actually won this year's *Celebrity Big Brother*.

I'm really pleased with my theory, but with hindsight I probably shouldn't have told it to Davina during the live interview; she didn't seem overly impressed.

At the end of the show my best mate, Charley, was waiting for me. She'd come along to the studio to be one of my 'family and friends' who I was supposed to run to when Davina had finished the interview and shown me my 'Best Bits' (which, incidentally, were disappointingly short). I'm glad Charley came because none of my other friends or family bothered to turn up, and the production team had to persuade a few random members of the public to pretend to be them just so they could get a shot of me running into their outstretched arms. It was all slightly embarrassing, especially when the show is supposed to be a popularity contest. Charley found the whole thing highly amusing, although she made me promise to tell the press that I was only joking about my claims that I should have won.

I think I've got a point though; look at who's left in the house: David Dickinson, Susan Hampshire and one of the bloody Chuckle Brothers.

I think the Great British Public have a very warped sense of humour.

3 JAN

The *Celebrity Big Brother* experience is not for the faint-hearted, weak-willed or thin-skinned. I'm all of those, so I found the whole thing very stressful. I couldn't get used to the fact that I was being watched twenty-four hours a day, which is strange because before I went in, that's what I thought I'd enjoy most of all. Once you're in there it's quite a scary thing, and I couldn't help feeling that I constantly had to perform. Then again, I've gone through my whole life feeling like that, so maybe it wasn't that different.

I spent today reading through all the press coverage I received while I was inside the house. There was quite a lot of it, but I can't believe the trivial stuff they picked up on. They seem to have totally ignored all the 'big' discussions I had in the house about life, the universe and my career and instead concentrated on the really minor details. A lot of it has been blown out of all proportion, so just for the record: I do not fancy Su Pollard and what happened with the vacuum cleaner was a genuine mistake. I'd simply spilled some salt on my lap and was trying to hoover it up. The top-of-the-range Dyson had more suction than you'd imagine, and it created a vacuum between the hosepipe and my private parts. It was actually very painful and even when I switched it off and disconnected the three-foot hose from the machine, the suction still remained. I looked like I had an elephant's trunk swinging between my legs, which might be impressive in some circumstances but when you've got twenty-eight cameras recording your every move, it's not to be recommended (I could actually hear the cameramen laughing on the other side of the mirrors). I had to go to the Diary Room where Su Pollard helped me to remove it. The fact that I was wearing a dressing gown with no pants underneath only seemed to make matters worse. I remember thinking at the time that it probably looked a little dodgy having Su Pollard kneeling in front of me, holding me down with one hand while yanking viciously at the hosepipe with the other, but because I was in such obvious pain I thought they'd edit that bit out. It didn't help that Su found the whole thing hilarious and at one point used the hosepipe as a trumpet and started playing the theme tune to *Hi-De-Hi!*

What I didn't realize (or maybe subconsciously, I did) was that the story would make the front page of every single tabloid newspaper. Something tells me that image is going to haunt me for years to come.

2.34 a.m.
I wonder how much it costs to buy a top-of-the-range Dyson?

5 JAN

Barry Chuckle has won *Celebrity Big Brother*.
Tonight was the big Winner's Night Party and all the

housemates were invited back to take part. As the firework display exploded overhead, we all had to act as if we were really pleased for Barry, but you could tell that Susan Hampshire was gutted.

Davina made me snog Su Pollard on camera and it was actually more pleasant than I expected it to be. Lots of the audience were waving vacuum cleaners in the air and a couple of guys had hoses attached to the front of their trousers. I saw a sign saying 'Simon Sucks', but I pretended not to notice.

7 JAN

Something very strange has happened. Since I came out of the house, the public reaction towards me has been incredible, and as I walk around my local high street, people come up to me, shake me by the hand and tell me how wonderful they think I am. Of course, I accept all their compliments with a modest smile and a humble nod of gratitude.

I hope this new-found superstardom isn't going to be too intrusive into my everyday life. I hope I'm not going to have to become a recluse.

8 JAN

Today I spent eight hours walking up and down the high street in my *Celebrity Big Brother* production jacket. I signed forty-eight autographs and posed for thirteen mobile-phone photographs. I think lots of other people recognized me but some individuals don't like to admit to it, do they? One old lady insisted she didn't want my autograph but I could tell that she did really. She got quite emotional when I signed the collar of her coat for her. She kept asking me if it would wash out but because it was indelible ink, I assured her that it wouldn't.

I just know that coat will be for sale on eBay tonight.

10 JAN

Mobbed!

I just happened to be passing the local school gates at twenty to four when all the kids were coming out. I had to walk past three times before they recognized me but once they did, it was chaos. I felt like a rock star; they were screaming and shouting and tearing at my clothes.

I'm going again tomorrow.

11 JAN

I have a new hobby. I really enjoy walking up and down suburban high streets where people don't expect to see a famous person and then watching their reactions when they see me.

Today I went to Crawley.

While I was there I carried out my own survey, and everybody I asked, agreed that I should have won *Celebrity Big Brother*. There were a couple of people who said they thought Susan Hampshire should have won, but when I pressed them on the subject they admitted that I should at least have come second.

12 JAN

Watford.

Twenty-one autographs and six photos. Not bad.

13 JAN

Luton.

Fourteen autographs, three photos and I had to sign my first naked breast. (It would have been better if it was a woman's.)

14 JAN

Milton Keynes.

Came home early as I couldn't actually find a high street.

15 JAN

Stevenage.

I was passing a building site.

'Simon Peters!' I heard someone shout. I looked up and saw a gang of builders leaning over the top of the scaffolding. The one who shouted was a large man and even though it was bitterly cold, he wasn't wearing a shirt. He was incredibly hairy and had a tattoo of an eagle on his chest.

'I saw you on that *Big Brother*.'

I was about to remind him that he'd missed the word *Celebrity* out of the title, but then thought better of it. I gave him a cool wave of acknowledgement and flashed him my best showbiz smile.

'You were a right twat!' he said.

For a moment I felt a stab of disappointment, but when I looked at him, I saw that he was smiling and putting his thumbs up. I looked around and all his mates were doing the same. They started cheering, waving and laughing and I realized that he'd meant it as a compliment, and even if he didn't mean it as a compliment, the fact that he thought I was a twat was obviously a good thing because at least it meant that he and his friends accepted me. That's the effect I seem to have on working-class people. They take the mickey out of me but they do it in a positive way.

I climbed to the top of the scaffold and shook their hands before the foreman came along and told me I had to get down because I wasn't wearing a hard hat.

'He doesn't have to follow rules,' said one of the younger builders. 'He's famous.'

How right he was.

God, I love being a celebrity.

16 JAN

I've been out of the *Big Brother* house for two weeks now and my agent, Max Golinski, has finally managed to arrange a meeting for me at ICE, one of the biggest and most well-respected independent TV production companies in the country.

Career-wise, I know that I have to strike while the iron is hot, so I've come up with a great idea for my own TV show. I've known for some time that developing formats is where the big money is, but in the past nobody has ever wanted to listen to my ideas. The good thing about *Celebrity Big Brother* is that it's raised my profile enough to get my foot in the door of the big players in the world of television, the people who can turn my ideas into reality and make my dreams come true.

At midday, I arrived at ICE's large, ultra-cool suite of offices in the middle of Soho. I pushed open the heavy glass doors, walked up to the receptionist and gave her my winning Simon Peters showbiz smile.

'Name?' she asked, uninterestedly.

I was quite taken aback by this; I thought she was joking and I laughed out loud. I gave her the smile again and this time I pointed at my face and nodded gently as if to say, yes it's OK, it really is me.

She stared at me blankly.

'Name?' she repeated, while continuing to chew her gum.

'You don't know who I am?'

'No.'

'Are you sure?'

'Yes.'

'Look at my face.'

'I'm looking.'

'And you don't know who I am?'

'No.'

This was embarrassing but there was no way I was going to back down.

'You've never seen me before in your life?'

'No.'

'Do you watch television?'

'Yes.'

'Did you watch *Celebrity Big Brother*?'

'No.'

I was genuinely shocked by this.

'You didn't see *Celebrity Big Brother*?'

'No.'

'Surely if you work for a TV company you should actually watch such things. I've just been a contestant on *Celebrity Big Brother*, it was the biggest show in the country. I'm actually quite famous; surely you recognize me . . .'

I noticed another receptionist sitting next to her who had just come off the phone. I turned to her.

'Have you seen *Celebrity Big Brother*?'

'Of course I've seen it,' she said.

'Thank you,' I said triumphantly. 'And do you recognize me?'

I turned back to the first receptionist, indicating that she should listen to her answer.

'No,' said the second receptionist. 'I didn't watch this series; I saw the one a couple of years ago with Les Dennis, he was really popular actually, I think he came third . . .'

'Thanks for nothing,' I said.

I knew I was a beaten man. Oh, the pain and humiliation of only being famous in the provinces.

'Name?' the first receptionist asked, as if the previous conversation hadn't happened.

'Simon Peters,' I said, flatly, while silently promising myself that one day everybody would know my name.

She picked up her phone and punched in a number; she spoke to someone and then, somewhat coldly, informed me that I'd have to wait. Opposite her desk there was a large aquarium which covered one whole side of the reception wall. I've always thought there was something incredibly calming and therapeutic about fish, so because I was feeling slightly stressed I walked over to it. The colours of the fish were extremely vivid and I was very impressed by the species they had. They had clownfish, New Guinea tiger fish, green flame angelfish and a couple of red-eye puffers, which I know are quite rare. Strangely, there was even a small squid in there. I passed the time by tapping on the glass, waving at them and giving them funny names and little comedy voices.

'Please don't touch the screen,' I heard the receptionist say.

At first I didn't think she was talking to me, but then

I glanced over my shoulder and realized that the whole aquarium was actually a projected image and that I'd spent five minutes pulling faces into a plasma screen. I didn't feel too bad because I imagined I wouldn't be the only one stupid enough to make that mistake but as I looked over at the two receptionists, their sniggering and giggling informed me that I probably was.

'They're not real,' said the first receptionist, now stating the obvious.

'Yes, it's just a TV programme,' said the second.

'I was aware of that,' I said, desperately trying to regain some dignity. 'I was just thinking of the parallels between this and the goldfish bowl that is the *Big Brother* house.'

'I see what you mean,' said the first receptionist sarcastically. 'Because in the fish world, all those fish are *actually quite famous.*'

I think she was trying to do an impression of me.

'Don't you recognize them?' said the second receptionist, who obviously considered herself to be a great wit. 'That one's Skate Moss and the other one is Kylie Minnow!'

They both burst out laughing at this.

'Oh look, there's Nicole *Squid*man,' said the first.

Just my luck to be landed with the French and Saunders of the receptionist world.

'And that shellfish at the bottom is Mussel Crowe!'

By this point they were in hysterics, and I was only saved from further humiliation by one of them taking a call and informing me that I was to take the lift to the second floor. As the lift doors closed their cackling continued and I heard mention of 'Cod Stewart' and 'Prawn Connery.'

My meeting was with the 'development team', or at least that's what he called himself. His name was Tristan Reece-

Davis and I found it incredibly depressing how young he looked; I own underpants older than he is.

Despite his youthful appearance, Tristan emanated a cooler-than-thou, ex-public-schoolboy air of superiority and a slightly edgy, taking-the-piss-type attitude. I got the distinct impression that he thought the meeting was a waste of his time.

He led me to a large conference suite. Inside, there was a plasma screen on the wall and two glass chairs positioned artistically in the middle of the room. That was it; nothing else. I couldn't work out if it was trendy minimalist or if it hadn't been decorated yet. I touched my chair before I sat down, just to make sure it wasn't a projected image. Tristan sat down opposite me, poured each of us a glass of mineral water and glanced down at my CV.

'So you came fifth in *Big Brother*?' he said, smiling at me condescendingly.

'Fourth,' I said, probably a tad too sharply. 'And it was *Celebrity Big Brother*, there is a difference.'

'Not much of one these days.'

He let his cutting remark hang in the air.

'So what do you see yourself doing next?' he asked.

'Well, I see my career moving in a more serious direction,' I said thoughtfully. I didn't want to feel belittled by him and wanted him to know I was his intellectual equal. Because of this, I'd stopped talking in my usual Yorkshire accent and was now sounding like someone who worked for the Queen.

'I want to prove that TV personalities don't have to have empty and ultimately vacuous careers . . .'

I'd rehearsed this speech all morning.

'. . . I want to become something of an Ambassador of Light Entertainment and do something important that makes a real difference to the world. I think it's time that I stood up and used my celebrity status and my position of influence to tell everyone what I really believe in.'

There was a pause.

'What is it you believe in?' asked Tristan.

'Nothing,' I said. 'But that's not the point; I've come up with an idea for a TV show that would give me the opportunity to pretend that I do.'

He'd just taken a mouthful of water and suddenly seemed to be having difficulty in swallowing it.

'Interesting,' he said unconvincingly. 'So what's your idea?'

This created something of a dilemma. Production companies like ICE are famous for hoovering up ideas, changing them slightly and then making millions of pounds when they sell the format rights all over the world. I knew my show could be a massive hit and that the format had the potential to sell internationally. It even lent itself to the possibility of a worldwide simultaneous telecast. I didn't know what to do: should I tell him my idea and run the risk of him stealing it, or not tell him and throw away the prospect of it ever being made?

'*Celebrity Peacemakers!*' I said.

I just couldn't resist it.

'Celebrity Peacemakers?'

He uttered the words as if he'd never imagined the two of them could be used in the same sentence.

'Yes, but it has to be *Celebrity Peacemakers* with an exclamation mark,' I explained. 'That's very important.'

I then went on to tell him how all the best light entertainment programmes of the last thirty years have exclamation marks in the title: *I'm a Celebrity . . . Get Me Out of Here!*; *You Bet! . . . The Shane Ritchie Experience!* The exclamation mark is

27

what made those shows great. *Celebrity Peacemakers* without the exclamation mark just wouldn't have the same impact. I was quite adamant about this but after a two-minute monologue on the subject, Tristan interrupted me and asked me what the show was actually about.

I took a deep breath and made him wait for it. I knew I was about to give him television gold and that put me in a position of power, something I really enjoyed. I spoke slowly and clearly.

'Two teams of celebrities visit the trouble spots of the world and try to negotiate peace, lobby for the release of political prisoners and try to eradicate Third World debt.'

I could tell he was impressed because he sat there staring at me with his mouth wide open.

'It's similar to the sort of thing that Bono does,' I continued, 'but with a game show angle and featuring Joe Pasquale and me as team captains. The Grand-Finale-Big-Money-Head-to-Head would be held at the United Nations. Of course, the floor would have to be a lot shinier but I really like the idea of the studio audience sitting there with those little headphones on as the questions are simultaneously translated into seventy-eight different languages.'

I then delivered the killer punch.

'I see Kofi Annan as the score keeper.'

I'd obviously touched Tristan at an emotional level, because by this point he was wiping the tears from his eyes and was obviously finding it difficult to contain his emotion. He even had to go out of the room to compose himself, and when he came back he had the two receptionists with him. He asked me to tell them my idea, insisting that I do it word for word, '. . . with the funny accent and including the stuff about the exclamation mark.'

When I got to the end, Tristan said that even though it

was one of the funniest things he'd ever heard (I'm not sure what he meant by that), ICE Productions wouldn't be able to develop my show because 'they weren't making that sort of television at the moment'.

I was incredibly disappointed. Couldn't they see that my idea was the future of British television? At that moment, I vowed to myself that one day I'd prove to them that *Celebrity Peacemakers!* would work as a TV format. I sensed that they hadn't taken me entirely seriously and that made me quite angry. I stood up, kicking my chair backwards as I did so, and strode towards the door as dramatically as I could.

'*Aren't making that sort of television?*' I said, spinning round to face them to emphasize my point. 'Well maybe you bloody well should be!'

As I slammed the door I heard Tristan shout, 'Is that *bloody well should be* with an exclamation mark?'

I took the Tube home, their laughter still ringing in my ears.

17 JAN

'It's obvious to me that I have to get more famous,' I said to Charley.

I heard her sigh on the other end of the line, but I carried on regardless; I had to get it off my chest. I was still quite upset at the fact that even though I'm more of a celebrity now than I've ever been in the past, I still don't seem to be taken very seriously in the world of television.

'I don't think they'd laugh at me like that if I was more famous.'

'Oh, I'm sure they would,' said Charley.

She's my best friend but she can be a little flippant sometimes.

Now it was my turn to sigh.

'I don't know why I feel this way,' I said. 'For as long as I can remember I've just wanted everyone to know who I am and I still feel like that now. It's like a disease with no cure; I want to be famous, I want to be more famous than anyone else in the country; in the world, even. I want to be a star: a real star who can't be ignored or ridiculed; a celebrity who is above derision and disdain; a serious artiste with genuine beliefs and—'

'Earth calling Simon,' she said, interrupting me with her best Ground Control to Major Tom voice. 'No it's no good . . . he's lost in the showbiz abyss . . . this time he may have gone for good. Over.'

This was one of the things Charley did when she felt I was getting a little too full of myself, or starting to gaze at my own navel a little too intently. That's the thing with Charley, I know her so well and she's such a good friend that I probably open up to her more than I should and say things I wouldn't dream of saying to anyone else. She works as a producer on the mid-morning TV show *Coffee Morning with Mike and Sue*. She's smart and sassy and I'm really lucky to have her as a friend, even if she sometimes tells me things I don't particularly want to hear.

'Simon, you have to stop wallowing in this pool of self-obsession.'

Occasionally she would dress it up a little to spare my feelings, but today she was telling it to me like it is.

'You have to face up to reality. You're not a huge star, you're just a jobbing TV presenter who came fourth in *Big Brother* . . . sorry, *Celebrity Big Brother*.'

She corrected herself before I had a chance to.

'You have to stop living in the pages of *Hello!* magazine

and start living in the real world. Simon, I mean this in the nicest possible way: you have to get a life.'

Charley's right; Charley's always right. I have to give up this empty and vacuous lifestyle. I have to stop gleaning comfort and security from the recognition of strangers; I have to stop putting so much emphasis on the cult of celebrity and pretending that I'm more famous than I actually am.

I have to start living in the real world. I have to get a life.

18 JAN

Went to a high street in Hemel Hempstead and signed nineteen autographs.

I just can't help myself.

4:

Dominic Mulryan interviews Charley O'Neil

When Simon Peters wrote the preceding entries in his diary, he didn't know that within six months he would go on to become a bigger celebrity than he could ever imagine.

For this book, as well as publishing extracts from Simon's diary, I've also interviewed his family, friends, colleagues, casual acquaintances and worst enemies, and what becomes clear is that it's sometimes difficult to distinguish which is which.

First I spoke to the person who knew Simon best, his good friend and confidante of ten years, Charley O'Neil.

DM
So Charley, when did you first meet Simon?

Charley O'Neil
There was a Saturday morning kids' show in the mid-nineties called *A.M. Mayhem*; do you remember it? No, not many people do, to be honest; God, it was awful. It was a typical kids' show of that time with lots of gunge and gaudy colours, pop stars who only ever had one hit single and

presenters who shouted a lot, you know the sort of thing. It was desperately trying to be original but was ultimately just a watered-down version of *Tiswas*. It was my first job in television and I was working as a junior researcher, which basically meant I was a glorified tea girl. Oh yes, I made tea for some of the biggest pop stars of the nineties; just listen to this for a list: Hanson, B*Witched, Chumbawumba and wait for it . . . Aqua! Do you remember them? They had a hit with 'Barbie Girl' . . . you're really impressed now, aren't you? Interesting to see that they're all still multimillion-selling artistes who are still topping the charts and filling stadiums on a regular basis. What? They're not? I think they can probably blame *A.M. Mayhem* for that.

Simon was one of the shouting presenters on the show, and I didn't like him at first because he seemed so showbizzy. I thought he was full of himself and a bit of a big-head.

DM
When did you realize he wasn't?

Charley O'Neil
Never. He was always a big-head but I just got used to it. Eventually I realized he was just like that because of his insecurities. I got talking to him at the wrap party for the show and I realized that once you got through all the layers of showbiz bullshit he had a vulnerable side which was actually quite sweet. We became friends and stayed close for the next ten years, right up until . . . well, you know what happened.

DM
What are your favourite memories of Simon?

Charley O'Neil

I've got so many but it's the really stupid stuff that makes me smile.

I remember that, when it first came out, Simon became obsessed with eBay and he was constantly checking to see how much his autograph was worth. For a while he even tried selling his own signed photographs on it, but I think he was slightly disappointed when he only got a bid of £1.53 for two. That was including postage and packing.

I remember laughing so hard when he told me that story; surely most people don't do that sort of thing and if they do, they keep it to themselves. Not Simon. He knew it was ridiculous and self-obsessed but he still told me about it. I loved the fact that he was so honest with me. Well, about most things anyway.

DM

Is it true that at one point, you shared an intimate relationship with him?

Charley O'Neil

I think the word 'intimate' might be pushing it a bit . . . Is that what it says in his diary? I look forward to reading that. I guess we were very close and for a while there might have been something more, but it wasn't to be. The problem was that Simon only ever really loved three things in his life: himself, his career and himself. I guess you could call it four things if you include 'himself' in that list. There really wasn't any room for anyone else. It sounds harsh but it's true.

I think it's probably best if you say we were just good friends.

DM

He was obviously very driven in his career, very often to the detriment of personal relationships. Where do you think his seemingly insatiable craving for fame and celebrity came from?

Charley O'Neil

I have absolutely no idea. What fulfilment does someone get from being a familiar face to a total stranger? How many total strangers does your face have to be familiar to before you're contented? I never understood it.

It was as if Simon was constantly seeking approval. He needed an audience to tell him that his existence on this planet was meaningful and worthwhile, and when that audience informed him that it was and showed their appreciation with warmth, applause and laughter, he didn't believe them and went in search of a bigger audience. The bigger the audience became, the less worthwhile he felt and eventually he forgot what it was he was searching for.

I think he felt that if he wasn't in the spotlight, he simply ceased to exist. What's that John Updike quote? *Celebrity is the mask that eats the face* – well, I think he was talking about Simon when he wrote that.

If you want to look at the psychology of it, I guess it had a lot to do with Simon's childhood. His mother died when he was thirteen and I know his father, who was a struggling stand-up comedian, didn't give him an awful lot of attention. I don't think there was much love lost between Simon and his dad, and I always got the feeling there was an awful lot of resentment there.

DM

I know this is difficult, but how did you feel when Simon died?

Charley O'Neil

Devastated. Absolutely devastated. I loved him; I genuinely loved him but it's difficult to say that without sounding all showbizzy. When he died there was lots of crap spoken by people who didn't really know him. Did you see that Trevor McDonald thing, *Death of a Game Show King*? Oh my God, Simon would have loved that title. Did you see all the sad old has-beens on it? I think they saw it as one last opportunity to get their face on prime-time television. Did you see the state of Billy Fox? He's let himself go, hasn't he? Was that a rug he was wearing or did he have a Shredded Wheat strapped to his head? Anyway, I really hated the show because everyone was so bloody insincere on it. They all spoke as if they knew Simon really well, but they didn't. Why does that happen? Why is it that when a celebrity dies, all the other celebrities have to say how wonderful that person was? Why can't they just tell the truth? Simon wasn't wonderful; he wasn't the nicest person in show business; he wasn't an icon or a legend or a . . . I don't mean to speak ill of the dead, I'm just trying to be honest here . . . he wasn't a genius. The word genius intimates a level of intelligence which he simply didn't possess. Simon was just *Simon*. If the truth were known he was a bit of an awkward sod, but no one knew that better than Simon himself. He always said he'd be difficult to live with because he had difficulty living with himself. I realize that I'm rambling here and that you probably won't use any of this . . . you probably just want me to say something like, 'Simon Peters was a great friend and I miss him dearly.'

Well he *was* a great friend and I *do* miss him dearly. It's just that sometimes he was a bit of a pain in the arse.

5:

Extracts from Simon's diary

20 JAN

Today the showbiz tide turned, and I felt an icy chill running through my career. For the first time in three weeks there hasn't been one single mention in any of the tabloids of any of the contestants who took part in *Celebrity Big Brother*. Quite rightly, they stopped mentioning Hampshire, Dickinson and Pollard pretty soon after they were evicted, but Chuckle and I had managed to keep some sort of profile going.

That is, until now.

Suddenly *Celebrity Big Brother* is old news and although it's very nice walking around the high streets and shopping centres garnering all the praise and recognition, the truth of the matter is that I haven't actually got any more work to further my career. I thought it would come rolling in but that just hasn't been the case.

To make matters worse there's a brand-new series starting next week on Channel 4 called *10 Celebs, No Toilet!* The show pretty much does what it says on the can (if you'll excuse the pun). Ten celebrities are locked in a house with no toilet and the idea is to see who can last the longest without having to go. It sounds completely hideous and tacky but I know that once it starts, us real celebs from *Celebrity Big Brother* will be completely forgotten by the public and, worse still, by the TV executives.

I can't let that happen.

I just can't.

The only reason for going into the house was to try to raise my profile so the bigwigs at Network Centre would start considering me for some of the top jobs. I just hope the plan hasn't backfired. I hope they realize I'm a serious artiste and not just some desperate wannabe who would do anything to get my face on television.

21 JAN

So far I've managed to last fourteen hours and seventeen minutes without going to the loo. I wonder if *10 Celebs, No Toilet!* would consider me as a contestant.

22 JAN

I can't believe it. Channel 4 have just announced that Billy Fox is going to be a contestant on *10 Celebs, No Toilet!* Has that man got no shame? And why on earth would they want him in there in the first place? Who wants to watch a seventy-two-year-old man not going to the toilet? Surely the public would prefer to see a younger man desperate for a poo?

I also read in *Broadcast* that ITV are thinking of recommissioning his show, *Foxy's One Last Chance!* How many years is that now? Thirty? Thirty-five? Please God, let me be hosting a game show in thirty-five years. Please God, let me have one shot at the big time. All I'm asking for is the opportunity to prove myself, but I know I'm never going to get that break while people like Billy Fox are still on the scene. I don't understand why the powers that be are giving *One Last Chance!* one last chance anyway. Everybody knows it's slow, dull and boring. The public acknowledge the fact that it should be put out to pasture, but the commissioning editors don't have the balls to cancel it. They think there's nobody out there to take Billy Fox's place. What is wrong with these people? Are they talent-blind? Can't they see that I'm here, waiting on the subs' bench, young, fit and raring to go?

He can't even read an autocue properly. I actually saw him read out the word 'ad-lib' once.

'This is Jenny Davies from Oxford Ad-lib.'

I think he thought she was from some sort of political party.

People criticize me for not being able to speak the English language, but he absolutely murders it. He stutters and stumbles and coughs and wheezes and I don't mean to bitch about a fellow artiste but *hello*? What colour is his skin these days? It's like those cheap baked beans that you buy in Netto (not that I go to Netto, of course). If his skin were available in the Dulux paint range, they'd give it a really subtle name like 'BRIGHT ORANGE'. And what about that wig he wears? How many hamsters had to die for that? It's as if he's got all of Paul Daniels' old rugs, stitched them together with a couple of Brucie's, dragged it through a hedge backwards, used it as a dishcloth, wiped his arse on it, plonked it on his head upside down and backcombed it with a hedge trimmer. The man's a mess and a disgrace to the entertainment profession. I'm all for longevity in a career, but don't let old people host prime-time game shows.

Put them on *Last of the Summer Wine* with all the other old duffers.

23 JAN

I must have a little star status left, because the charity Barnardo's have asked me to be a celebrity runner in the London Marathon in April. I immediately said yes, as it's something I've always wanted to do. Every year I sit in front of the television and watch thousands of people pushing themselves to the limit, and I always vow to myself that one day I'm going to enter. Then I forget all about it until it's on telly again the next year, when I say exactly the same thing all over again.

Now is my opportunity to actually take part and at the same time raise some money for all those poor little children (Barnardo's is a children's charity, isn't it?).

When I told Charley, she obviously saw the funny side.

'You do realize the marathon is over twenty-six miles?'

'Of course I do,' I said. 'As long as I do lots of training for it, I could run twenty-six miles.'

'Simon, you couldn't run to the end of your road.'

I decided to prove Charley wrong and immediately went to the local sports shop where I bought a luminous green Lycra all-in-one running suit ('as worn by the winner of last year's London Marathon') and a brand-new state-of-the-art pair of trainers, which cost £150. I asked the shop assistant for some advice on running a marathon. He was actually about fifteen stone and would probably have been happier giving me advice on where the local McDonald's is.

'It's all about fitness and training,' he mumbled.

'No shit, Sherlock,' I said.

I told him not to bother wrapping the shorts and trainers as I would start my training regime straight away with a gentle jog back to my flat, which was about a mile away.

With hindsight, I was probably a tad too ambitious, as a mile is actually a bloody long way. I had to stop three times to get my breath back, the trainers started giving me blisters and I ended up getting a taxi home.

As long as I keep up the training, I'm sure I'll be all right by April.

24 JAN

Couldn't move all day.

25 JAN

I think I'll leave the training regime until next week.

26 JAN

Ha ha! I don't know why I get such juvenile pleasure out of this, but Billy Fox was the first one to have to leave the *10 Celebs, No Toilet!* house. You should have seen the look on his face. He must have been desperate and I mean that in more ways than one.

27 JAN

It's the end of an era.

Today I was only asked for my autograph three times. Three times! That's despite spending five hours walking up and down the aisles of Waitrose in Rickmansworth. Maybe I should start going to Asda again, that's always full of working-class people and they're more likely to remember me. Actually, I think the Waitrose shoppers remembered me, but the horrible truth is they just weren't that bothered.

I can't believe it. When I first came out of the house I was mobbed; three and a half weeks later I'm completely ignored. The British public are so fickle. Is the average shelf life of a celebrity now only twenty-five days? I didn't realize my celebrity status would have a sell-by date. If I'd known it was only going to last this long, I'd have spent much less time impressing the public and more time impressing the people who really matter: i.e. the TV executives. I'd have pressed the flesh and networked and done whatever else was needed to get the next gig. I just hope I haven't missed my chance.

Maybe I should really start pushing my format for *Celebrity Peacemakers!* I know it would make a great show. Billy Fox famously devised *One Last Chance!* and everybody knows that he made an absolute fortune from selling the rights worldwide. That's obviously where the real money is.

Surely I should have been offered my own show by now, but nothing seems to be happening for me; nobody really seems to be biting. There was an initial furore when I came out of the *Celebrity Big Brother* house and lots of talk of the possibility of prime-time shows, but the wind changes so quickly in show business, and I can feel the opportunity slipping from my grasp.

28 JAN

Why isn't anything happening for me? Why has everything suddenly stalled? I can't help but blame my agent, Max. I would call him but I know he'd fob me off with some excuse and tell me to be more patient.

'Patience is a virtue,' he'd say in his thick Jewish accent.

Max isn't actually Jewish, you understand, he just started talking as though he is when he became an agent.

For some time I've been thinking that I should leave him and get a new agent, but I'm not 100 per cent sure it's the right thing to do. People say that leaving an agent is like changing deckchairs on the *Titanic*: ultimately a complete waste of time. Anyway, where would I go? Who would want to take me on? There's only one agent who's bigger than Max, and I'm sure Annie Reichman wouldn't even consider me.

Leaving an agent is a very precarious business. It's OK to leave when your career has gone cold, but if you leave when you're on the way up there can be hell to pay. I'm probably somewhere in the middle at the moment, so I don't know how Max would react. In truth, I'd really love to get the big break while he's representing me, but it just doesn't look like it's ever going to happen.

Why am I so desperate to please Max Golinski? Surely it should be the other way round? Every time the phone rings, the first thought to hit me is 'I hope it's Max', and no matter who it is, there's always a slight piercing of disappointment when it isn't him. For years I've craved his attention like a little boy trying to impress his father, but he's made me feel like a bastard son who's an embarrassment to the family.

All I've ever wanted is for Max to believe in me enough to send me for the big auditions, the big meetings, the big lunches. The trouble is that he never has and I know that when it comes to his clients, I'm always near the bottom of the list, and I don't mean alphabetically. He's always had his favourites, the ones he socializes with, the ones he plays golf with, and more importantly the ones he gets jobs for.

When I question Max about why I'm not working, he always says it isn't the right time for me and that broadcasters aren't making the sort of shows I'm suitable for. When I tell him I'm desperate, he calls back ten minutes later and offers me panto in Bognor Regis with The Krankies.

That's the level that Max thinks I play at.

29 JAN

'Can we have a meeting?' I asked him.

I'd finally plucked up enough courage to call Max and I was desperate to have a conversation about my career, or more to the point, the lack of one.

'Well, the thing is, my boy,' he said and I sighed, knowing what was about to follow.

Very often I can't understand a word that Max says to me. When he speaks, he spits his words out like bullets from a machine gun and his speech is peppered with Yiddish expressions (half of which I'm sure he doesn't understand, the other half he just makes up). He's always mixing his metaphors, has an analogy for absolutely everything and uses twenty words when the sound of silence would suffice. He loves to give the impression of processing a vast general knowledge and never fails to employ a trivial piece of information in his wordplay. He seems to speak without taking a breath and tries to blind (or deafen) you with his verbal dexterity.

Of course, a lot of the time he just talks complete bollocks.

'Well, the thing is, my boy,' he said. 'Meetings are like a large funnel into which the parties concerned pour all their ideas. Now what comes out the other end of the funnel is like what happens when you eat a piece of food. You put it in your mouth, you chew it for a while, you savour the flavour and then you swallow. But that's not the end of that particular meeting. Oh no, slowly it navigates its way through your digestive system like a world-weary old sea dog sailing along on an ocean of half-digested mush. The gastric muscles mix and grind these nutrients of ideas like an electric blender whisking the ingredients of a small child's birthday cake . . .'

At this point he was starting to lose me.

'. . . the pancreas and the kidney throw in their twopennyworth and all the facts are chemically aggravated and violently absorbed. Slowly but surely the meeting lumbers along to the final stages of the large intestine, where everybody sits and broods for a while and all you get is a lot of hot air. Very often they stay there too long, and nobody wants to be the first to leave until eventually the meeting erupts. Some people storm out while others have to be ejected with force and that can be a strain for all parties concerned. One thing's for sure, what comes out the other end isn't always a good thing. Very often what comes out the other end of a meeting is shit, Simon, just shit.'

There was a long pause.

'So we can't have a meeting then?'

'No.'

'Thanks, Max.'

I asked him if he could get me appearances on any chat shows to help to promote my book, *Diary of a C-List Celeb*, which the publishers have reprinted in an attempt to cash in on the back of *Celebrity Big Brother*. Max said he was 'working on it'. I tried another tack and pitched him my *Celebrity Peacemakers!* idea, but he just pooh-poohed it and said that it needed work.

'It needs to be more aspirational,' he said. 'That's the buzzword in TV at the moment. Every show has to be *aspirational*. The viewers have to believe that they stand a chance of appearing on the show, they have to think that it could be them . . . There, that's a good title . . . *It Could Be Them* . . . no, even better . . . *It Could Be You!* Quick, write that down.'

I did as he said and wrote it down, but when I hung up the phone I didn't feel any happier. He just doesn't seem very interested in my career. If that's what he's like, why do I feel so guilty about my thoughts of leaving him?

6:

Dominic Mulryan interviews Simon's former agent, Max Golinski

DM
Max, what are your memories of Simon Peters?

Max Golinski
I know you're putting this book together and you're expecting me to say nasty things about Simon but I will not speak ill of the dead, so help me God. Let me start by saying this . . . is this thing on? . . . One two, one two, check . . . here we go then . . . ahem . . . Simon Peters was one of the greats and will go down in the anals of television history.

There. You can quote me on that.

DM
Do you mean annals?

Max Golinski
Sorry?

DM
Annals as opposed to anals?

Max Golinski
Anal Schmanal. Whatever. I knew the moment Simon Peters walked into my office that he had what it takes to get to the top of that precarious hierarchical structure that is the show-business ladder. He was a nobody then. You couldn't pick him out of an identity parade. But I knew that with my guidance he could be a *groyser tzuleyger*, a big shot. I've represented many clients over the years and I pride myself on being able to smell raw talent and believe me, I could smell Simon Peters a mile off. This boy was drenched in talent. He was covered in it. I tell you, he sweated charm and it was dripping from every orifice. When he leant back in his chair and put his hands behind his head, you could see the charisma stains under his armpits.

On the first day I met him, I sat him down and said '*Kaddishel*, within a year you will be a big star.' Of course it took a lot longer than that, because the *shmucks* over at Network Centre wouldn't know talent if it came up to them wearing a great big flashing neon sign saying 'Get Your Talent Here!'

DM
Is it fair to say that, at first, you struggled to find Simon work?

Max Golinski
Struggled? Couldn't get him a gig, you say? I couldn't get him arrested. He was a *nishtikeit*. For years nobody was interested in the boy. He was on the fast train to anonymity and in his pocket was a one-way ticket to obscurityville. He was dead in the water . . . sorry, that's a bad turn of phrase

considering the circumstances surrounding his death . . . *a schwartzen sof* . . . you won't put that in the book, right?

I'm a big believer that you can't suppress talent and I never lost confidence in the boy. I always had faith in him. Despite what he thought, I was always out there batting for him. I did so much batting I should have had an office at the Oval. I was doing what a good agent should do. I was working the phones and fielding offers. If you think I only got him shitty little jobs, you should have seen the crap I turned down for him. I've always said that cream rises to the top and Simon Peters was la crème de la crème. He was the *chaye baitism*.

That's Yiddish, by the way, for 'the dog's bollocks'.

DM
But did you actually like Simon as a person?

Max Golinski
'Like'? What is 'like'? I like Cohiba cigars and the girls in Spearmint Rhino, but I wouldn't invest the time in them that I did in Simon.

On second thoughts, maybe I would.

Let's say I 'admired' Simon as an artiste. All the things that would deter most people from a career in show business, the rejection, the failure and the fear of abject poverty, never seemed to affect him. Instead he had this inner drive and this deep-rooted burning ambition which I found quite infectious. The problem was that the boy was so impatient. He didn't appreciate that it was difficult to recognize exactly what sort of show would make him a star, but I knew deep in my heart he would crack it eventually.

Celebrity Big Brother had put him on the show-business map, but he wasn't yet a major city on that map. At the time he was probably the equivalent of, let's say, Wolverhampton . . . and let's be honest, not many people want to go there. But despite that, people were finally starting to take notice of him, just as I always said they would. Producers would actually call and ask for his availability which, for Simon, was a first.

Even though they were calling for him, we had to be careful about what he did next. I'd realized at an early stage in Simon's career that the talent he possessed was a very unusual one; the sort of talent you don't often come across in this business. He couldn't sing or dance or tell jokes or do impressions or juggle or eat fire, or any of those other things which might define him as 'talented'. But what he did have was that indescribable something that you can't really put your finger on and find difficult to explain in words exactly what it is.

DM
If you had to describe Simon's talent, what would you say?

Max Golinski
If I had to describe it, I'd say it was an incredible flair of the indefinable and an unbelievable talent of the imperceptible. Not many artistes have that. Are you getting all this? I'm giving you nuggets here.

Now the danger with Simon's talent, of course, is that some people would just think he was untalented. You have to admit, there's a very fine line between talented and untalented. Now, I didn't want the public, and more importantly the TV executives, trying to analyse Simon's talent too deeply, so my plan was not to overexpose him when he came out of the *Big Brother* house. The one way to ensure this was to limit his appearances and to be very choosy about the work we accepted for him. I was absolutely 100 per cent adamant that I didn't want him to do just any old crap. I wanted him to do quality crap and there's a big difference between the two.

I explained this to Simon and he agreed with everything I said. We were strong. We were a team.

'Together, *chavva*,' I'd say to him, embracing him to my bosom like a long-lost son. 'Together we will make it.'

It was around that time I realized the vultures were starting to circle. Those *schmucks* thought I wouldn't notice, but you can't piss on my back and tell me that it's rain. I knew what they were up to.

7:

Dominic Mulryan interviews Simon's agent at the time of his death, Annie Reichman

Annie Reichman of Reichman Associates is known as one of most successful agents in show business. With a lightning-quick brain and a razor-sharp tongue, Reichman, who gained a First in law at Oxford and then went on to study corporate law at Harvard, has negotiated some of the biggest deals in the history of British television. The Sunday Times *called her the most powerful woman in the entertainment industry and if you name a major A-list star in this country, the chances are that Reichman represents them. Notorious for her ferocious temper and vicious outbursts, Reichman is a formidable agent with a fearsome reputation. Max Golinski famously once said of her: 'She's like Adolf Hitler but with a bigger moustache.' She attempted to sue but ultimately lost the case when Golinski proved that she did indeed have the bigger moustache of the two.*

DM
Ms Reichman, when did Simon Peters first come to your attention?

Annie Reichman

Celebrity Big Brother. I wasn't aware of his existence up until that point but when I saw him on that show I knew that with the right marketing and the right packaging, he had what it takes to get to the top. The very top.

DM

Did you consider it a risk to take him on to your books?

Annie Reichman

I don't take risks.

I had access to in-depth research from focus groups which reported that the public had grown weary of seeing presenters who seemed intellectually superior to them. They were bored of watching performers who were more talented, more interesting and more fashionable. Most of all, it seems, they didn't want to watch people who were better-looking.

That's when I knew that Simon Peters could be a big star.

DM

So did you think Simon was a good presenter?

Annie Reichman

Totally irrelevant. Let's just say his presenting technique was interesting. He often came across as awkward and self-aware; he wasn't particularly good-looking and his dress sense was laughable. He lacked intelligence and his command of the English language was totally inadequate. The more I saw of him, the more I realized he was the future of British television.

DM
How could you be so sure?

Annie Reichman
It was all about timing. Six months earlier or six months later and he'd have been just another desperate wannabe. It just so happened that at that time the television industry was starting to use a lot of people with what I called NDT – No Discernible Talent. It seemed that every TV show being made needed someone with NDT to host it. Commissioning editors, executive producers and programme makers were crying out for presenters who appeared to be ordinary. They'd normally have to make a whole series of reality-TV shows to find someone, but here was a celebrity who already had NDT in abundance.

DM
So your idea was to market Simon as being 'ordinary'?

Annie Reichman
Absolutely, and I knew it wouldn't be difficult. He was very similar to another of my clients at the time, Billy Fox, but Simon was forty years younger and television is very much a young man's game. I knew it would be easy to market Simon as being in touch with his working-class roots; he didn't really have anything that would set him apart from the man in the street, and that was his unique selling point. The public would feel he was one of them and in many ways they were right, he *was* one of them.

DM
The only real difference was that within six months of joining your agency, he would have forty million pounds in his bank account.

Annie Reichman

I don't like to talk about artistes' personal finances.

DM

When you first approached Simon he was actually represented by Max Golinski?

Annie Reichman

Yes, you could say he was the right man with the wrong agent.

8:

Extracts from Simon's diary

30 JAN

Annie Reichman is my new agent!

I can't believe it. Reichman is the country's top über-agent, she's the best there is and every one of her clients is a successful household name. This is the break I've been waiting for all my life.

It's slightly ironic that I should meet Reichman on the day that Max finally got me an appearance on another TV show. He called late last night to say that I'd been booked as a guest on *Trisha* on Channel 5. I was slightly worried about this, but when I turned up at the studio the researcher told me that they now have celebrities reading out the results of the DNA tests. She also let it slip that I was actually a last-minute replacement for Bobby Davro.

'We had a real panic,' she said. 'You were the only person who was available.'

'Thanks,' I said, with more than a hint of sarcasm. 'My agent makes sure I'm always available just in case Bobby's busy.'

So, the only work that Max can get me is standing in for Bobby Davro. Great!

I was quite upset but because I was already there I decided to make the most of it and give it my best shot. During the recording of the show, when it got to the part where I had to reveal the results of the DNA test, I decided to inject a bit more showbiz razzmatazz. As Trisha handed me the envelope I thought some audience participation was needed, so I got everyone in the studio to do the equivalent of a drum roll by stamping their feet continuously. Trisha shot me an evil look as if to say, 'We don't do that sort of thing here, this isn't *The Jeremy Kyle Show*!'

I thought it worked well and really helped to build the tension. I paused before slowly opening the envelope and removing the card. The studio audience fell silent. I took a deep breath and for maximum impact I looked straight at the camera.

I paused again.

'Negative,' I said.

'Noooo!' screamed the pregnant sixteen-year-old girl, and the studio audience erupted. The guy with the bad teeth and the baseball cap started cursing the girl and saying that he'd known all along that the baby wasn't his. She implied that if it wasn't his, it must be his *brother's* baby. The respective families were obviously in the studio audience and they all started arguing and fighting amongst themselves. Trisha put her finger to her ear and looked confused and I could see the production team frantically running around behind the cameras.

I knew the reason for their panic was because the card actually said 'Positive', and I was only joking when I announced 'Negative'. Comedy is all about timing, and I couldn't help feeling that the moment to tell them this had probably gone.

I'd decided before the show started that I was going to use my appearance to try to publicize my book, *Diary of a C-List Celeb*. But when it came to it, it was quite a difficult thing to do, especially considering the chaos I'd just created by announcing that someone wasn't the father of an unborn child when actually he was. I decided the only way to get a good plug in was to offer the guy a copy of my book as a consolation prize. He wasn't very interested and instead seemed intent on strangling his brother in the audience. Luckily for me, they cut to a close-up of the book before an enraged Trisha snatched it away. I tried snatching it back again and something of a scuffle broke out. It must have been quite a bizarre sight to see Trisha and me rolling around on the studio floor, me desperately trying to show my book to the camera while Trisha tried frantically to wrestle it from my hands. It made quite a change for the large bald-headed security man to have to restrain the host of the show and to hear a pregnant sixteen-year-old chav shouting, 'Leave it Trish, he's not worth it!'

I was in the green room after the show and for some reason, everybody seemed to be ignoring me. Everyone, that is, except for the guy in the baseball cap and his brother. They tried talking to me but luckily the bald-headed security man held them back.

Within a few minutes the green room was deserted, and the temperature seemed to drop by a good few degrees. I heard a loud crack of thunder overhead and through the window I saw a fork of lightning illuminate the sky. I turned around and suddenly, as if out of nowhere, Annie Reichman was standing next to me. She scared the life out of me. I recognized her from her photograph in *Broadcast* (at the time, I remember thinking that it must have been a particularly bad photograph of her, but seeing her in the flesh I realized that it had actually been quite flattering). I wasn't sure where she came from or why she was there, but she looked me straight in the eye. Or at least I think she did: Reichman suffers from exotropia and has a divergent squint where her left eye is constantly looking off to the left. It's rather disconcerting, and you can't help but look over your shoulder to see if she's staring at someone else. That, coupled with the large mole on her chin, made her quite a fearsome sight . . . Oh, and it's true what they say about the moustache.

'I enjoyed your performance,' she said, lighting up a black Gitane and exhaling a long plume of grey smoke.

I glanced over my shoulder just to be sure that she was actually talking to me.

'Thanks very much,' I said, inhaling some of the smoke and then starting to cough slightly. The green room is obviously a no-smoking area, but Annie Reichman is not the sort of person you would mention this to.

'I think it's time you started being more successful in your career, what do you think?'

I'd been waiting my whole life for someone to say something like that to me, and now I couldn't believe it was Annie Reichman who was saying it.

'I agree,' I said. 'I've always thought I could be a huge star, but no one's—'

'I think you might be with the wrong agent,' she said, interrupting me.

As she spoke I was desperately trying to focus on her one good eye. It was almost hypnotic.

'I can't just walk out on Max,' I said, but my words were

drowned out by the thunder and lightning which seemed to fill the room.

'I have a vacancy on my books, if you'd be interested?' she said, matter-of-factly.

She held out her hand. I hesitated. I think I saw her wink. Did she wink, or was it the squint? I couldn't be sure. Before I knew it, I was holding out my hand. She had long thin bony hands, but a surprisingly firm handshake. There was another loud crash of thunder and as we shook, I couldn't help thinking that I was selling my soul to the Devil.

Having said that, it's probably worth it to have Annie Reichman as my new agent.

All I've got to do now is tell Max.

9:

Dominic Mulryan interviews Max Golinski

DM
Max, how would you describe your relationship with Simon at the time that he decided to leave your agency?

Max Golinski
Well, Dom . . . can I call you Dom? Thank you. Well, Dom, an artist's relationship with his agent is like a marriage, and that marriage is like a house. It has to have good solid foundations built on loyalty and devotion. Honesty is the sand and fidelity is the cement. If those foundations start to crumble you don't just leave the house, check into a motel and go screw some *maidel mit a klaidel* on a cheap and tacky one-night stand. What you do is strengthen the basic structure of the building. You talk through the problems and you work at it and try to make it better. That's what a partnership is all about.

Simon didn't want to work at it. Simon wanted the *maidel mit a klaidel.*

DM

What did you think of Annie Reichman approaching your client?

Max Golinski

Rule number one of show business:

'Never bitch about another agent!'

Having said that, Reichman is a *kushinyerkeh*, a no-good cheapskate, a woman who comes into your shop and asks for tuppenceworth of vinegar in her own bottle. She's so full of shit her eyes are brown. May that moustache of hers never be bleachable.

She shouldn't have done what she did and she knows it. Client larceny is the worst kind of crime. There should be honour among thieves . . . not that agents are thieves, of course, but you know what I'm saying here. Annie Reichman broke the unwritten rule, the unspoken code of conduct that no agent should ever break. Rule number two of show business:

'Thou shalt not steal clients from other agents or thou shalt rot in Agent Hell!'

And believe me, Agent Hell is worse than any other kind of hell. Imagine it already, an eternity of bullshit!

DM

Were you upset when Simon left the agency?

Max Golinski

Was I upset when Simon told me he was leaving the agency? *Oi vai*, if I had a pound for every person who asked me that question, I'd have more money than the Bank of Israel.

Of course I wasn't upset.

C'est la vie, live and let live, *abi geznut*! Life isn't all about making money, you know. If it was I'd have become a plumber, the thieving *mamzers* that they are. No, being an agent is all about personal relationships, it's about one on one, it's about trust, it's about commitment. If Simon wasn't happy with me looking after his interests then so be it.

When he told me he wanted to leave I was honest with him; I said his judgement shouldn't be clouded by the fact that I'd sweated blood and tears and invested time and money in his career. I told him he shouldn't stay just because I'd slogged my *kishkehs* out for him and treated him like a son for all those years. Simon had to do what he thought was right for him, and I supported that decision 100 per cent.

I shook his hand and wished him good luck.

10:

Extract from Simon's diary

31 JAN

Hell hath no fury like an agent scorned.

I suppose I could have taken the easy way out and just phoned to tell Max I was leaving, but for me, that was a no-no. I'm a big believer in confronting your fears head on and doing business, no matter how difficult, on a face-to-face basis. Maybe it's the Yorkshire pride in me, but I was brought up to believe it's the man's way of doing things. For me to hide behind the security blanket of a phone call would be the ultimate act of cowardice and prove an indelible sign of weakness. There was no way I was going to do that.

Besides, every time I called, he was engaged.

I went to the office with every intention of having a dignified and civilized conversation with Max. We'd sit down, I'd tell him I was leaving and he'd shake my hand and wish me all the best for the future. He'd then pour me a whisky and we'd spend the afternoon reminiscing about the good old days of television when there were only 150 channels to choose from.

Of course, it was never going to be like that.

Max's assistant, Scary Babs, showed me into the inner sanctum of his office, flashing me a smile as she did so. Actually, it's unfair to say she flashed me a smile as, since the unfortunate incident with the Botox, Babs can't do anything *but* smile. To be honest I don't think she can even blink these days. She was recently the subject of an ITV2 documentary, *When Botox Goes Bad*, and also took part in a beauty competition on Bravo for the over-sixties called *Never Mind the Botox*. She came third.

'Max will be with you in a minute,' she said.

At least, that's what I think she said; it's very difficult to understand her due to the collagen implants in her lips. She looks like that bloke from Papua New Guinea who Sting used to bring over when he was trying to save the rainforest.

'Thanks Babs.'

'No problem,' she said, sounding like someone farting in a bath: a sort of 'Blub-blubbler', if you can imagine.

'Peters, my boy,' said Max as he finally swept into the office. He was wearing a yellow Pringle sweater and had an expensive set of Calloway golf clubs casually slung over one shoulder. 'I've just been playing at Wentworth with Bruce. You really must join us sometime. How are you fixed next week?'

It suddenly hit me that two years ago I would have given anything to go and play golf with Max and Bruce. Now I couldn't think of anything worse.

'I'll check my diary,' I said.

'What's your handicap?'

'My agent.'

He laughed because he thought I was joking. He was about to find out that I wasn't.

'You're looking very sharp,' he said, fingering the lapel of my slate-grey single-breasted suit. 'Prada?'

'Primark!' I answered.

I wanted him to know that was all I could afford.

'Cigar?'

He opened a wooden box full of Cuban Cabañas and offered them in my direction. Obviously, this was no time to be smoking cigars. I'd come to the office to tell Max that he no longer represented me, so I felt it was unfair to take advantage of his hospitality. Having said that, I've never been one to miss the opportunity of a freebie, so I took one (I should point out that I feel very guilty about this now). Max leant forward and lit my cigar with a solid gold Zippo lighter. He held it in such a way that I couldn't help noticing that it bore the inscription:

To the wonderful Mr Golinski, thank you for all your help and guidance over the years. Long may it continue. Best wishes, Orlando.

I know that Max wanted me to see this and think that it was a gift from the Hollywood superstar, Orlando Bloom. This is what he wants people to think and he always leaves the lighter lying around for everyone to see. I know for a fact that Max has never represented Orlando Bloom and that the lighter was actually a gift from one of his real clients, The Great Orlando: Children's Entertainer and Balloon Modeller extraordinaire.

That's when I knew I was doing the right thing in leaving him.

'I'm glad you came in, my boy,' he said, lighting a cigar for himself and blowing a plume of smoke in my direction (why does everyone do that?) 'I've been wanting to talk to you about this format idea of ours that we've been working on, I think it's a real winner. I may have a production company interested.'

Format of *ours* that *we've* been working on? This was so typical of Max. He hasn't contributed in any way to the development of my idea. OK, he suggested that it should be 'aspirational' and the viewers should think that 'it could be them'. He also suggested a title but that was about it. This was more fuel to the fire. I knew I had to tell him and I had to tell him at that moment. There was nothing he could say that would make me change my mind.

'You're like a son to me, you know . . .'

Oh God.

'. . . and there's nothing I'd like more than to see you succeed. Now, what did you want to see me about?'

For the briefest moment, my confidence deserted me and I was sucked into the World of Max. I looked into his eyes. I'd always thought he had ice-cold killer eyes like Clint Eastwood in *Dirty Harry*, but today there was warmth there and more than a flicker of compassion. I looked at his lips and they creased into a great big smile, which spread across the lower part of his face causing the skin on his cheeks to appear all wrinkly. As he smiled, he raised his thick bushy eyebrows at me in a friendly inquisitive manner. This was a side of Max I hadn't seen before, the soft and caring side. He was tender, loving and comforting.

Paternal, almost.

All this shot through my mind, quickly followed by the thought that Max Golinski could never make me a big star but Annie Reichman could.

I took a deep breath.

'I'm not happy, Max,' I said, desperately trying to say it all, and nothing at all, at the same time.

Max stared at me blankly. I'd obviously picked the nothing-at-all option.

'I think it's time for a change.'

'What? . . . A change of cigar?'

He wasn't making this easy for me.

'What do you prefer, my boy? A Cohiba?' He pressed the button on his intercom and leant into the microphone. 'Babs, bring in that box of the finest Cohibas.'

'Not that sort of change, Max.'

'Well, what sort of change?' he asked. 'A change of car? A change of scenery? A change of underpants?'

He chuckled at his own joke.

'A change of management,' I said.

He looked at me for the longest time. A million expressions spun across his face, like a one-armed slot machine waiting to reveal the jackpot: anger, hatred, contempt and betrayal flew by, but the emotion that appeared was one of sorrow.

'You're leaving me?' he whispered. He seemed genuinely upset. His voice was hoarse and brittle with pain. He was like a little puppy dog whining for its owner, and I swear I saw a tear in his eye.

'Why now, when things are finally starting to happen?'

'I just think it's time to move on.'

'Was it something I did wrong?'

This was the opportunity I'd been waiting for. I would tell him everything I'd wanted to say for years but had been too scared to, because of the fear of what it might do to my career. In the past I'd always held my tongue because I needed Max more than he needed me.

Now it was different.

Now it didn't matter what I said, so I had every intention of saying it. I would spell out to Max exactly what I thought of him. How he'd been a terrible agent for me and always treated me like an also-ran; how he'd never pushed me or promoted me and never fully appreciated the possibility that I could be a success in this business; how for a long time he'd made me feel like a failure and how he'd ultimately held me back in my career. I'd tell him all these things and more.

In the words of the great Martine McCutcheon: *This was my moment.*

I would flick the switch of animosity and pull the lever of antipathy. I would push the button marked loathing and turn the key of detestation. I would open the valve marked bitterness and stand back as all the vitriolic bile I'd been bottling up over the years gushed over Max, the sheer power of it pushing him to his knees, forcing him to apologize and repent.

Of course, this being show business I didn't do anything of the kind. This being show business, where nobody says anything with any degree of sincerity, I said the exact opposite of everything I wanted to say. I told him I thought he was a wonderful agent and that I was grateful for everything he'd done for me. I then used a line which anybody who's ever had to split up with somebody in any capacity will be familiar with:

'It's not you . . . it's me.'

Maybe Max had been right all along, maybe an agent/artist relationship is like a marriage. This was certainly starting to feel like a divorce. I knew it wouldn't be long before we'd be arguing over who got custody of the 10x8 publicity shots.

'I think it's time I moved on.'

He can keep the CVs and biogs as long as I get to see them every other weekend.

'I just need a little bit of space.'

The showreels are mine, though; there's no way he's having those.

'But what about the plans we made for the future?' he cried.

This was affecting Max more than I thought it would. Either that or he was employing a little bit of psychology and taking me on a day trip to Guilt City.

'Well the thing is, Max . . . it's just that . . . it's just that . . .'

The words wouldn't come, but my silence betrayed the truth.

'You've met another agent, haven't you?'

I nodded my head silently.

'Who is it?' he hissed. 'Who is it?'

This was more like the old Max we knew and loved (or hated, depending on how you look at it).

'Annie Reichman.'

I knew he had a temper but I've never seen him lose it like that before. He went from millpond calm to ocean-like anger in the space of a millisecond. It was like watching a bomb go off. He was purple. Literally purple. Due to the high blood pressure he's always been a strange sort of puce colour, but this was bordering on violet. His eyes were bulging so brutally and his temples throbbing so violently, I thought his brains were going to explode. If he had been a cartoon, steam would have been coming out of his ears, but as this was real life all he did was throw his Executive Stress Reliever out of the window and swear at me in Yiddish.

'*GEHAGET ZOLSTU VEREN!*' he screamed, his face contorting into a mask of ferocity.

When I got home I looked up what it meant in my *Big Book of Yiddish Expressions*, and it really wasn't very pleasant. *Gehaget zolstu veren* means 'you should be killed!'

I hope he was speaking figuratively.

11:

Dominic Mulryan interviews former TV star Ricardo Mancini

When Simon joined Reichman Associates, it sent shock waves throughout the world of entertainment and for the first time in his career, people started to sit up and take notice of Simon Peters.

Ricardo Mancini is a TV presenter whose career, by his own admission, has seen better days. Simon and Mancini had a long history of being competitors for the same jobs and up until the time that Simon joined Annie Reichman, Mancini had always been the more successful of the two. Tall, tanned and handsome, he was everything that Simon was not, and at one point he seemed destined for the glittering career which Simon would ultimately enjoy. However, as so often happens in show business, things quickly changed and Mancini, once the Golden Boy of British Television, seemed to suffer a complete reversal of fortunes.

Mancini currently works for the home shopping channel, Going Gone TV!

DM
Ricardo, during your career, did you see Simon Peters as competition?

Ricardo Mancini

No . . . no way . . . For a long time he wasn't even in my league. Does that sound conceited? I guess it does, but to be honest I don't care cos it's true. Ask anyone.

DM

Do you think you had similar careers?

Ricardo Mancini

I suppose you could say that towards the end we started doing the same sort of stuff. He appeared on *Celebrity Big Brother*, I appeared on *I'm a Celebrity . . . Get Me Out of Here!* He hosted a game show on ITV; I hosted a quiz show on BBC. He ended up dying in a horrific helicopter crash, I ended up on a home shopping channel.

Yeah, I guess career-wise, we were very similar.

DM

How did you feel when you heard that Simon had signed with Annie Reichman?

Ricardo Mancini

I have to admit that I was jealous. Annie Reichman is a very scary woman but there's no doubting she's the best in the business. She knows everyone there is to know and does whatever it takes to make things happen for her clients. She's got this incredible focus and inner drive and when you look at her, you can see the burning ambition in her eyes . . . well, one of them, anyway.

If Annie Reichman represents you, you've got a winning lottery ticket. She's very proactive as opposed to my agent WHO JUST SITS ON HIS FAT ARSE WAITING FOR THE PHONE TO RING! You will make sure you print that bit, won't you? . . . Can you write it in capitals so he knows that I shouted it? You can also mention that besides the shopping channel, I HAVEN'T WORKED SINCE PANTO. You'd think somebody with my CV would be able to get a decent job somewhere, wouldn't you? I came third in last year's *Celebrity Dominoes* for Chrissakes, doesn't that mean anything in this industry? Now I have to sell pots and pans and fucking Mickey Mouse watches on Going Gone TV. Do you watch Going Gone TV? No, exactly. Do you know anyone who watches it? No, exactly. That's what my career's come to . . . ARE YOU READING THIS, MAX GOLINSKI?

Sorry, I get a bit angry sometimes. I've been to anger-management classes but they didn't really work. They just made me realize how angry I am at my management.

DM
What's the difference between Annie Reichman and Max Golinski?

Ricardo Mancini
Annie Reichman is a major player in the industry whereas Max Golinski is just the great pretender, a wannabe, a could-have-been, A NEVER-REALLY-WAS!

I've always been a big football fan and to put it in foot-balling terms, Annie Reichman is the Manchester United of show business, whereas Max is the Accrington Stanley. Yeah, Accrington might make the play-offs one year, they might even get promoted, but they're never going to play in Europe, are they?

Come to think of it, Reichman actually looks a bit like Sir Alex Ferguson.

Except Sir Alex hasn't got a moustache, of course.

DM

What was the reaction in the industry when Simon joined her agency?

Ricardo Mancini

I think people were really surprised because there was a feeling that SIMON PETERS WAS A TALENTLESS LITTLE SHIT WHO DIDN'T DESERVE ANY KIND OF SUCCESS! I'm sorry . . . don't put that in capitals, will you? I don't want to give people the wrong impression.

There was definitely a heap of resentment. It's a well-known fact that in show business artistes don't like to see other artistes doing well; there's always a lot of 'why him and not me?' going on. I never felt like that personally but now you mention it, why was it him and not me?

I mean, seriously . . . why him?

DM

Is it true that you approached Reichman to be your agent?

Ricardo Mancini

Well, I had a meeting with her last year on the back of *Celebrity Dominoes* where I came third . . . I came third, you see, Peters only came fourth in his show; I couldn't understand it. *Dominoes* had been Living TV's surprise hit of the summer and I thought it was all going to start happening for me in a big way.

I walked into Reichman's office and within thirty seconds she told me she wouldn't take me on. When I asked her why, she said that I had the right sort of talent . . . 'NDT' or something she called it . . . but she thought that I was 'too good-looking for television at the moment'. I was quite shocked; how can you be *too* good-looking for television? Surely that's what people want? I said to her that I must be right for some sort of show and she said she thought I'd be perfect on a home shopping channel. When I told her there was no way I was ever going to do that, she just smiled at me knowingly. Normally I'd have been really upset about that sort of thing, but to be honest she frightened the life out of me and I just wanted to get out of there. Have you seen that mole on her chin? I swear to God she's growing another head.

DM

Do you think Simon would have been as successful if he hadn't joined Reichman Associates?

Ricardo Mancini
Absolutely not. Max Golinski is officially THE WORST AGENT IN THE WORLD! – you can use capital letters on that one – but with hindsight, leaving him was the biggest mistake that Peters made.

If he'd stayed with him, he'd probably be the same as me and working on some crappy satellite channel now. If that was the case he wouldn't have been as successful, so he wouldn't have been as rich, so he wouldn't have been able to buy a helicopter, so he'd still be alive today.

Having said all that, joining Reichman Associates was an opportunity which anybody would have jumped at, and I'd have done exactly the same thing.

I just wouldn't have bought the helicopter.

12:

Dominic Mulryan

Career-wise, signing with Reichman Associates was obviously a major step in the right direction, but at that point in his life, what was Simon thinking deep down? What were his quirks and foibles? What were his fears and ambitions? On the surface, everything was going well. He was sailing on very calm waters and had obviously realized he was within easy grasp of achieving his lifelong ambition. So if this were the case, what demons lurking below would, within the space of two years, drive this seemingly successful man to supposedly commit suicide? And if that wasn't the case, what terrible deed could he have performed to give cause enough for someone to murder him?

What follows are the entries from two consecutive months in Simon's diary, a period which seemed to have been a crucial turning point in his life.

At this moment the format for the TV show which, in a short space of time, would make him his millions was just the seed of an idea (although exactly whose seed it was, remains a vital question). He had just joined Reichman Associates and there was a general consensus in the entertainment industry that Simon Peters was going to be the 'Next Big Thing'. After finally managing to escape the crushing anonymity of the C-list, Simon was about to be accepted as one of the beautiful people (allegorically if not aesthetically). It was all very exciting and Simon seemed to relish every moment of it. He was now on the B-list, but he was at the top of it and pushing for promotion. To use one of Ricardo Mancini's football metaphors, if this were the FA Cup, he was the underdog who'd made it to the semi-final, the crowd were behind him and there was every chance he was going to lift the trophy. Simon Peters was, slowly but surely, on his way to the big time . . .

13:

3 FEB

Today is the day I know that I've finally made it.

When I'm an old man – I'm talking a really old man, i.e. in my mid to late fifties – my ten loving grandchildren will sit at my feet and gaze up at me in wonderment, amazed that their grandfather still looks so youthful. Their eyes will be full of admiration and awe as I regale them with stories and anecdotes of show business in the early days of the twenty-first century. I'll tell them how I used to do panto in places like Grimsby, and personal appearances at Butlins in Bognor Regis. I'll tell them how tough it was to land your own prime-time TV show, and how I occasionally had to appear as a guest on daytime game shows just to make a living. They won't believe me, of course, and they'll fire a constant barrage of questions at me about my career, and at that point I'll be thankful I kept a video of every single TV appearance I ever made. They'll gladly spend their six-week summer holidays glued

79

to their TV set watching endless reruns of my early work on Challenge TV.

Then, one day, they'll ask me the question I'll have been waiting for.

'Pops,' they'll say (I'm pretty sure I'll be the sort of grandfather whose grandchildren will call him Pops). 'How did you know when you'd actually made it as a big star?'

Looking wistfully into the middle distance, I'll take out a leather tobacco pouch and start to fill my pipe. I'll probably be really famous for smoking a pipe by this point, and will have been, on more than one occasion, voted Celebrity Pipe Smoker of the Year.

'Was it when you hosted that daytime game show *Simon Says*?' asks Peter. He's not the brightest kid, which means he'll probably end up being a professional footballer. He'll play for England and score the winning goal in the World Cup or something.

'Although that was extremely popular for a daytime game show, Peter,' I'll explain patiently, 'it wasn't really what I'd call *making it big*.'

'Was it when you did *Slebs*? People still talk about that today.'

God, I love my granddaughter Simone. She'll be the sort of grandchild who will always say exactly the right thing.

'Well, *Slebs* was a massive show of course, but it wasn't really *my* show. I was just the co-host. We all know what "co-host" means, don't we?'

'Is it the bitter and twisted person who thinks they should be the main host?'

'That's right, Simon Jnr.'

Simon Jnr will be my favourite grandchild. He's the one who'll take a real interest in show business and show signs of wanting to learn to play the piano, join amateur dramatics societies and go to ballet and tap-dancing lessons. He won't be gay or anything, though.

'I know the answer, I know, I know!' This would be Simeon, jumping up and down with his hand in the air, his spectacles getting steamed up with the excitement of it all. He'll be the intelligent one who will be destined to be a television producer or, better still, the Director General of the BBC. I won't mind, of course, as long as he still gives me work. 'Was it when you appeared on *Celebrity Big Brother*, which incidentally was one of the most successful shows ever commissioned?'

Bless him, I'd think. He's only four and he already knows words like 'commissioned'.

'Well actually, it was just after that, Simeon.'

All the grandchildren would point at Simeon and take the mickey out of him for getting it wrong. They'd call him 'specky' and 'four-eyes'. He'll get his own back on them one day by cancelling their favourite soap opera and commissioning highbrow TV shows which they won't understand.

'Are you sure you want to hear this?' I'll say, getting the attention back on to me (you can do that sort of thing when you're a grandfather . . . personally, I can't wait).

'Yes,' they'll yell. 'Please tell us, Pops. Please!'

'Well, the day I knew I'd really made it was the day I was invited to . . .'

I would pause to relight my pipe.

'Invited to where?' they'd scream in unison, barely able to conceal their eagerness.

'The day I was invited to . . .'

'Yes?'

'The day I was invited to play in my first Celebrity Golf Day.'

'Hurrahhhhhhh!' they'd all shout, little SimSim nearly wetting his nappy with the relief. 'Tell us about it, Pops!'

And I *will* tell them about it and I'll be able to remember every single detail because today is that day . . .

I'd had a call from Lucy in Annie Reichman's office. Lucy is Annie's assistant and the complete opposite of Scary Babs, Max's assistant. For a start, she's never had a boob job, Botox, collagen implants or HRT. She doesn't drink, smoke, cough or wheeze and I can't imagine her swearing at her clients, which was one of Scary Babs' trademarks. I think the biggest difference is that Lucy always seems really happy on the phone and genuinely enthusiastic about her work. She's intelligent, courteous and professional, as opposed to Babs who has a severe personality disorder and gets people to pull her finger when she's about to fart. I have a theory that Babs is secretly in love with Max and that her nastiness was born out of sexual frustration. Excuse me for a moment, the thought of Scary Babs being sexually frustrated has left me feeling quite queasy. One day Max and Babs will end up together in the biblical sense, and I'm sure they'll make each other thoroughly unhappy.

I've only been with Reichman Associates a couple of days but I'm already very impressed with the whole set-up. When I joined the agency, Annie and Lucy asked me what I wanted to do with my career and I told them that I wanted to be a proper celebrity. I told them that I wanted to move up the showbiz ladder and drop the C-list tag, which I seem to have been stuck with for some inexplicable reason.

'I want to raise my profile,' I said, 'and be the sort of person who gets invited to charity golf tournaments.'

They didn't laugh at this and just nodded their heads

as if they totally understood and would be able to make it possible.

Now, two days later . . .

'You've been asked to play in the Billy Fox Celebrity Pro-Am Golf Classic.'

This was very exciting news, if not a little surprising. I've heard on the showbiz grapevine that since Annie took me on to her books I'm not exactly Billy Fox's favourite person. A lot of people say we have a very similar presenting style, and apparently he's claiming that I've stolen his act (as if he's got an act to steal).

I think he's just jealous of me. Admittedly he's been the so-called King of Light Entertainment for four decades now, but that's two decades too long and it's only a matter of time before I steal his crown. I know it, he knows it, and the world of television knows it. I'm up and coming and he's been and gone.

'Did Billy Fox himself ask me to play?' I asked Lucy.

'No,' she said. 'The people who run the charity have invited you. Billy doesn't have anything to do with the organization of it. He just lends his name to it and turns up on the day and plays.'

*Note to self: Lend name to golf day. The Simon Peters Celebrity Pro-Am Golf Classic has a real ring to it.

What does Celebrity Pro-Am Golf Classic actually mean? It just looks like a random collection of words desperately in need of punctuation. Surely they can be rearranged in any order and make just as much sense: Pro-Am Golf Celebrity Classic. Classic Pro-Am Celebrity Golf. Golf Classic Celebrity Pro-Am. What is Pro-Am short for, anyway? Maybe it's Prozac and Amphetamines? Prozac on the first nine holes, amphetamines on the second. Now that would make golf more interesting.

I've never actually played golf before and don't really know much about it, but I didn't tell Lucy this as I didn't want to appear too negative. I saw it on the telly once; how difficult can it be? The most important thing is that I've been accepted on to the golfing circuit, which is a definite nod of recognition and approval from the world of entertainment. I imagine 'Celebrity Golf' to be an elite clique where business is talked, deals are struck and jokes are told about the state of Jimmy Tarbuck's backswing. I think it's like the showbiz equivalent of the Freemasons and if that's the case, I'm quite prepared to roll up my trouser leg and learn a funny handshake.

Maybe that's why golfers only wear one glove?

'The tournament is the day after tomorrow at Wentworth,' said Lucy. 'You have to be there for nine and you're teeing off at ten.'

There was a pause.

'What does teeing off mean?' I asked.

Lucy laughed. I think she thought I was joking.

5 FEB

Charley agreed to come with me to be my caddy. I picked her up at eight o'clock and she spent the first five minutes in fits of hysterical laughter at the clothes I was wearing.

Last night I went to one of those discount golf shops and asked the two young lads who worked there to make me 'look like a golfer'. I was there for about three hours and as they handed me different clothes to try on, they kept nudging each other and sniggering and giggling. I thought it was just because they recognized me from *Celebrity Big Brother*, but this morning, as I drove along with Charley in my bright pink sweater, puce roll neck and purple plus fours, I started to think maybe they'd taken the piss slightly.

'So, what's your handicap then?' asked Charley as we headed out into the Surrey countryside.

'Well I suffer from an ingrowing eyelash occasionally.'

'Simon . . .'

'I know it doesn't sound much but it's actually bloody painful. Every time I blink it feels as though I've got something in my eye . . .'

'No Simon, I mean in golf. What do you play off?'

'It's called a tee, isn't it?' I said, feeling rather pleased with myself that I knew the answer (I'd actually looked it up on the Internet last night).

Charley stared at me. It was a look she often gave me, one of sympathy and pity mixed with a hint of incredulity.

'In golf, you have a handicap system,' she explained slowly, the way a teacher might tell a four-year-old how to tie his shoelaces. 'My dad used to play all the time and he told me all about it. If, for instance, you play off six, it means you're a six handicapper and you get six free shots per round. If you play off eighteen it means you get eighteen shots. It basically determines how many free shots you get per round.'

'I play off one hundred and fifty.'

'It only goes up to twenty-eight.'

'Bugger.'

'Simon, have you ever played golf before?'

I had to think about it.

'I played pitch and putt once.'

'When was that?'

'1981.'

Charley looked at me.

'Why do you want to do this?' she laughed. 'Why would you want to put yourself through the shame of it all?'

'I don't know; it's just that anybody who's anybody in show business seems to play golf. I just want to be part of the gang . . . Brucie, Tarby, Lynchy . . .'

'Foxy.'

His name hung in the air. I didn't rise to the bait but Charley knew she'd hit a nerve.

'This isn't anything to do with your lifelong obsession with Billy Fox, is it?' she asked.

'I am not obsessed with Billy Fox,' I said, and it's true, I'm not. 'I just think everything he does I can do better and surely it's only a matter of time before the public and, more importantly, the TV executives realize it.'

Charley had heard this record before and knew it was time to change the subject.

'So if you've got Brucie, Tarby, Lynchy and Foxy, what's your nickname going to be?'

'I don't know . . . Simsey? Petersey? Neither of them sound right really, do they?'

'What about Slimey?'

I took a deep breath.

'I don't think you're taking this very seriously,' I said. 'The reason I'm appearing here is because it's for charity and I think it's good to give something back to the community. It's a moral responsibility to contribute to a charitable organization in any way you can. I don't have a lot to give but what I do have is my time, my energy and my celebrity status, and one could argue that's more valuable than donating money. Wasn't it Emanuel Swedenborg who said *True charity is the desire to be useful to others with no thought of recompense*?'

'So how much are you getting paid for appearing?'

'Two hundred and fifty quid.'

'And what's it in aid of?'

'I haven't got a clue.'

Charley shook her head and let out a snort of disbelief as we passed a sign informing us that Wentworth Golf Course was two hundred yards ahead on the right.

'Aren't you nervous?'

'Of course not,' I said. 'It's only a small event. It's not as if there's going to be anybody watching.'

As we turned into the drive at Wentworth, I couldn't believe what I saw. Thousands of people streaming over the fairways and jostling for position; TV cameras on cranes and soundmen with backpacks and boom poles; large advertising hoardings, refreshment stalls and marshals with walkie-talkies. There was a tannoy system, a leader board and a grandstand which overflowed with even more spectators. They had picnic hampers and carried large umbrellas and looked more like golfers than I did. Many of them wore clothes which were truly ridiculous, and I couldn't help thinking that they'd probably been helped by the same two seventeen-year-olds who served me.

I swallowed hard and glanced at Charley. She smiled and squeezed my hand reassuringly and I was pleased that she was there with me. I felt confident that with her help, I'd be able to get through this with the minimum amount of embarrassment. She then burst into a fit of uncontrollable laughter. Me being in that sort of predicament really appealed to her warped sense of humour.

I was about to slam the car into reverse and wheelspin away when one of the marshals came running over.

'Simon . . . Simon Peters,' he shouted, tapping on my window. 'I'm a big fan of yours. I'm so glad you could make it.'

Of course, this immediately made me want to stay. I wound down the window.

'I'm Phil . . . Phil Dunn,' he said, leaning into the car and shaking my hand. 'I'm one of the organizers of the event. Thanks for coming. So what made you want to support our charity?'

'It just seemed so worthwhile,' I said without missing a beat.

'Well, as you can see we've had a great turnout and it's wonderful news that the BBC have agreed to broadcast it live on *Sport on Sunday*. It's great publicity for the charity because it's the Beeb's most popular sporting show at the moment. I think it gets something like four million viewers every week.'

I didn't want to look at Charley but I could sense the biting of the lip, the shaking of the shoulders and the tears of laughter that were filling her eyes.

'If you'd like to park your car and go into the clubhouse, you can meet the rest of your four-ball. Today's tournament is an individual Stableford event with the best two scores counting from your team. There's "out of bounds" down the right on the first, you get a free drop on the third and watch out for the G.U.R on the twelfth. Oh and we've got a longest drive on the seventh and a nearest the pin on the thirteenth.'

I didn't have a clue what he was talking about and I was half expecting to see subtitles. Four-ball? Stableford? Free drop? Nearest the pin? Surely you'd never be able to find a pin on a golf course?

'Nearest the flag,' he said, sensing my confusion. 'By the way, what's your handicap?'

'An ingrowing eyelash,' shouted Charley, before I could stop her.

'Eight,' I said.

'Very impressive.' he said.

With hindsight, maybe I should have said twenty-eight, but at the time I didn't want to appear amateurish.

'Your team will be teeing off second, so if you'd like to get your clubs, I'll put them in the buggy for you.'

There was a pause.

'Clubs?' I said.

There was another pause, this one in the early stages of pregnancy.

'You haven't got any clubs, have you?' said Charley.

'No clubs?' said Phil.

'THE DOG ATE THEM!' I shouted in a state of panic.

I don't know where that came from. It must have been some sort of knee-jerk reaction from somewhere deep in my schoolboy psyche. The truth of the matter is that the two seventeen-year-olds who served me said I wouldn't need clubs; they said that nobody in golf used them these days.

'Well, not to worry,' said Peter calmly. 'I'm sure we can get you some from the pro shop.'

Charley and I parked the car and made our way into the clubhouse, where I was introduced to the rest of my team. They were three businessmen who'd paid £150 each to play in the tournament, and for that they got to play with a celebrity, i.e. me.

I flashed them a showbizzy smile and shook their hands.

'Great to meet you guys,' I said in a don't-be-nervous-about-meeting-me-I'm-just-a-normal-bloke-out-for-a-game-of-golf-type way.

They all stared at me blankly, and I got the distinct

89

impression that for £150 they were hoping to get Bruce Forsyth.

'I'm afraid I don't watch much television,' said one of them.

That was his polite way of saying he'd never seen me before in his life.

'You were on *Big Brother*, weren't you?' said another one.

'*Celebrity Big Brother*,' I said, correcting him. 'There is a difference.'

'I hope you're good,' laughed the third. 'We had Billy Fox himself in our team last year. He plays off twelve and we won the tournament. What do you play off?'

'A tee,' said Charley and that got a big laugh from all of them.

'She nicks all my gags,' I said. 'Actually I play off eight.'

They were obviously impressed by this.

'Yeah,' I said, feeling I was on a bit of a roll. 'In the last tournament I played in, I actually won the longest-pin competition and the nearest the drive.'

They laughed, but I'm not entirely sure why. At that moment Phil, the organizer, came over and handed me a small tatty golf bag.

'I'm afraid they only had a junior set of clubs left.'

That set Charley off again.

'Don't worry about it,' she said, 'I'm sure an eight handi-capper can manage.'

One of the marshals called out my name and informed us that our team would be the next to tee off. The three businessmen collected their expensive-looking clubs and made their way through the door. I slung the junior set over my shoulder and followed them.

When we got outside, I didn't like what was waiting for me. There were a thousand people, three TV cameras and a collection of journalists and photographers surrounding the first tee. If that wasn't bad enough, who should be in the middle of them all, about to take his first shot?

Billy Fox.

There was a squeal of feedback and a hiss of static as the tannoy system burst into life.

'Ladies and gentlemen, please welcome on to the tee, the man responsible for everything you see today, that legend of light entertainment, playing off a handicap of twelve . . . Mr Billy Fox!'

I hate to admit it but the crowd went wild. There was cheering, whistling, whooping and hollering, all of which Fox acknowledged with an air of mock modesty and his trademark wink and point. The noise quickly subsided as he coolly pushed a tee into the ground and placed a ball on top of it. He looked at the flag some four hundred yards away.

'Pull,' he said, putting the golf club to his shoulder as if he was about to do a clay-pigeon shoot.

This got a big laugh from the crowd. A much bigger laugh than it actually deserved. I think it was a touch of the Prince Charles syndrome. People always feel compelled to burst into hysterics at his jokes even if they're not even remotely amusing.

Billy looked back at the ball. He bent his legs slightly and adopted a position which led me to believe he'd probably played this game before. God, I hated him.

Suddenly there was complete silence.

He looked at the ball for what seemed an age. There was a twitch of his head and a slight movement in his hands, but other than that he just carried on staring at the ball.

Still complete silence.

It was unbearable.

I had an overwhelming urge to shout out, 'GET ON WITH IT YOU TALENTLESS OLD HAS-BEEN, GIVE SOMEONE ELSE A GO!' and I wouldn't have just been talking about his golf shot.

I managed to restrain myself and Fox finally hit the ball. He caught it beautifully and it sailed majestically down the fairway. In the words of Bing Crosby it went straight down the middle, and the crowd erupted into a spontaneous round of applause. The rest of Fox's team took their shots and then it was our turn.

'Next on to the tee,' said the voice over the tannoy, 'From *Celebrity Big Brother* and *Slebs* please welcome . . . Simon Peters.'

There was a polite round of applause and a few cheers, but not as many as there had been for Billy Fox. Even though it was his charity day, I still couldn't help feeling disappointed at this.

'Simon Peters is playing off a handicap of eight,' said the voice from the tannoy.

'Oooooooooohhhhh!' said the crowd.

It was at that moment it finally hit me that I didn't have a clue what I was doing. Sure, I'd managed to look good in my pink Pringle sweater and purple plus fours and yes, I'd even made the whole junior-golf-bag-thing work for me, but the truth was that I didn't actually know how to hold the stick or the bat or whatever it was called.

I froze.

From the tannoy I heard my name again.

'Simon Peters!'

There was another round of applause, but not quite as loud this time and without the cheers. Charley gave me a small push and I staggered on to the tee in a state of shock.

People were nudging each other and I could hear them whispering.

'*Slebs.*'

'*Big Brother.*'

'*That jumper doesn't go with those trousers.*'

I tried to remember everything Billy Fox had done. I took out a plastic tee and pushed it into the ground, but my hands were shaking so much I couldn't put the ball on top of it. The audience laughed. They thought I was doing a comedy routine, so I looked up and laughed with them to pretend that I was. I eventually got the ball to stay there. I looked at the flag and then back at the ball and then just for good measure back at the flag again. I decided to continue with the comedy option.

'Who'll give me a tenner if I can hit Billy Fox from here?' I joked, looking around with a cheeky smile. Admittedly I stumbled over the 'if I can hit Billy Fox from here', but I still thought it was quite a funny gag.

Silence.

Not even a titter.

I'm more famous now than I've ever been, but I'm still not quite famous enough to enjoy the Prince Charles syndrome.

I adopted what I thought was a good golfing stance. I then realized that the junior golf club I had to use was much too small for me and meant that I had to bend over quite a long way to reach the ball. It felt very awkward and I couldn't help thinking that I probably looked quite ridiculous.

I then started staring at the ball.

Billy Fox had stared for about thirty seconds, but I knew I could last a lot longer than that. I twitched my head, wiggled my hands, shook my leg and wobbled my club.

Once I'd finished this little routine I started it all over again in a different order. I wiggled, twitched, wobbled and shook pretty much every part of my body, while all the time staring at the ball intently. I was there for what must have been a good two minutes before one of the marshals coughed politely and told me there were another twenty-three teams waiting to play.

Charley had given me a little pep talk on the way from the clubhouse. She said her father had told her one very important thing about golf.

'Don't try to hit the ball too hard,' she said.

This, to me, sounded like complete nonsense. Surely it's all about power, I thought. I drew the club back, swiped viciously at the ball and then using my hand to shield the sun from my eyes, I adopted the classic pose of a golfer looking into the distance to see how far the ball had gone. I held the pose for what was probably a couple of beats too long, but I wanted to make sure that all the cameras had got a good shot of me. The ball must have travelled quite a long way because I couldn't even see where it had landed. I felt completely exhilarated. I'd done it. I'd managed to hit a golf shot in front of one thousand people without making myself look stupid. What's more it was being broadcast live to millions of viewers on *Sport on Sunday*. This golf malarkey isn't as difficult as everyone makes out, I thought.

At first I wasn't aware of the laughter. When I eventually heard it, I thought somebody else had come on to the tee: Tarby or Lynchy maybe, acting the fool as they came up to congratulate me on a great shot. I spun around but there was no one there. Still the laughter continued. I smiled and acknowledged their appreciation with a nonchalant wave of my hand, the way I'd seen Tiger Woods do it. This just made them laugh more, so I did the one thing that came naturally: I bowed in a theatrical fashion. As I was bending over, I noticed Charley, who was subtly pointing at my feet. I looked down and there, still on the tee, was my ball. It hadn't moved an inch.

What followed was the longest day of my life. I noticed the TV cameras stopped focusing on me after the second hole, but to be honest I couldn't really blame them and I was actually quite relieved. When I occasionally managed to hit the ball, I sliced it, hooked it, topped it and duffed it and at one point managed to hit it 180 yards in totally the wrong direction. Anger and frustration eventually gave way to hilarity as Charley and I couldn't stop laughing at just how bad I was. I hit the ball into the trees, into a lake and in one freak accident into an open-top double-decker bus which just happened to be driving around the perimeter road. (The bus was on its way to Windsor, surely that would qualify for the longest drive?) I lost twenty-three balls, four spectators were taken to the first-aid tent, and the three businessmen who I was playing with stopped talking to me after the third hole and started mumbling something about asking for their money back.

Although it was a totally humiliating experience, Charley was there to share it with me and things never seem quite so bad when she's by my side. We've been best mates for ten years now, and in all that time there's been a gentle under-current of feelings telling me that it could be more. We've been seeing an awful lot of each other lately and getting on better than we've ever done before. On days like these, I look at her and think we're perfect together, and I know today will be the sort of thing we'll laugh about in years to come.

Maybe we'll tell our grandchildren about it.

It's strange, but whenever I think about my imaginary grandchildren, I always think of them being Charley's grandchildren as well. I'm not sure she feels the same way about me, though. I think she just sees me as a good friend and, as it turns out, possible business partner. That was one of the good things to come out of today's round of golf. As we were looking for one of the numerous lost balls, Charley told me she was thinking of leaving *Coffee Morning with Mike and Sue* and setting up an independent production company. Surprisingly, she said she wants me to join her; she thinks it's time we started trying to make some of the programme ideas we've been talking about. She thinks that with my name and her production skills, we could be quite a formidable team. I think she could be right.

'I've got a brilliant idea for a TV show,' I told her, while trying to retrieve a ball from the middle of a prickly gorse bush.

'Not *Celebrity Peacemakers!* again?'

'No, this one's different, although I still maintain that *Celebrity Peacemakers!* would make a great show . . . Of course, it's got to have an—'

'An exclamation mark,' she said, interrupting me. 'I know. What's the new idea?'

'It's called *It's All About Me!*'

'What's it about?' asked Charley.

There was a pause.

'Me!' I said.

There was another pause.

'Yeah but what's the actual format?'

I hadn't actually thought of a format, so I stayed quiet and pretended to look for my golf ball.

'I think it probably needs a little bit of work,' said Charley and we agreed to meet up next week for a brainstorming session (at the moment we always seem to find some reason for meeting up).

After the humiliation of the golf had finally ended, there was a prize-giving ceremony and what my mother used to call 'a bit of a do'. It was very posh with silver service, five courses and lots of wine. Charley agreed to drive home so I set out to forget just how bad the day had been by getting very drunk, very quickly. Obviously, drink affects people in different ways. Some people become morose, some people violent, some people overfriendly and some people antisocial. I'm always very funny when I'm drunk, or at least I think I am at the time. I always spend the next day having flashbacks and thinking I didn't, did I? I feel what happened at the golf dinner will be a flashback that haunts me for a long time to come.

During the second course, Des Lynam came over to our table and shook my hand. He told me he was a big fan but warned me to watch my back because Billy Fox wasn't very happy about my behaviour on the golf course. I didn't care; I was just happy that someone like Des Lynam knew who I was. This was a bit of a first for me. Usually, people only seem vaguely aware of my existence. They'd know my name but would probably get it slightly wrong, or they'd recognize my face but think I went to the same school as them. At the golfing party, everybody seemed to know my face *and* my name. I certainly wasn't the most famous person there, but all the people who were more famous than me knew who I was and that was very important to me. I said this to Charley and she was fascinated by it. She kept asking me why it was so significant, but in my drunken state I couldn't really explain it to her. Something to do with my mother dying when I was thirteen, leaving me with a lifelong sense of abandonment and emptiness, mixed together with the fact that my father's own quest for fame and fortune left me lonely, unloved and psychologically damaged, which resulted in an insatiable thirst for recognition and acknowledgement from strangers, which I know ultimately can never be quenched.

It's either that or I just like showing off; I'm not sure which.

After dinner, Bruce Forsyth stood up and proceeded with the inevitable charity auction. There's a real knack to being a member of the audience involved in a charity auction, especially if you're a celebrity. You're expected to bid for stuff because ordinary members of the public think you've got loads of money. This isn't necessarily a bad thing, in fact it's good to bid because . . .

a) It shows willing.

b) You get a namecheck from the auctioneer.

The real trick, of course, is not to get caught having to actually buy anything. Bidding, just like comedy, is all about timing, and I managed to time my bid beautifully. The first lot was for a pair of chopsticks signed by the Chinese celebrity chef Ken Hom (these are the sorts of things you get at these auctions). Brucie informed us that the sticks came with a 'certificate of authenticity'. Well that's all right then, I thought. Surely if you're going to go to the trouble of forging Ken Hom's signature on a pair of chopsticks, you wouldn't have any qualms about forging a certificate of authenticity. Maybe the certificate of authenticity should have a certificate of authenticity. But then how would you know that was real? Where does it stop? Some items come with a photograph of the famous person actually signing the object to prove that it's authentic. But how would you know the photograph was genuine? How do you know they haven't superimposed

Ken Hom's face on to somebody else's body, or got a Ken Hom lookalike to pose with a pair of chopsticks? On second thoughts, it's probably easier just to get the real Ken Hom to sign them in the first place.

Well, quite naturally, there wasn't a huge demand for this particular item, and despite Brucie's best efforts he couldn't get anybody to open the bidding. I saw my opportunity, put my hand up and offered one hundred and fifty quid. Brucie looked in my direction.

'A very generous bid of one hundred and fifty pounds from Mr Simon Peters. Give him a big round of applause.'

The audience obeyed and I stood up and waved, just in case there was anyone in the room who didn't know who Simon Peters was.

'A hundred and fifty?' said Brucie. 'Wasn't that his golf score?'

Brucie's delivery was immaculate and it got a really big laugh. I acknowledged the gag by miming a golf swing and then covering my eyes as if I'd just played a terrible shot. More huge laughs from the audience (maybe my forte is physical comedy?) I sat down again, thrilled that my little ploy for a namecheck had worked. The bids started rolling in, just as I knew they would. Somebody came in with a bid of £175 and in no time at all it had moved up to £350. They eventually went for £425. Even though it wasn't me who actually paid the money, I couldn't help feeling rather pleased with myself. Those crappy chopsticks had obviously raised so much money because of my input, and they wouldn't have raised half as much without it. That's the sort of good work we celebrities do. I said this to Charley but she just laughed.

Other items in Bruce's auction included a chair from the set of *EastEnders*, a pair of tickets to sit in the directors' box at Stamford Bridge (unfortunately not when there's actually a game on) and a signed David Beckham shirt. It's compulsory that every charity auction has a signed David Beckham shirt, but this one was different because it wasn't actually signed by David himself; no, this one was signed by 'H' who used to be in Steps, and that, Bruce reliably informed us, made it a collector's item. The final item was a DVD of *The Wizard of Oz* signed by Judy Garland. The fact that Judy Garland died about thirty years before the invention of DVDs worried me slightly, but didn't seem to bother anyone else.

The evening was turning out to be good fun and I slowly got more and more drunk on the free wine. The only downside was when Billy Fox got up to do his speech. His jokes were corny and his presenting style was laughable. He kept tripping over his words and messing up the punchlines. Why on earth do people keep comparing him to me? It didn't help when Charley leant across and said she thought I looked like a younger version of him; it's better than looking like one of the Chuckle Brothers, I suppose, but only just. He kept saying how this golf day was the most important day of his year and he went on and on for what seemed like an age about the charity, which was something to do with children or donkeys or both, I couldn't quite make it out from his inaudible mumblings.

'Speak up,' I shouted.

Charley later claimed that I added 'you boring old fart' but I have no recollection of that whatsoever. She also claimed I shouted that his rug needed a trim and offered to go and get my Flymo lawnmower, but once again I dispute this. Whatever I said, Billy was obviously thrown by the heckling and seemed to lose the thread of his speech. He started saying that even though the day had been successful, it had been marred by certain people who didn't really understand the etiquette of golf.

'Bloody Lynchy!' I shouted and this got a laugh, although admittedly only a small one. A couple of people tutted and it was at this point that Charley suggested we go home. I agreed with her and as Billy continued his speech, I whispered my goodbyes to Des Lynam. Thinking about it, I must have whispered quite loudly because he was actually sitting on the other side of the room and several people told me to be quiet. Charley and I started to creep towards the door but found the route to the exit blocked by several long tables. I looked around and there was no way out. Suddenly from somewhere deep within my drunken stupor, I had a brainwave. I grabbed Charley's hand and dragging her down with me, dived under the first of the tables. Laughing as we went, we belly-crawled our way past several pairs of shoes and a plethora of dodgy golfing trousers. We started humming the theme tune to *The Great Escape*, pinching a few calf muscles as we went and even finding time to stop and tie a pair of shoelaces together (it was obviously a small person because whoever it was, his feet didn't quite touch the ground). People were jumping and screaming and banging their knees on the underside of the table in shock and surprise. I managed to negotiate a route along the floor from one table to the next and when our faces eventually emerged, blinking into the light, we could see there was only one more table between the exit and us. I signalled for Charley to make a dash for it. In one swift movement she was up and sprinting for the door with the speed of a gazelle and the heart of a fearless warrior. I took a deep breath, stumbled from beneath the table and tripped over Ricardo Mancini's leg. With hindsight I think he may have done this deliberately, and it caused me to spin around and bump into

Sir Henry Cooper's table. As I desperately tried to regain my balance and avoid Sir Henry's outstretched arms, I inadvertently tugged at Tim Brooke-Taylor's tablecloth, dragging it with me as I fell. Chaos ensued as three bottles of wine, six half-filled glasses and countless items of cutlery crashed to the floor in a cacophony of sound. I darted for the door, dodging Rick Wakeman as I went and neatly sidestepping Peter Shilton (it's compulsory to have an ex-professional footballer at a celebrity function). As I got to where Charley was standing, I looked around and was quite surprised to see the trail of anarchy and destruction we'd left behind. There were upturned tables, celebrities throwing food at each other and Ronnie Corbett running around in circles with his shoelaces tied together. As I was about to leave, I caught Billy Fox's eye. I smiled at him, waved politely and thought I'd help alleviate the gravity of the situation by giving him my own version of his trademark wink and point. It didn't seem to work and he shot me a really evil look. Charley spotted it.

'If looks could kill,' she said.

I was too drunk for it to bother me and slept like a baby in the car on the way home.

I wonder when the next Celebrity Golf Day is.

6 FEB

Today I spent the morning in Hangover Central, the afternoon in Flashback City and the evening in the small Welsh village of Ididn'tdothatdidI?

7 FEB

Surely hangovers shouldn't last two days.

9 FEB

My brother David has just called me, which came as something of a surprise. We don't exactly see eye to eye and even though we're brothers we couldn't be more different. There's always been a personality clash: I've got one and he hasn't. I don't really like speaking to him on the phone because he always quotes the Bible to me and informs me that I'll end up burning in hell.

'I've done panto in Grimsby,' I tell him, drolly. 'Burning in hell will be a walk in the park compared to that!'

He doesn't laugh. Then again, he never laughs at any of my jokes.

Today he asked me if I'd called Dad recently, but he knew what the answer would be. Dad and I have never really got on; I thought he'd have at least called me to congratulate me when I came out of the *Celebrity Big Brother* house, but he just didn't bother; David said that he didn't even watch it. Apparently he's really angry because in the house, I'd told Su Pollard that my dad was a comedian but his style of comedy was old hat and outdated now. I did say something similar to that, but the producers edited the conversation and used it out of context. David wants me to apologize to him but I'm not going to because I don't think it's such a bad thing to say (and what's more, it's the truth).

Anyway, it's created something of a Mexican stand-off between my dad and me, and we're both so stubborn that neither of us wants to call the other one. Deep down it upsets me because, despite our differences, I know that one of the driving forces in my life has been to try to make my dad proud of me. The problem is that whatever I do, it's not quite good enough for him, and no matter how successful I am, he always manages to make out that I'm only being successful to spite him. He feels I'm rubbing his nose in it. He thinks I'm constantly trying to prove that I'm better than he is, and secretly laughing at the fact that he didn't make it as a big star. That couldn't be further from the truth. I want him to share my success and feel that his son has done well. I want him to be proud of me like any father would be, but for some reason he just doesn't seem to feel like that.

David always makes a half-hearted attempt at trying to keep the family bond going but he does it in such a pious way, it makes me want to fight against it. During our conversation he asked what I was up to at the moment, and when I told him I'd signed with the top agent in London and that there was a good chance she could make me rich and famous, he said:

'*And I say unto you: it is easier for a camel to fit through the eye of a needle than for a rich man to enter the house of God.* Matthew 19:24.'

I haven't got a clue what he meant by that. I don't want to enter the house of God and I certainly don't want a camel, I just want a flashy sports car. I sometimes think David is a little bit of a loony. Is it wrong to think that about your own brother? Then again, he probably thinks the same about me.

David then went on to tell me how awful he thinks television is these days and how even *Songs of Praise* has gone downhill. The only thing my brother has ever done remotely connected to show business is when he appeared on *Songs of Praise*, or more to the point *didn't* appear. They put him at the back of the church because they said his singing was a little 'too enthusiastic'. My guess is that it had more to do with David's mad, staring eyes. I don't think it's too much of an exaggeration to say my brother looks like an axe-murderer. I think the producers were probably worried that he would give religion a bad name. Two weeks later they filmed a *Celebrity Songs of Praise*. I'm not actually religious myself, but because it goes out prime-time on a Sunday night I thought it might be good for the profile. I managed to get in the front row and there were several close-ups of me singing 'Onward Christian Soldiers'. I don't think David's ever forgiven me for it.

'There's so much negativity on television these days,' continued David. 'I think it should be positive and serve the community more . . .'

I knew this was the beginning of one of his long rants so I started to switch off.

'I'd like to see an uplifting, feel-good show where people are given the chance to achieve their lifelong ambition . . . it should be heartening and enriching; spiritual, almost. Everyone has the opportunity to appear, everyone thinks it could be them . . .'

There was that phrase again: *it could be them*.

The problem is that David doesn't know the first thing about television; that type of programme went out of fashion years ago. The only thing like it at the moment is Billy Fox's *One Last Chance!* and everybody knows that's rubbish. I let him continue and after another ten minutes of rhetoric and Bible quotes, David finished the conversation by promising me that he would pray for my soul.

I asked him if he'd pray for a prime-time game show for me, but I don't think he was listening.

10 FEB

I don't believe it! Are you sitting comfortably? Fanfare please . . . *dur dudulur dur dur dur duuuuuuuuuuur . . .*

105

Billy Fox's *One Last Chance!* has been cancelled!

I'm thinking of throwing a party, letting off some fireworks and cracking open a bottle of champagne. I know I shouldn't wallow in someone else's misfortune but to be honest, I can't help it. Surely he knows it's the end of his career. Surely he knows it's time for him to remove his rug, wash off his perma-tan, hang up his spangly gold jacket and join all the other past-their-best game show hosts in the Bitter and Twisted Retirement Home for Sad Old Has-Beens. Maybe I'm being slightly harsh on him. I'm sure there might be a late-night spot for him hosting *Call-a-Quiz* on Channel 895 but for prime-time television, it's Goodnight Mr Fox and Hello Mr Peters.

Annie Reichman called me and told me she'd had a conversation with Michael Rimmer, the Head of Programmes at ITV (I love that I've now got an agent who can speak directly to the Head of ITV; I know for a fact that Rimmer used to avoid phone calls from Max Golinski like the plague). He told Annie that *One Last Chance!* is not going to be recommissioned, and that the network are actively looking for a new show to replace it.

Wait! It gets better.

They want format ideas to help resurrect the Saturday night schedules, and following my success on *Celebrity Big Brother* (strange that coming fourth is suddenly considered a success), he's asking independent production companies to develop ideas with me in mind.

'That's brilliant,' I said, not quite believing the holy grail was finally within my grasp. I don't know what my brother said to the Big TV Commissioner in the Sky, but whatever it was, it must have worked.

'It would be even better if we could develop our own format,' said Annie. 'The future of television is in worldwide sales and globalized packaging. What we need is a really strong brand which we can develop here and then sell into the international marketplace with you attached.'

I only understood every other word of what she was saying, but guessed that she was asking me if I had any programme ideas. I told her about *Celebrity Peacekeepers!* but she said it wasn't the right time for a show like that, with or without the exclamation mark. I mentioned my other idea, *It's All About Me!*

'What's it about?' she said.

'Me,' I said.

'Yes, but what's the actual format?'

Why can't people accept that it's just about me? Once again, I hadn't really thought of anything more than the title, but suddenly I remembered what my brother had said.

'It's an uplifting, feel-good show where I get to achieve a different lifelong ambition each week.'

There was silence on the other end of the line and I could tell Annie was thinking about it.

'It would be heartening and enriching . . . Spiritual, almost . . .'

I was starting to struggle but then I remembered what Max Golinski had said was the buzzword in television at the moment.

'And aspirational,' I added. 'It would definitely be aspirational.'

'We have to be careful,' said Annie sharply. 'It all sounds very similar to Billy Fox's *One Last Chance!*'

'Yes, but that's tired and dated and all about the public. This one's fresh and new and all about me. Hence the title.'

'Have you mentioned this to anyone else?' asked Annie.

I had to think about it. I'd told Charley the title of it at the golf day and my brother might have inadvertently helped with the actual concept, but he doesn't work in television so he doesn't count.

'I haven't told anybody,' I said.

'Good, if this thing takes off we don't want anyone else claiming they had input into it.'

Annie said the concept was a good one but she thought it needed work. She asked me to go into the office next week for a brainstorming session where we could work on the format. She also mentioned that we should set up a production company together.

Alarm bells immediately started to ring, and I thought of my conversation with Charley on the golf course. Obviously the best thing was for me to be totally honest and tell Annie that I'd already agreed to set up a production company with somebody else.

'A production company?' I said. 'Great idea.'

Annie's a very scary woman, so I'll cross that bridge when I come to it.

'With the right show and the right branding, I think you could be the person who brings Saturday night television back from the dead,' said Annie. 'This could make you very rich.'

I've never been that financially motivated, so Annie saying I could be very rich didn't really register with me. Me being the Saviour of Saturday Night Television did.

Now that's something I would like as an epitaph.

3.17 a.m.
Billy Fox must be furious.

11 FEB

I'm hosting a TV game show.

It's obviously a very popular one with a big budget. There's a large expensive set with a chrome-effect backdrop, plush velvet sofas and a shiny black floor. The shiny black floor can only mean one thing, it's Saturday night and it's prime time. Several cameras glide silently across the floor in perfect choreographed synchronicity, all of them pointing in the same direction, each one focused on the most important thing in the studio:

Me.

Members of the production team, young, talented and vibrant, each one carrying a clipboard and with headphones slung casually around their necks, gather around a monitor and watch the proceedings, full of admiration and grateful to be involved in what is obviously such a successful show.

My show.

I'm tanned and healthy, wearing a sharp dark suit and a crisp white shirt. I'm carrying a hand-held microphone and commanding the stage like the star that I am. I talk about my life, my career, my hopes and my ambitions. I love this show and the reason I love it is because it's about me.

It's All About Me.

I'm a natural at this. Born to do it. As my stream of consciousness continues, I'm getting big laughs from the studio audience and I'm on a roll. I'm funny. Really funny. Funnier than I've ever been in reality and that's how I know it's a dream.

My dream show.

Suddenly the dream changes from bright and sparkly light entertainment to dark and moody film noir. I see a pair of black-leather-gloved hands placing a leather case on the metal floor of the lighting gantry. Then, just like in a movie, the action cuts back to the TV show and I'm interviewing a contestant.

'Contestant number one, what's your name and where are you from?'

'Hello Simon,' she says in a strong Midlands accent. 'My name's Cheryl and I'm from Dudley.'

'Sorry?'

'From Dudley.'

'I heard what you said, I'm just sorry!'

A tidal wave of laughter washes over me and I know I can do no wrong. But what's this? I seem to have two different dreams running at the same time. I see the gloved hands again and this time they open the leather case to reveal a soft red velvet interior, which neatly cushions a black and silver Heckler & Koch sniper rifle, broken down into three pieces.

'So let's meet our next contestant. Contestant number two, what's your name please?'

Twist. The gun barrel is slipped into position.

'Hello Simon, my name is Peter Van-Hyer.'

Click. The telescopic sight is slid into place.

'Ah Mr Van Hyer, I know your brother . . . Hertz!'

Clunk. The magazine clip is snapped into its hold.

'*Hertz Van Hire*, dear,' I say, explaining the gag to the only member of the audience who isn't convulsed with laughter. 'Oh suit yourself!'

The butt of the rifle is placed against a leather-jacketed shoulder and a pair of hate-filled eyes blink away a bead of sweat.

'I also know your other brother, *Budget*, and your little-known sister, *Thrifty*!'

As the audience erupts in an explosion of hilarity, I see

myself in the cross hairs of the telescopic sights and at this moment I realize this isn't two different dreams, it's the same dream and in it, somebody's about to kill me.

There's a finger on the trigger, a licking of the lips.

Suddenly, a telephone rings loudly and it makes the sniper jump.

BANG!

The scoreboard behind me explodes. Confusion. A moving camera shot. I'm not too sure what to do.

'Well, we seem to be having a slight problem with the scoreboard . . . we'll try to get that fixed . . .'

BANG!

The podium in front of me smashes and bursts into flames.

'Oh my God!'

BANG!

There goes the toaster on the prize carousel.

BANG!

Pandemonium in the studio. People shouting, screaming and running for cover. Ever the pro, I do what comes naturally. I put my finger to my earpiece and continue to broadcast.

'Somebody seems to be shooting at me on live television,' I inform the viewing millions. 'This has been happening to me a lot lately.'

Still the telephone rings, louder now, almost deafening.

'Will somebody answer that bloody phone!' I scream.

BANG!

More confusion. A camera whip-pans along the audience, looking for the sniper. I notice movement high up in the lighting gantry. My dream-vision fast-tilts up, crash-zooms in and freeze-frames on the face of the would-be assassin. I recognize him immediately. It's a face I've known for years.

A face I've loved and hated in equal measure. A face that many people have said is very similar to my own. I realize I'm in his sights and there's no escape, nowhere to run, nowhere to hide. I'm frozen to the spot. As he pulls the trigger and the bullet heads for my heart, Billy Fox gives me one of his trademark winks.

'NOOOOOOOOOOOOOOOOOO!' I screamed as I woke up, panting and covered in a sheen of sweat. I was lying on my sofa in a pair of boxer shorts, surrounded by empty beer cans and pizza boxes. The phone was ringing and I picked up the receiver and placed it to my ear.

'Simon?' said the voice on the other end of the line.

I was still in a state of shock from the dream. The television was on in the corner, the volume turned up to full blast. My face filled the screen and I realized I must have drifted off while watching videotapes of my old daytime game show, *Simon Says*.

'Simon?'

I was surprised at how much younger and thinner I looked in those days. I vowed to lay off the beer for a while and stop eating all the junk food.

'Simon . . . it's Charley. Are you OK? You haven't had the Billy Fox dream again, have you?'

'He tried to assassinate me on live television.'

'That's awful,' said Charley.

'Do you think so?'

'Yes, he should use poison. Much more subtle. What's that noise?'

'Sorry?'

'That noise?'

'What noise?'

'That noise in the background?'

I quickly tried to turn the volume down with the remote

112

control but to no effect. The button seemed to be stuck.

'Simon, what exactly were you watching when you fell asleep and had this dream?'

'What? Erm . . . yes I was watching . . . erm . . .'

'Simon?'

I panicked. Charley would never let me hear the end of it if she knew I'd been watching old videos of myself again. Especially if she knew I'd been doing it in my boxer shorts.

'I'm watching porn!' I screamed in desperation.

'I can hear applause.'

'It's Japanese porn, they'll clap at anything.'

'Simon, I can hear your voice.'

I paused.

'Yes . . . erm . . . I did a voice-over for a Japanese porn film.'

'Simon?'

'I was young, I needed the money.'

'Simon?'

'What?'

'You're watching old tapes of *Simon Says* again, aren't you?'

'It relieves the stress.'

'You'll go blind.'

Some people will probably think that it's an outrageous act of vanity for me to be watching myself on television, but I want to make it clear that I do this purely for research purposes. I believe it helps me to learn my craft, especially if I view the tapes over and over again. I particularly find that using the jog-shuttle slow motion really helps me to analyse my performance.

'Listen,' said Charley. 'I just want to make sure you're OK for this meeting tomorrow morning. I'll come over to your flat and we'll sort everything out. I'm really excited about it, Simon, I think us setting up a production company is the right thing to do.'

This was obviously the moment to tell Charley that Annie Reichman has asked me to set up a production company with her.

'Me too,' I said. 'I can't wait.'

'Now go back to watching yourself on television and make sure Billy Fox isn't hiding behind the sofa. See you about elevenish.'

As she put the phone down I suddenly felt very excited about seeing Charley. I also checked behind the sofa just in case.

1.32 a.m.
Surely I shouldn't feel this excited about meeting Charley tomorrow morning?

2.46 a.m.
Surely she's only a mate?

12 FEB

'If we're going to do this we've got to do it properly,' said Charley, all brisk and businesslike. 'This morning I had a meeting with an accountant who said it's more tax-efficient to set up as a limited company. To do that we need to open a business bank account and register the name at Companies House. We'll both be the company directors and if it turns over a profit we'll take a fifty-fifty split of the dividends.'

God I love it when she talks dirty.

We were sitting at the breakfast table in my flat and in front of her, Charley had a slim leather briefcase crammed with pieces of paper. She'd obviously been doing a lot of research and was taking it all very seriously. I know Charley well and I can tell she's determined to turn this production-company idea into reality. As she talked me through what the accountant had said, I couldn't stop staring at her. She'd obviously made a real effort with her clothes. Whether it was for me or the accountant I couldn't be sure, but she was wearing a dark two-piece pinstripe suit and underneath was a white V-neck T-shirt, which showed off the remainder of a winter tan and offered an occasional tantalizing glimpse of her cleavage. She'd had her hair straightened and highlighted and it framed her face with a golden glow. She wore glasses, which I'd never seen before; they really suited her and seemed to accentuate her emerald-green eyes. She looked stylish and sharp, every inch the young, successful independent producer.

She also looked very sexy.

It made me wish I'd made more of an effort, but as I'd only managed to drag myself out of bed five minutes before she arrived I hadn't had time for a shower, so I was still padding around in my tatty old dressing gown and slippers. I offered her a beer but she refused, saying it was too early for her. Not wanting to appear like I needed alcohol at eleven o'clock in the morning, I only poured myself half a glass.

'Right,' she said. 'Let's get the important stuff out of the way first. What are we going to call the company?'

'Simon Peters Productions,' I said without missing a beat. Charley laughed, even though she knew I wasn't joking.

'I thought we could do something where we combine our two names,' she said. 'Maybe use our middle names? Mine's Catherine.'

'Oh no,' I said. 'My middle name's awful.'

'Why are people always so embarrassed about their middle name?' asked Charley. 'Whenever you ask someone what it is, they always giggle, go red and refuse to tell you as if it's the most stupid name in the world. And then, when they eventually tell you what it is, it's something really dull like Susan. So what's your middle name?'

'Susan,' I said.

Charley laughed at that. I seem to make her laugh a lot lately.

'Simon Susan Peters?'

'My mother had a wicked sense of humour.'

'What is it really?'

'Thomas.'

'That's your dad's name, isn't it?'

'He wanted it to be my first name so I'd be known as Tommy Jnr; I think that tells you a lot about my dad's ego. Luckily my mum wouldn't let him, thank God.'

'So what have we got? Catherine Thomas . . . Not very exciting, is it? Sounds like an author of crappy romantic novels.'

'I've got it,' I screamed, barely able to contain my excitement. 'You take the Tom from Thomas and the Cat from Catherine. Join them together: TomCat Productions.'

There was silence.

'That's crap,' said Charley, bursting my balloon, raining on my parade and weeing on my bonfire, all at the same time. 'Maybe we could use our porn names.'

'Porn names?'

'Yes. You take the name of your first pet and your mother's maiden name, and put them together. We had a rabbit called Bunty and my mum's maiden name was Hunter, so my porn name would be Bunty Hunter. Not a very good name for a production company but quite funny all the same. What was your first pet called?'

'Little Baby Jesus.'

Charley just stared at me.

'It was a Siberian hamster. My brother named him – he looked like he had stigmata on his little paws. Long story, don't ask. My mum's maiden name was Smith.'

'Little Baby Jesus Smith Productions? I don't think that would get us many commissions. Plus the fact it wouldn't fit on the credits.'

We both stared at the table in silence.

'Simon Peters Productions?' I suggested again, thinking it was worth another try.

Charley ignored me.

'What about Ego Productions?' she said.

I don't know where she got the idea from but it certainly worked for me. We both nodded our heads in silent agreement.

'Ego Productions it is, then.'

'Do I have to sign anything?' I asked.

'No, I'll get all the formal paperwork together and we'll sort it out next week.'

Having finished the first can of beer, I went to the fridge and grabbed another. It's not every day you set up a production company, and I thought it was something that was worthy of celebration. As I sat back down I couldn't help noticing that Charley was staring at my waist area. At first I thought she was checking me out, but then I realized that my dressing gown had come undone and I wasn't wearing any boxer shorts.

'Excited about this production company, are you?' Charley asked with a great big smirk on her face.

'Very cold in this flat, isn't it?' I said, covering myself

up and quickly taking another slug of beer. I desperately wanted to change the subject. 'So let's talk about some programme ideas, shall we?'

'What about *Dressing Gowns from Hell!*?' said Charley.

'Very funny.'

'*Confessions of a Serial Flasher!*'

'Any more?'

'*When Penis Reductions Go Wrong!*'

I let her enjoy her moment of hilarity.

'All right,' she said, suddenly clicking into business mode. 'We need to write up some of our ideas into proper formats. I've been thinking about *It's All About Me!* It's good but I think we need to change the title.'

'That's the best bit,' I protested.

'Yes, but I think it should be all about the public. I like the aspirational thing, but I think it should be the viewers who get to achieve their lifelong ambition . . .' She paused. 'Not you.'

I knew she was right but I didn't want to give it up without a fight.

'But that makes it the same as Billy Fox's *One Last Chance!*' I said.

'Yeah but that's been cancelled now, and the difference is we broadcast live and give it a bit of a twist.'

'What's the twist?'

'The viewers don't know who's going to be getting the chance to fulfil their dreams. The beauty of it is, they're sitting at home watching the TV, there's a knock at the door and suddenly they're appearing on the show. One minute they're viewers, the next they're contestants.'

Charley handed me a piece of paper with some suggested titles: *Maybe, Just Maybe*; *DreamTicket*; *Dreams Incorporated* and *Saturday Night Dreaming*.

'I think they're all good,' she said. 'But personally, I don't think they quite sum it up. It's got to be a title that encapsulates the idea that when they're sitting at home watching the show, it could be them appearing next.'

'I've got it,' I said.

I leant over to the phone and rummaged through the large pile of paperwork next to it. I found the scrappy piece of notepaper which I'd used when I scribbled down the title that Max Golinski had suggested a few weeks ago.

'*It Could Be You.*'

'Perfect,' said Charley. 'Well done, Mr Peters.'

I was about to tell her that it was actually Max's idea but then suddenly, with blinding clarity, almost as if I could see the future, I realized that if the show was made and was a success, Max might be able to claim that he had input into it. I needed to change the title slightly.

'I think it should be *It Could Be You* with an exclamation mark,' I said, hoping this would do the trick but knowing deep down that it probably wouldn't.

'Well . . . *all the best light entertainment shows of the last thirty years have exclamation marks,*' said Charley, in what was more than a passable impression of me. '*It Could Be You* with an exclamation mark it is, then.'

'Great. So how's the show going to work?' I asked.

'Viewers phone in to nominate someone who they think deserves to have their dreams come true.'

'Brilliant.'

'On the live show, you're in the studio and you surprise four different people at four different houses by having camera crews turn up on their doorsteps.'

'Excellent.'

'Throughout the course of the programme we keep cutting back to the different households, and through

119

a series of elimination rounds you slowly get rid of the contestants until there's just one remaining.'

Charley paused.

'And then what?' I said.

'Well, that person gets to achieve their lifelong ambition.'

'Genius!'

I love this sort of meeting when we're both cooking on gas and bouncing ideas off each other.

'What else?'

'Well, we need a game how element to help us eliminate the other three contestants. Maybe they have to complete a series of tasks or answer general knowledge questions, that sort of thing.'

'I'll work on it,' I said.

Charley looked at her watch and said that she had to leave. I felt disappointed and offered to make her some lunch.

'Difficult as it is to resist you in that dressing gown and slippers, unfortunately I've got a meeting with a financial advisor and then I'm going to see about getting some headed paper printed.'

I walked her to the door and as I opened it, she turned around and pecked me on the cheek. Charley's pecked me on the cheek a thousand times before, but this time it was different; maybe it was my imagination but I couldn't help thinking that she held the kiss for a moment longer than usual.

Did she do that deliberately?

Her lips felt soft against my skin and a drift of her perfume danced delicately around my senses. As she slowly pulled her head back, her hair gently brushed against my cheek and the tingling sensation of it sent a shock wave pulsating to my nerve endings. Goosebumps erupted all over my skin and I felt a cool tremor shoot through my entire body.

'Wow,' I said. 'I felt a real shiver when you did that.'

'You would do,' she said. 'Your dressing gown's come undone again.'

I quickly pulled it together and tied the belt in a double knot. She gave me another peck and told me to call her if I came up with any good ideas for the show. After she'd gone I felt hot, sweaty and light-headed. My heart was thumping and I was so excited that I couldn't stop myself. I immediately went to the back of the video cabinet and pulled out one of my special videos . . .

Two episodes of *Simon Says* and a box of Kleenex later, I'd finally managed to calm down. I felt ready to give my full concentration to *It Could Be You!* By now, I was really starting to like the idea. Although the show was no longer all about me, there was obviously going to be lots of scope for interaction with the public, and that's a real forte of mine. I also liked the idea that Charley trusted me to come up with the game show element. If there's one thing I'm good at, it's coming up with unique and imaginative ideas.

13 FEB

Who can say where truly great inspiration comes from? Who can say where each individual finds their muse, where brilliance is conceived, where genius is born? All I know is that mine hit me in the middle of the night. From out of the darkness came a blinding flash of creativity and I saw the name blazing before me in huge 20-foot-high neon lights.

Ricardo Mancini!

That wasn't the idea, you understand, that's just who I nicked it from.

I'd been hitting my head against a brick wall all night trying to come up with a truly original idea (it's actually a lot more difficult than you think). I suddenly remembered that Mancini had been at the Celebrity Golf Day at Wentworth. The only thing we have in common is a mutual hatred of each other, but in true showbiz fashion we always pretend to be the best of friends. In the locker room, as we were getting ready for the evening's entertainment, I asked him what he was up to at the moment and he said he was 'writing', which basically meant he was unemployed. When I asked him what he was working on, he told me that it was a format idea for a nostalgia quiz called *The Retro Show*. His idea was to have lots of questions about the toys we used to play with when we were kids, mixed together with clips of old TV shows from the 1970s.

'People love nostalgia,' he said to me. 'They can't get enough of it.'

PING! went the cartoon-comedy light bulb that appeared above my head when I remembered this.

'People love nostalgia,' I said to Charley on the phone, when I called her first thing this morning. 'They can't get enough of it.'

'Good idea,' she said.

'We could have lots of really cool questions about sweets and toys from the seventies and eighties, and lots of clips of old adverts and TV shows. We could call it the Retro Round.'

This made me feel a lot better. Because I'd opened it up to the eighties, added 'sweets' and 'old adverts' and changed the name from *The Retro Show* to Retro Round, technically I wasn't stealing Ricardo's idea. This is what we call 'redevelopment', and in the television industry it's perfectly legal. Everyone does it.

'Retro Round?' said Charley. 'Yeah, I like the sound of that.'

'Maybe we should meet up and have a chat about it.'

I wasn't sure if I was saying this because I wanted to discuss the idea, or just because I wanted to see her again. Luckily, Charley sounded really keen and we agreed to meet in Soho House at lunchtime. At first she suggested meeting in the King's Arms on Poland Street, but that's just a normal pub, and I had to remind her that following *Celebrity Big Brother* I was too famous to go into normal pubs now.

'But Soho House is really showbizzy and full of egotistical wankers,' protested Charley.

'I always feel really at home there.'

Her silence said it all.

In the end I managed to persuade her, and when we got there we sat in two big leather sofas on the second floor. I put my baseball cap on and pulled it down low over my eyes to make it difficult for anyone to recognize me. After about half an hour it became clear that nobody could recognize me, so I took it off again to make it easier for them.

I ordered a couple of drinks. Charley had a white wine which cost £4.80, and I had a large gin and tonic that came in at a whopping £7.50. At least with prices like that I wasn't going to get drunk.

We started talking about the Retro Round and both agreed it was a great idea. This led on to a discussion about nostalgia, and we spent the afternoon reminiscing about all the great things that we remembered from our childhood (although to be perfectly honest it was me who did most of the talking). I'm only four years older than Charley, so it's strange that some of the things she mentioned I'd never heard of, and a lot of the stuff I got so enthusiastic about made her just look at me with a puzzled expression on her face. We still had a great time, though, and I got particularly animated talking about toys that I'd desperately wanted for Christmas when I was a kid. I got a piece of paper and a pen from the waitress and insisted that we make a list.

'Chopper bikes, Raleigh racers, Grifters, Scalextric, Hungry Hippos, Buckaroo, Operation, Mousetrap, Mastermind, Cross-fire, Tin-pan Alley, Ker-Plunk, Etch-a-Sketch, Rubik's cube, frisbees, Clackers, Space Invaders, Atari computerized tennis that you could play on your telly . . . beep . . . beep . . . beep . . . be-beep.' I made the sound so Charley would know exactly what I was talking about. 'Action Man with moving eyes and gripping hands (or was it the other way round?) Evil Knievel Stunt Bike, Panini football stickers of Kevin Keegan and John Toshack, Airfix models, Top Trumps, Swingball, catapults, cap guns, spud guns, pogo sticks, Space Hoppers, *The Blue Peter Annual 1978* and Rolf Harris' Stylophone, which never sounded as good in real life as it did on the advert. Come to think of it, it sounded crap on the advert.'

'My Little Pony!' said Charley, and I smiled, giving her a nod of recognition. I didn't actually add it to the list, though, because it didn't get me excited the way real nostalgia should. I guess that's the thing about nostalgia: it's very personal. One man's nostalgia is another man's long-forgotten memory. The greatest nostalgia is the really trivial stuff.

'Sweets!' I said. 'Spangles, Space Dust, fizz bombs, lemfizzes, Flying Saucers, Sherbet Dip, Refreshers, Pacers, Chewits . . .'

'Parma violets,' said Charley.

'Yeah but Parma violets were girls' sweets,' I said. 'I'm talking about real sweets here: Texan Bars ("sure is a mighty chew"), Milky Bars (I wanted to be the Milky Bar Kid), Curly-Wurlys (they were much bigger in those days, of course), Cadbury's Creme Eggs (they were four times as big), Marathons (not Snickers), cola bottles, black jacks, liquorice imps, liquorice pipes, chocolate cigars, sweet cigarettes (you wouldn't believe how cool I looked with a sweet cigarette in my hand. Why on earth did they stop making those?), traffic-light lollies, gobstoppers, aniseed balls, pineapple chunks, cough drops, herbal twists, cola cubes, fruit salads, rhubarb and custard . . .'

'Rhubarb and Custard? That was a kids' TV show, wasn't it?' said Charley.

'Kids' TV!' I said. '*Bagpuss, Pipkins, Morph, The Flumps, The Herbs, The Clangers, The Magic Roundabout, Hector's House, Fingerbobs, Captain Pugwash, Rentaghost, Rainbow, Rod, Jane and Freddy, Jackanory, Camberwick Green, Trumpton* – Pugh, Pugh, Barney McGrew, Cuthbert, Dibble and Grub – *Play School, PlayAway,* Floella Benjamin, Brian Cant . . .'

'Legend!' said Charley. 'It can't be easy carving out a career in show business with a name like Cant. It's crying out to be misspelt.'

'Yes, he's just an apostrophe away from being Brian Can't.'

'And a vowel away from being something completely different.'

She lost me there so I carried on regardless.

'*Crackerjack!*' I shouted.

I paused but she didn't say anything.

'You're supposed to shout *Crackerjack*!'

'*Wacaday!*' she said, obviously trying to get the conversation back to her own frame of reference.

125

'*Jim'll Fix It*,' I said, wanting to keep it within my own. 'Classic television. I wrote in but they never replied.'

'What was it you wanted to do?'

I paused. I didn't want Charley to know that I'd asked Jim to fix it for me to meet Billy Fox.

'I wanted to be on *The Muppet Show*,' I lied.

'*The Muppet Show*!' she screamed, obviously relieved that we finally had a show in common. '*Ma-na-ma-na doo doo do do do . . .*'

I joined in and we sang it at the tops of our voices. By this time, you understand, it was about six o'clock in the evening and having forgotten how expensive the drinks were, I'd ordered a couple of bottles of wine and we were drinking them on empty stomachs. Admittedly Charley only drank two glasses, but she still seemed quite tipsy. At some point during the conversation she had moved next to me on my sofa, and I couldn't help noticing that whenever she said anything to me, she touched my arm. Occasionally she'd leave her hand there and would only take it away to pick up her glass of wine. Subconsciously I started doing the same, and pretty soon we were touching each other's arms continuously and giving them a little squeeze every time we laughed. And we laughed an awful lot.

We were probably being quite loud and raucous, but when you're young and famous and sitting in Soho House, that's what you have to be. The singing of the *Muppets* soon led on to other TV theme tunes including *Hawaii Five-0*, *du du du du duu duuuu, du du du duu duuuu*; *The Banana Splits*, *tra la laa, la la la laa, tra la laa, la la la laaa* and the famous raunchy guitar riff from the beginning of *Grange Hill*, *DA DUM DANG DAANGGG*! Before long we were belting out a series of songs made famous by TV adverts, a selection of which were the song from the fudge advert (little boy with a high-pitched voice singing about a finger of fudge), the song from the McCain's Oven Chips advert (a load of builders in the back of a van hoping 'It's chips, it's chips') and the song from the Smash advert (four Martian puppets singing 'For Mash get Smash!'). We both did the metallic Martian laugh and it went on for about five minutes.

'What has a hazelnut in every bite?' sang Charley.

'Squirrel shit!' I shouted and we did the Martian laugh again.

Before we knew it, it was eleven o'clock at night. One thing I've noticed when I'm drinking quite heavily (which I seem to do a lot lately) is that time just seems to disappear. By this point I was feeling quite drunk, and Charley reminded me that she had to work in the morning. She still works on *Coffee Morning with Mike and Sue*, but the show has been coming in for a lot of criticism from the press lately (Mike in particular). Charley has a feeling it's not going to be recommissioned, and I think that's one of the reasons she wants us to set up our own production company.

I asked for the drinks bill and when it arrived I was shocked to see that it came to £146.53. I asked Charley if we could put it on the company expense account, but she pointed out that we didn't have a company yet, let alone an expense account.

'We will have this time next week, though,' she said and laughed excitedly.

I felt it would have ruined the moment to tell her about Annie Reichman wanting me to set up a production company with her, so I paid the bill and we stepped into the cool night air, laughing and giggling like two teenagers on a first date.

Once we were outside there was a slightly awkward

moment when we didn't know what to do next. Even though Charley had to work in the morning, it was obvious that neither of us wanted the evening to end. We stood there in silence for what seemed an age, shuffling our feet and looking at our watches. I started to say something at exactly the same time as Charley.

'Sorry,' I said.

'No, you go first,' said Charley.

I couldn't remember what I was going to say.

There was a pause.

'Good fun today, wasn't it?'

'Great fun.'

There was another pause.

'We must do it again sometime.'

'Definitely.'

Silence. I think it's good if men and women can have pauses in their conversation without feeling they have to fill them with inane small talk.

'Cold tonight, isn't it?'

'Freezing.'

'I suppose you'd better call me a cab.'

'You're a cab,' I said. 'Whey hey! Morecambe and Wise, 1978.'

Charley laughed, and using the humour as a shield against the possibility of rejection, I seized the opportunity.

'You can come back to mine if you want . . . just for a coffee, of course.'

I've asked Charley back to my flat a million times before, but this time, just like yesterday's peck on the cheek, it was different. This time I couldn't help making it sound like a loaded suggestion.

'Simon Peters, you're not getting all flirty with me, are you?'

She said it in a way that made me think she rather hoped that I was.

I looked up to the sky and noticed there was a full moon. It was a shimmering soft milky-white colour, and it looked bigger and closer than I'd ever seen it before.

'Make a wish,' said Charley, taking my hands in hers.

She closed her eyes and I did the same. I started whispering under my breath; I wished harder than I've ever wished for anything in my life. When I opened my eyes I saw Charley staring at me with a big smile on her face.

'What did you wish for?'

'I can't tell you that,' I said. 'It won't come true.'

'You wished for me to kiss you, didn't you?'

Damn.

'How did you know that?'

'I heard you muttering it under your breath. *Pleaseletuskiss pleaseletuskiss pleaseletuskiss.*'

'Was I that loud?'

'I think the whole of Soho heard you. The manager of that strip club came over and asked if you could keep the noise down.'

I felt foolish and embarrassed and muttered something about finding a black cab to take her home.

'I wished the same,' said Charley, and at that moment the moon started to work its magic.

She took my arm and I knew this was it. My head began to spin and I was breathing hard. She gently pulled me towards her and everything blurred into slow motion. As her lips touched mine I took a deep breath and London came to a standstill. A shower of roses fell from the sky and covered the streets in a carpet of petals, the fragrant scent rising up and swirling around our bodies. The city stopped as she opened her mouth and the world fell silent as her soft tongue came in search of mine. It was the perfect kiss, sexy but gentle, passionate but tender. Just Charley O'Neil and me under a beautiful moon.

Nothing could spoil that moment of paradise.

Nothing, that is, apart from the fact that I hadn't breathed for about a minute and a half. Like a wrestler admitting submission, I tapped Charley on the shoulder to let her know I needed a break. I opened my eyes, pulled my head back and took a gulp of air. It proved to be a big mistake. In that moment, paradise disappeared and I crashed back into the reality of London life: noise, music, sirens, car horns, shouting, screaming and whistling. There were workers, clubbers, drinkers, tramps, prostitutes, rent boys and drug dealers. The stench of urine and kebabs filled the air and the carpet of petals had vanished, only to be replaced by a layer of litter and dog turds.

I looked at Charley but I didn't know what to say. What can you say when you've just spent an intense 90 seconds playing tonsil tennis with someone who, up until that point, had just been your best friend?

'Come on,' I said. 'I'll find you a cab to take you home.'

I didn't want to push my luck and have Charley thinking I was trying to take advantage of her, so I thought this was the proper thing to say. I wanted to show her that I was a gentleman and what had just happened wasn't going to affect our friendship. Just because she'd kissed me, it didn't mean she wanted to take things any further. She'd been my friend for ten years and if there's one thing I knew about Charley O'Neil, it's that she wasn't that type of girl.

She looked at me and smiled.

'I thought we were going back to your place for a shag,' she said.

14 FEB

As I stumbled my way towards consciousness, I slowly became aware that something was different. The dull thud of pain in my temples informed me I was suffering from another hangover, but that wasn't it; I was getting used to that feeling these days and I'd taught myself to ignore it. By this point I hadn't opened my eyes, so I knew it was one of my other senses notifying me of change. Taste maybe? My mouth was dry and the sour metallic tang of stale alcohol was a flavour I was familiar with, so I knew it wasn't that. Was it the sound that was strange? I listened hard, but the continuous growl of traffic from Chiswick High Road and the excited squeals of schoolchildren in the nearby playground was the same as it ever was. Perhaps it was the smell? I inhaled slowly. That was it: my room smelt different. It was sweet and fresh and it took me a couple of moments to realize it was the enticing scent of a woman's fragrance.

I opened my eyes, and the first thing I saw on the bedside cabinet was a piece of lined paper which had been folded in two. It had obviously been ripped from a notepad.

Happy Valentine's Day was scrawled on the front in red biro. A large love heart had been drawn around it with an arrow protruding from the side. I leant over, picked up the piece of paper and opened it. Inside was a big question mark. Maybe it was the hangover or maybe I wasn't fully awake, but for a moment I wondered who it was from.

Then it hit me.

Oh my God.

I'd slept with Charley.

Again.

I say *again* because we'd slept together when we first

131

became mates. It was one of those awful drunken fumbling occasions, the sort of thing that happens when you're single and you first become friends with a member of the opposite sex. It helps you decide between 'yes, I quite liked that, let's have another go', 'no, that didn't feel right, let's just be friends' and 'God, that was awful, I never want to see you again'. Some people have several drunken fumblings before they find the answer, but with Charley and me it only ever happened the once.

Until now.

Last night was different. Yes, in many ways it was still a drunken fumble (having drunk three bottles of wine and four gin and tonics, I wasn't performing at my physical peak, you understand), but that seemed irrelevant. It *felt* different. It felt real; it felt as though it actually meant something.

Charley had obviously left early in the morning while I was still asleep, but there was an indentation in the pillow where her head had been, and when I spotted a long strand of golden hair it made me feel all gooey inside. I haven't felt like that for a long time; in fact, I don't think I've ever felt like it. I've always been so driven to make a success of my career that I've never had much time for relationships; I've always felt slightly wary of them. I've never let anyone open the door to my heart in case they didn't like what they found in there, or more importantly, in case *I* didn't like what they found. I think that's why, in the past, I've always gone for the unattainable: the supermodels, the actresses and the dancers who are far beyond my reach. These are the girls who are far too interested in themselves to ever want to get too deep and personal with me. My theory has always been: if they're not too close, they can't hurt you. I don't feel like that with Charley though, I want her to be close. I want to open the door and let her in.

Surely I shouldn't feel like this?

Surely this should be the classic scenario where you sleep with your best friend and then wake up the next day and immediately start regretting it. Surely there should be a feeling of awkwardness, which eats away at the friendship until there's nothing left except spiteful words and bitter memories. But there is no awkwardness and I don't regret it, and judging by the note that Charley left, she doesn't regret it either. I picked up the piece of paper again and noticed she'd written something on the back.

Dinner it said with another big question mark.

I texted her immediately.

I say *immediately*; it actually took me a long time to compose. I was entering unknown territory in my relationship with Charley, and I wanted to get the tone of the text just right. It needed to be flirtatious without being presumptuous, suggestive but not smarmy. Every word was vitally important and I didn't want anything to be misinterpreted. I agonized for at least thirty minutes on how many kisses I should add. I tried it with one kiss, but that's what we used when we were just friends. Two kisses seemed incomplete so I eventually settled on three. Because it was Valentine's Day, I toyed with the idea of adding a mysterious and sexy pet name at the end of it. I tried Cuddles, Snugglebum and Lover Boy, but none of them looked right. At one point I nearly added PS. U WER GR8 LST NGHT but I thought it sounded a little sycophantic (plus I couldn't be 100 per cent sure that she had been that GR8).

After forty-five minutes of typing and retyping (so much for texts being a fast and spontaneous form of communication), the message I eventually settled on was:

DINNER AT MINE 8PM? SIMON (PETERS) XXX

With hindsight the 'Peters' part probably wasn't that necessary, but I wanted her to be sure it was from me. Charley obviously didn't suffer from the same texting anxiety because she replied immediately with:

C U THERE X

I noticed that she only used one kiss. I hope I hadn't been too pushy.

I really wanted to spoil Charley, so I spent the rest of the day preparing for her arrival. I started by cleaning my flat from top to bottom. I often sympathize with those people who appear on that TV show, *Living in Squalor.* Obviously, I'm nowhere near as bad as they are, but I don't mind living with a bit of mess as long as it's my own. Having said that, I didn't want Charley to think that I was dirty, so I cleaned absolutely everything. I hoovered with my brand-new top-of-the-range Dyson (the suction is excellent!), dusted, polished, mopped, rubbed, scrubbed, brushed and bleached. I even cleaned the grill pan, which is something I haven't done in the four years that I've lived here. That's not as bad as it sounds, by the way, as I don't think I've ever actually grilled anything. On second thoughts, maybe it *is* bad because it means all that burnt-on grease was somebody else's.

When I'd finished, I went to Waitrose to buy ingredients for the meal I was planning on cooking. I quite like going to my local Waitrose because that's where all the other celebrities who live in the area go to shop. In the past week alone, I've seen Bill Oddie, Lorraine Chase and Christopher Biggins in there. I even saw Dale Winton in the cheese section once, but I think I was the only one who appreciated the irony of it. If a bomb dropped on our local

Waitrose on a Saturday afternoon, it could set the British pantomime industry back several years.

I'm not really a very good cook but if there's one thing I've learnt from my limited experience, it's this: if you cook a meal for a girl, they'll be impressed and stay impressed for a very long time. Even when they realize it's the only meal you can actually cook, they still appreciate you trying. The one meal I can cook is spaghetti Bolognese, but I do it with a totally unique twist. As well as minced beef and onions, I also add some red wine and garlic. It's bloody gorgeous, honest. I'm thinking of writing my own cookbook.

I wanted this to be a Valentine's Day that Charley would never forget. I wanted to do something romantic but also something totally original. Then I had an idea . . .

Charley rang the doorbell at eight o'clock on the dot. I was slightly nervous about seeing her again. What if the whole thing had been a big mistake? What if she was embarrassed about what happened and regretted it all? What if I didn't fancy her any more and worse still, what if she didn't fancy me? Luckily, all my fears were laid to rest when I opened the door. Charley looked stunning in a short cream jacket, brown trousers and matching boots. She'd obviously made a real effort but without going over the top. This was typical Charley. Sexy yet modest; casual but cool. As a joke I'd worn my tatty old dressing gown and slippers.

'Hello, TV's Simon Peters,' she said, handing me a bottle of wine. 'You look nice.'

'I didn't realize we were dressing up,' I said.

In one fluid action, I undid the belt and whipped open my dressing gown to reveal my tuxedo and dicky bow underneath. I felt like James Bond as I slowly let the gown fall to the floor. I felt even cooler when I whipped out a single red rose and handed it to Charley.

'Happy Valentine's Day,' I said, kissing her on the cheek.

'That's really sweet,' she said, taking the rose and stepping inside. She sounded as if she meant it. 'Something smells nice. It's not spaghetti Bolognese by any chance, is it? What a surprise.'

I'd forgotten that this wasn't like a normal first date and that I'd cooked for Charley on several occasions, always the same meal. Luckily I knew she loved it.

I lit a couple of candles and opened Charley's bottle of wine, but I was determined to go easy and not get too drunk. I wanted to enjoy the night just as it was. I feared we might be slightly awkward together and self-conscious over what had happened, but it wasn't like that all. It was just how it always had been, only better. We were relaxed and comfortable in each other's company and it felt as if we'd been 'a couple' for a long time. In many ways, we had. We laughed and joked just as before, but now we did it with little looks and touches and playful nudges. Charley still took the piss out of me but I didn't mind (she wouldn't have been Charley if she hadn't). In return, she had to listen to me talking about my celebrity lifestyle and my hopes and fears for the future of my career. We also talked about a lot of stuff we hadn't discussed before. Charley said she'd eventually like to give up television and could imagine herself living in a remote village on the east coast of Australia and working as an artist: painting landscapes, sculpturing and making pottery. I told her I'd like to present my own Saturday night TV show. OK, I've probably mentioned that to her a couple of times in the past, but tonight's the first time I've gone into so much detail.

Towards the end of the evening, Charley proposed a toast.

'To Ego Productions,' she said, raising her glass. 'Showing the world how to make great television.'

She stretched out her hand, which I shook enthusiastically.

'Ego Productions,' I echoed.

'And to Simon Thomas Susan Peters, because this is going to be your year.'

She raised her glass again.

'Our year,' I said, and she seemed to like that. 'To Simon Thomas Susan Peters and Charley Catherine O'Neil.'

'Charlotte Catherine O'Neil,' said Charley, correcting me. 'You might as well know my terrible dark secret now. My first name is really Charlotte.'

I'd known her all this time and I'd always assumed her name was just Charley. I liked the fact I was still finding out new stuff about her even after ten years.

'But of course if you ever call me that I'll be forced to kill you.'

'I wouldn't dare, Charlotte.'

Charley was out of her seat in a flash and shot to my side of the table, but I was too quick for her and darted out of the kitchen and into the hallway, shrieking with laughter as I went. She was hot on my heels and in one swift movement she tripped me over and dived on to my back, causing us to crash on to the stairway in a breathless heap. This started a frenzied bout of tickling, which led to uncontrollable hysterics on both our parts. As the laughter subsided I grabbed Charley's hand.

'Come with me,' I said. 'I've got something to show you.'

'It's not the framed photograph of you and Chris Tarrant again, is it?'

I didn't say a word. Instead, I slowly led her upstairs and opened the door to my bedroom.

'My God!' she screamed, when she saw what was inside. 'That's not over the top at all. Where did you get that idea from?'

I wasn't sure whether to tell her. But then I thought, why not?

'When you kissed me last night I imagined a shower of roses falling from the sky and covering the streets.'

If the streets of London couldn't be carpeted with petals, I'd made sure the floor of my bedroom was. I'd bought twelve dozen red roses from the florists and scattered the petals all over the room. Charley looked genuinely touched. Normally she'd have made a really cutting comment about the whole idea being a bit cheesy, or said something cynical like, 'When you kissed me, I was just watching out for the dog shit.' But she didn't. She just stared at the petals and I could see she was moved. I've never seen Charley react like that before; then again, she's never seen my bedroom covered in roses before. She looked quite emotional; either that or the flowers had set off her hay fever.

Suddenly, she kissed me, and it felt the most natural thing in the world. My only disappointment was that we could have been doing this for the last ten years. Charley was obviously thinking the same.

'I've wanted this for a long time,' she said, looking me in the eye.

'Really?'

She nodded.

'But why would you be interested in me?' I asked. 'I'm selfish, self-obsessed and egotistical.'

I said all this hoping she'd tell me I wasn't.

'I know you are.'

'Thanks, Charley.'

'But that's why we make such a good team. I balance out your defects by being kind, generous and wonderful.'

'And modest,' I said.

'Thank you, Simon. And modest.'

'And in no way sarcastic.'

'Absolutely not. I mean, let's be brutally honest here, I'm quite possibly the nicest person in the world and you're very lucky to know me.'

This caused another session of tickling, screaming and riotous laughter, which inevitably led to us falling on to the bed and doing a bit more snogging and fumbling, which as Tony the Tiger used to say was Grrrrrreat! After a while Charley pulled gently away and looked at her watch.

'I've got to go,' she said, sounding disappointed.

'You can stay the night if you want to?'

I didn't feel nervous about saying this and there was no fear of rejection, it just came out in a matter-of-fact-type way.

'I can't, I'm producing an OB for Mike and Sue tomorrow morning and there's a cab picking me up from my flat at five-thirty.'

Normally my insecurities would have kicked in and I'd be thinking I'd done something wrong, but with Charley, I didn't feel like that. Everything was cool and I knew we didn't have to rush anything. I called her a cab. Then after I'd done the old gag again, I picked up the phone and booked her a taxi. When it arrived, I helped her on with her jacket and walked her to the door.

'What are you doing tomorrow?' she asked.

'I've got a meeting with Annie Reichman. We're supposed to be talking about "the future".'

'I meant what I said earlier,' she whispered as she kissed

me on the cheek and walked towards the waiting cab. 'I really think it's going to be your year.'

As the taxi's lights disappeared into the distance, I started thinking that with Charley by my side, it just might be.

15 FEB

Annie immediately picked up the telephone and punched in a number. I'd only just finished telling her about *It Could Be You!* and already she was making a call about it. That's what I admire about Annie Reichman. As soon as she hears something she likes, she acts on it. Some agents sit around waiting for the phone to ring, but Annie is 100 per cent pro-active and makes things happen.

'It's Annie calling for Michael Rimmer,' she said into the mouthpiece and then after a short pause, 'thank you.'

She was obviously being connected. They didn't ask 'Annie who?' and she wasn't told he was 'in a meeting' or to 'call back later'. She was actually being transferred directly to the Head of Programmes at ITV.

As she waited to be put through I couldn't stop staring at her moustache. Surely she could shave it or have it plucked or waxed or bleached, or whatever it is that women do when they have a problem with facial hair? Instead she seems to be actively encouraging it. She has a strange habit of stroking it when she speaks, and she occasionally twiddles the ends like a villain in a Victorian melodrama.

'Michael,' she said, in a businesslike manner, 'I think I might have the answer to your prayers.'

Reichman started pitching him the format. She mentioned that the show would be broadcast live and that we'd surprise four different households in four different towns each week. She stopped for a moment.

'How about if we have one household in each of the four home nations?' she said. 'England, Scotland, Northern Ireland and Wales. That certainly ticks a lot of boxes.'

This was Annie's own idea, and it immediately struck me as a stroke of genius. Anything that guarantees an audience throughout the whole of the UK is going to be looked on favourably by the advertisers, and I knew Michael Rimmer would love it. She then told him about the Retro Round and the elimination process. It sounded really good coming from Annie, and she made it sound like a proper TV show. There was pause, and I guessed Rimmer was giving her some comments and suggestions of his own.

As they talked, I looked around Annie's office. It was large and impressive, but the decor was surprisingly old-fashioned and masculine. There was a heavy mahogany desk and bulky green leather seats, which gave the impression of a gentlemen's drinking club. It made me feel I should be wearing a velvet jacket and a cravat while sipping brandy and smoking a cigar.

Hanging from the dark, wood-panelled walls were framed photographs of Annie's clients, every one of them a household name and a multimillionaire. There were several smaller pictures of her standing next to major Hollywood stars including Arnold Schwarzenegger, Bruce Willis and a young Tom Cruise (Annie had started her career as a junior agent with ICM in Los Angeles. She'd moved back to England twelve years ago to set up their London office and then started her own agency three years later).

On the shelves were a number of self-help books with titles like *How to Get Ahead in Business*, *Winning at All Costs* and *The Power of Self-Belief*. I also noticed one called *I Am Beautiful* and another one called *Skin Deep: Beauty Tips for the Aesthetically Challenged*. Acting as bookends and scattered around the office were several awards and accolades, which had obviously been presented to her by grateful clients. Looking at the office, the one thing that struck me was the absence of family photographs or anything else that would indicate an existence outside the agency. For Annie Reichman, the business was her life and her life was the business. She was a major player in the world of entertainment, but at that moment I felt quite sorry for her.

'Thank you Michael,' said Annie into the mouthpiece. 'Yes . . . yes . . . we'll discuss that . . . he's here with me now, I'll tell him.'

She placed the receiver back in its hold.

'He loves it,' she said. 'He wants to see it as a written proposal with budgets and sponsorship suggestions, but from what he said, I think he's going to give it the green light.'

'Wow.'

Michael Rimmer is renowned in the television industry for going on his gut instinct and making snap decisions. It's a method that's served him well, and during his short reign he's already had big hits with the teatime soap opera *Trafalgar Way* and the interactive game show *House of Pain*, where celebrities are locked in a medieval torture chamber for a week and viewers have to vote for which form of torture should be inflicted on them. The show has proved to be a massive ratings winner, and Rimmer had famously commissioned it on the strength of a one-line pitch:

'Noel Edmonds in a torture chamber.'

Rimmer is a populist who knows exactly what the public want to see. He's turned around the fortunes of the ITV network, and the only area where he's failed to have any success is Saturday night. A hit show is something he desperately craves, and he's promised the City analysts and advertisers that he'll deliver.

'He was talking about making this show the lynchpin of Saturday nights and building the schedule around it . . .' continued Annie.

Things were moving very fast and my mind started to spin. I couldn't believe I was on the verge of fulfilling my destiny. This was it, this was the moment I'd dreamt of since I was a small boy. I was about to achieve my goal and step into the role I've always known that I was born to play. I was finally going to get to host my own Saturday night prime-time TV show. And it literally was *my* show. A format idea *I'd* come up with and developed myself.

'. . . six episodes starting in May and, if it's successful, a further twelve before the end of the year . . .'

A show I'd nurtured from a small seed of inspiration. I'd watched the buds of creativity blossom and now I was about to enjoy the fruit of my artistic labours.

'. . . a one-year exclusive contract with an option for a further two . . .'

Despite all my excitement, I had a slight nagging doubt at the back of my mind, but I couldn't put my finger on exactly what it was.

'It will depend on the ratings of course, but this show could run and run . . .'

It felt like guilt but what was there to feel guilty about? Surely this should be the happiest day of my life?

'I told Michael we were going to set up our own production company to make it.'

Suddenly it hit me and an explosion of panic detonated in my mind. What about Charley? There's no denying that her input on the format had been valuable, and she should be involved in this. My brother David, Max Golinski and Ricardo Mancini might recognize certain elements of it but I don't care about them; surely what they say is negligible.

But with Charley it's different. I'd agreed to set up a production company with her; we were a team. I couldn't just go into partnership with Annie and cut Charley out of it. That would be the ultimate betrayal.

'What do you think, Simon?'

I swallowed hard. I knew I was now in a position of power, and I was adamant the only way I was going to make this television programme was with Charley and Ego Productions.

'Simon?'

The problem was how to tell Annie.

'Simon?'

Reichman is one of those people that, when she says something, it's very hard to disagree with her. I nodded my head and then shook it, while at the same time making a strange humming noise that I hoped sounded confirmatory and negative at the same time.

'After I spoke to you last week, I had a solicitor draw up a contract,' she said, pulling out a piece of paper from her desk.

I couldn't believe the speed this was all happening.

'You'd own 80 per cent of the company, I'd own the other 20 per cent. It would be just like paying me a commission.'

Charley had only suggested a fifty-fifty split, so with this deal I'd be better off. But obviously that wasn't the point. My loyalty lay with Charley. I needed to be strong on this; I needed to stand up and tell Annie that I was sorry but I wanted to make the show through Charley's company.

'If we set up this company,' continued Annie, 'it will own the copyright on the show and one of the priorities will be to sell the format into other territories.'

She started twiddling her moustache again and I couldn't help feeling that I was in a silent movie and that *I* was the damsel in distress. I half expected her to kidnap me and tie me to a railway line.

'This programme has universal appeal and I'm confident that with my contacts we can sell it worldwide, especially to America. Chad Kowalski at NBC will love this, and Todd McLooney at CBS.'

NBC? *CBS*? I didn't know who Chad Kowalski and Todd McLooney were, but they both sounded very American and very important. Obviously Charley doesn't have those sorts of contacts but once again, that wasn't the point. Charley trusts me and she's the possible grandmother to my future grandchildren and there's no way I want Annie Reichman to ever be that (for a start, I'm not sure how strong the moustache gene is). Even placing that to one side, I'd shaken Charley's hand and, to me, that meant something. I'm a Yorkshireman and I'm a big believer that my word is my bond.

'I think this show could make you a big star,' said Annie. 'A bigger star than you ever imagined.'

'So if we set up this production company,' I asked matter-of-factly, 'what would we call it?'

'Simon Peters Productions,' she said, without missing a beat.

'Where do I sign?' I said.

16 FEB

I'm going to be a star.

18 FEB

Me, Simon Peters, that skinny, spotty lad from Rotherham, a star.

21 FEB

Surely I should feel happier than this, but instead there's just a sense of emptiness. I keep waiting for the euphoria to kick in and to start feeling like a different person, but it doesn't seem to be happening. Instead I can hear the black dog of depression barking at the back door. He's growling and howling and scratching to get in, but I'm determined to keep him at bay. I must stay in a positive frame of mind and not start wallowing in my own self-pity.

22 FEB

I can't eat. My appetite's disappeared and all my taste buds have gone on strike, giving everything I digest the flavour of cardboard.

I can't concentrate. I sit in front of the television in a subdued daze, blurred images flashing before me without meaning and sounds crashing together without sense. Still, I guess that's what happens when you watch MTV.

I can't sleep at night. Thoughts go tearing through my mind at a million miles an hour, and I can't hold on to them long enough to discover what it is I'm actually thinking about.

I've started to drink. Well, I've been drinking for a while but suddenly I've started to drink more. I told myself I was drinking to celebrate the fact that I'd got my own TV show. Congratulations to me! Whoopee! Let's have a party! It didn't take long for me to realize the real reason I was drinking was because I don't like myself, and the reason for that is because of my disloyalty to Charley. I know I've let her down but, being the big coward that I am, I've done what my father always used to do in situations where grown-up emotions were involved: I've run away and hidden at the bottom of a bottle.

She's tried phoning me several times and I know she came round to the flat last night. I didn't answer because I wasn't brave enough to face up to the truth and explain to her what I'd done. Maybe it's because I don't know why I did it. The only reason I can think of is that my quest for fame and recognition is stronger than any love I might carry in my heart.

Surely that's a terrible thing?

The irony is that if I explained this to Charley she'd understand and make me feel better, but part of me doesn't want to feel better. I know that letting her get too close was a dangerous thing so I've slammed the door on my emotions, padlocked it and thrown away the key.

Career-wise, I'm at a crucial point right now, and I don't want to do anything that would unbalance my priorities. If I start falling in love with Charley, I know she'd bring everything into perspective for me, and if there's one thing a celebrity doesn't need, it's perspective. She'd make me feel secure and persuade me that the celebrity lifestyle is ultimately an empty existence that has no worth in the real world. This would eventually cause my craving for recognition to dwindle away, and I worry that without that I'd be a nobody, and that's something I've always promised myself I'd never be. If I let love into my heart I'll never achieve my goal; I'll fail, and failure is not an option. I *need* my insecurities. Without that feeling of inadequacy spurring me on I'll be just like everyone else. Doesn't she realize that a sense of loneliness and desperation is what drives me on, and because of that I can never let myself be fully happy and emotionally fulfilled? On Valentine's night, that's exactly what I started to be. With Charley it

147

felt good, really good, and my life's not supposed to be like that. Is it?

23 FEB

The shame of my betrayal is unbearable; the remorse I feel, immeasurable. I am drowning in a sea of sorrow and regret; a strong undercurrent of deceit sweeps me along and treachery sucks me ever deeper into a vicious whirlpool of penitence.

The water is cold and dark except for a shaft of light being shone from the surface.

I glance to my right and notice what looks like the wreckage of a helicopter. Even though I'm underwater, the sharp blades are still turning and they're coming towards me. I swim away from them but it's no good, the faster I swim, the closer they seem to get. I panic and start thrashing around, desperately trying to reach safety. I try holding my breath but my lungs begin to fill with salty water and I gradually sink into the abyss.

Suddenly, illuminated by a beam of light, I see a black-leather-gloved hand reaching into the water, quickly followed by another one. Somebody is trying to rescue me. I grab for them, but instead of pulling me to the surface they push my hands away and press down on my head with an incredible strength, forcing me towards the helicopter blades. I frantically try to fight them off. I flail my arms, punching, clawing and biting at the hands, swallowing yet more water as I do so. Their grip is too strong and I can feel my energy sapping away. I can't hold my breath any longer.

A stream of bubbles escapes from my mouth and my lungs rapidly fill with water. My body goes limp and I know this is the end. My whole life flashes before me and it's still boring; I suddenly realize that up until that point I've led a vacuous life of failure, and this is enough to spur me on. With one last effort I grab the wrists of the would-be killer's hands, and using all my remaining strength I use them to catapult me towards the light. As I crash to the surface, desperately gasping for air, I catch a glimpse of the person the hands belong to. The face is set in a murderous grimace and in one sadistic movement they violently push me back underwater. This time I'm too weak to fight it. My only thought as I plunge to my inevitable death is that I can't believe Charley O'Neil would do such a thing.

'Forgive me!' I screamed at the top of my voice as I woke up breathless and fighting for air.

Being sad and alone (as I fear I will be for the rest of my life), the only thing to hear me was my own guilty conscience.

14:

Dominic Mulryan interviews Charley O'Neil:

DM
Charley, how do you feel when you read that?

Charley O'Neil
I can't believe that he felt so guilty and was beating himself up like that. It's interesting to read it now, because at the time I guessed he'd started to regret the whole 'sleeping with his best friend' scenario, or found another girl or just decided he didn't want to be with me. The truth is, he thought I'd try to put him off fulfilling his ambition, which of course is nonsense. I would have supported him, but he just couldn't see that. Well, he could see it, but it's not what he wanted. It's terrible to think that at his very core he was so insecure that he was incapable of allowing anyone to love him. It's sad, isn't it? He never acknowledged that it was possible to have a successful career and be in a successful relationship at the same time; he never realized that the two aren't mutually exclusive.

When I think about it, it's a shame; a real shame.

DM

Were you upset when you found out that Simon had set up a production company with Reichman?

Charley O'Neil

Well, I wasn't as upset as everyone thinks. You have to remember that at that point, nobody knew just how successful *It Could Be You!* was going to be. At the time, it was just an idea on a piece of paper. To be honest, I was quite philosophical about the whole scenario and when I analysed it, I realized he'd probably made the right decision. Annie Reichman had all the contacts, and there's no way the show would have been the massive phenomenon that it was if Simon and I had produced it without her involvement.

DM

Forgive me, but I can't believe you weren't upset in any way? Hell hath no fury, etc . . .

Charley O'Neil

Maybe I was upset on a personal level, but not professionally. I think the one thing that *did* hurt me was the way Simon told me about it; or more to the point, the way he didn't tell me. After his meeting with Annie, he avoided my calls for a couple of weeks and I wasn't able to contact him. He just disappeared. I tried phoning, texting and emailing him but he didn't reply. I even went to his flat a couple of times but he wasn't there. Well, now I know he was there but he just didn't answer the door. Obviously I was very confused; I thought I'd done something to upset him, but then I discovered the truth.

151

DM
How did you actually find out?

Charley O'Neil
I read it on the front page of *Broadcast*.

DM
That must have hurt.

Charley O'Neil
As I say, I was very philosophical about it.

DM
What did you think of Simon's dream?

Charley O'Neil
Which dream?

DM
The dream in which you killed him.

Charley O'Neil
Oh, *that* dream? Sorry, it had slipped my mind for a moment. Well, it doesn't make for very pleasant reading, does it? I know he had a lot of bad dreams but he never told me about that one. I guess a psychologist would say something about him feeling suffocated by the possibility of an intimate relationship. If I had to analyse it, I'd say that it was obviously born out of guilt, but I really don't know why he felt like that. I know nobody believes me, but my first reaction when I learnt that the show had been commissioned was one of joy. I was genuinely pleased for him because I knew how much it meant to him; it was all he

ever wanted and all he really lived for. It was as if he'd spent his whole life gearing himself up for that one moment. That might sound a bit sad to you and me, but you have to admire his single-mindedness and his tenacity. There aren't many people who actually get to live their dream.

DM
Or indeed, their nightmares?

Charley O'Neil
I don't know what you mean by that.

DM
I mean that Simon seemed to have a lot of nightmares where he appeared to be murdered by people he knew.

Charley O'Neil
Everybody has nightmares.

DM
Yes, but Simon's nightmares came true.

Charley O'Neil
And your implication is?

DM
I'm not implying anything, I'm just trying to establish who might have had a motive . . .

Charley O'Neil
Oh I see . . . I'm now suspected of murdering my best friend because he had a bad dream about me? Wow, you're very good, Monsieur Poirot.

DM

Moving on . . . Do you think you weren't as upset as you might have been about Simon's disloyalty because you were soon offered a dream job yourself?

Charley O'Neil

Well, it certainly softened the blow, let's put it that way.

Do you think we could open a window? It's getting very hot in here.

15:

Dominic Mulryan interviews Annie Reichman:

DM
Once you had the green light to go ahead with It Could Be You! *you obviously had to put together a creative team to actually produce the show. What made you think Charley O'Neil would be right for the role of Executive Producer?*

Annie Reichman
Instinct. When I saw her CV, I was very impressed. She'd been a senior producer on *Coffee Morning with Mike and Sue* and she'd managed to guide that show through some very troubled waters. I imagined producing a show like that was all about keeping egos in check, and I knew this job was going to be very similar.

We needed someone young and energetic with an assertive personality who could shape the show and steer it in the right direction, but ultimately still answer to me. More importantly, we needed someone strong enough to handle Simon and his mood swings. They weren't a problem at the time but I envisaged, quite rightly, that they soon would be.

DM
Did you know that Charley had been romantically involved with Simon and ultimately spurned by him?

Annie Reichman
Totally irrelevant. I might have been aware of the fact but it had no bearing on my decision. When Charley came in to meet me, I knew she was the girl for the job. She was smart and sharp and seemed to have an instant understanding of the show. She grasped the concept immediately and was full of ideas as to how we could improve it. I knew she'd be able to pitch the show at the level I wanted, which was 'Highbrow-Dumb-Down', as I like to call it; television for the masses but with a hint of culture to keep the broadsheets happy. When I asked her how she'd achieve a slightly more intellectual feel, she said that she'd throw in a few aerial shots of castles and play some classical music under it. I recognized her talent immediately and I had no qualms in offering her the position.

DM
Was Simon aware that you were offering Charley the job?

Annie Reichman
Yes, but when I told him he asked me to pretend that *he'd* suggested her for the job.

DM
Some people found it strange that you also gave Simon an Executive Producer credit.

Annie Reichman
That was just to keep him happy. I don't make many
mistakes, but with hindsight that was probably one of
them. To be honest, I don't think he actually knew what an
executive producer does. Then again, not many people in
television do.

16:

Extracts from Simon's diary

3 MARCH

I'm really pleased Charley's on board and that she doesn't seem too upset about what happened. Hopefully we can go back to how we were before: best friends who just have an occasional snog.

I can't believe how quickly everything's happening. *It Could Be You!* has been brought forward and now starts broadcasting live to the nation on 1st April. I've got a feeling that it's going to be huge; everywhere I go people are asking me about it, and it's already generating a phenomenal amount of press interest.

Antonio Bassani, the extremely camp and slightly controversial PR guru, is handling the publicity. Everybody calls him a genius but personally I think he's a bit of a loony. Apparently, the whole slant of the campaign is about living your dreams, but to be honest I don't quite get it. The newspaper adverts are going to be full-page black and white photographs of what, according to Bassani, are iconic, inspirational images: Judy Garland in *The Wizard of Oz*, Barbra Streisand in *Funny Girl* and Liza Minnelli in *Cabaret*. Each image is accompanied by a one-word tagline like 'Fulfil', 'Achieve' and 'Aspire'. When they showed me the proofs for the adverts, I pointed out that they didn't mention the name of the show, what it was about or more importantly the name of the presenter (i.e. me), but Bassani just tutted and said something in Italian.

He seems to do that a lot.

4 MARCH

As well as the press advertising, there will be a series of promos running on ITV1, which will start going out this week. It's quite unprecedented for the network to start running trailers for a brand-new series four weeks in advance, but it just goes to show how much faith they have in the format.

I've spent the last three days filming the trailers and they cost an absolute fortune (the most expensive ever made, according to a Bassani press release). They're shot on 35mm film and directed by Jean-Claude Beauchamp who directed the infamous *G.A.Y. Parfum pour Homme* commercials, and the cult French film *Maurice et Philippe: Un Affair d'Amour.* I thought Bassani was camp, but Jean-Claude makes him look like a Glaswegian docker.

The promos are a little surreal and hallucinatory and have a strange quality that I can't quite put my finger on. The idea is that we see a top celebrity asleep in bed, dreaming of achieving their lifelong ambition. With the use of computer-generated imagery, it then mixes through to see them actually fulfilling that dream. Annie managed to persuade some genuinely well-known names to participate. When I say 'persuade', she offered them bucketloads of cash and they agreed to do it. Personally, I thought the promos should be all about *my* dreams, but Bassani overruled me and said that using really big stars would add a touch of kudos. I reminded him that I was about to be a top celebrity myself but he just laughed. In fact, I'd call it a snigger.

Having said that, I do actually make an appearance in the promos. I'm in every dream sequence in a different guise and, apparently, part of the fun for the viewer at home is to try to spot me. In the Elton John promo, he's dreaming of playing tennis at Wimbledon and when it mixes through to reveal him actually living his dream, I'm dressed as Evonne Goolagong, the person he's playing against.

The other promos have Sir Alan Sugar dreaming of appearing in a 1950s Hollywood musical (I'm his leading lady, Doris Day), and Robbie Williams holding up the FA Cup at the new Wembley stadium (I'm dressed as the Queen). The dressing up in ladies' clothes was Jean-Claude's idea, and I'm guessing it's the French sense of humour. He thought it was hilarious, although I wasn't quite so sure. Having said that, Elton was quite handy with a racquet and there was something rather liberating about wearing a short white tennis skirt. The promos end with the camera pulling back from the sleeping celebrity to reveal me in bed next to them. I have a great big smile on my face as if I've just arranged the dream to come true for them (at least, I think that's the idea).

I have to admit, I wasn't entirely happy about being filmed in bed with Elton John but Charley said it was an innocent bit of fun and that Morecambe and Wise used to do it all the time, Annie Reichman said it would bring in a whole new audience and Bassani said the public probably wouldn't be that surprised.

I'm not sure what he meant by that.

17 MARCH

Two weeks to go and the countdown continues.

The show is promising to be one of the biggest light entertainment programmes ever broadcast live on a Saturday night, and I'm going to be the person at the centre of it all. I have to admit that I'm starting to feel a little nervous about the whole thing; in fact, I find the sheer scale of it terrifying. There are about eighty people already working on the show, including producers, associate producers, directors, production managers, production assistants, set designers, set builders, lighting designers, researchers and runners, many of whom are already out on location in various parts of the country shooting the VTs, which will eventually be inserted into the show.

I'm glad that I'm working with Charley because she doesn't seem to be intimidated by it all; she really is brilliant at her job and seems to know exactly what she's doing. Nothing fazes her and she's always totally in control. I have to admit that it scares the life out of me, and I occasionally get a little stressed and start shouting at some of the runners and PAs. When this happens, I immediately feel guilty about it and have to buy them croissants, muffins and cheesecake to make them like me again and make sure they don't bitch about me behind my back. Charley doesn't seem to have that problem; she's a really good people person and everyone warms to her. She never raises her voice but always seems to get exactly what she wants. I don't seem to be able to command that sort of respect unless I start yelling at people.

I'll have to be careful; I don't want to start getting a reputation.

18 MARCH

I was in the production office but I didn't seem to have very much to do. Everyone else was running around but I just got a bit bored and had to pretend to be busy. I ended up changing the combination number on my briefcase seventeen times. There's nothing actually in the briefcase, but I carry it around with me because that's the sort of thing that executives do. It's actually called an Executive Briefcase and that's the only reason I bought it.

I realized I couldn't just sit around doing nothing the whole time, or the production team might start to resent me; I knew I had to begin proving my worth as an 'exec', and contributing towards the production of the show. What is it the public really wanted to see? I thought to myself.

Then it hit me.

'I've been struck by inspiration,' I said to Charley as I bounded into her office, full of enthusiasm.

'Really?' she said, seemingly uninterested. She didn't even look up from her laptop.

'It's a great idea for the show,' I continued.

She mumbled something and continued to type.

'How about a Simon-cam?'

She stopped typing.

'A Simon-cam?' she asked flatly.

'Yes, basically it's a camera that is constantly on a close-up of me during the show.'

She looked up from the laptop and sighed.

'No . . . listen,' I said. 'If at any point I turn to the Simon-cam, the vision mixer cuts to it and I can give a knowing look or a funny line to the audience at home. It's a good device for letting the viewers in. It's very conspiratorial, Brucie used to have one on *The Generation Game*.'

'Yes, and Billy Fox had one on *One Last Chance!*'

There was a pause.

'Did he?' I said. 'I never really noticed.'

Charley gave me a look which suggested she didn't believe me.

'We can also take it one step further,' I said. 'We could have some sort of red-button symbol like they have for the football on Sky Sports. The viewer at home can press the button and have the option of watching the close-up of me for the whole programme. It's like a player-cam but it's a *Simon*-cam. What do you think, Charley? . . . Charley?'

By this point she'd returned to her laptop.

'Charley?'

She exhaled slowly.

'The red-button thing is never going to work because of the technology involved in setting it up,' she said. 'But if you want a Simon-cam, you can have a Simon-cam. Just don't keep looking into it all the time trying to get a close-up.'

As if I'd do that.

19 MARCH

'How about I sing the theme tune?'

'Oh God,' said Charley, throwing her head back and looking up at the ceiling.

I was back in her office again first thing this morning, just to prove how keen I was.

'No . . . listen, I think the public like it when the host of

163

the show sings the theme tune, just like Cilla on *Surprise, Surprise!*'

'Yes and just like . . .'

'Don't say it,' I said. 'I know Billy Fox sang his theme tune but he didn't *write* his, so that makes this one different.'

There was a pause.

'You've actually *written* a theme tune?'

'Yes,' I said.

'Oh God,' she said, throwing her head back again. '"Write the theme tune, sing the theme tune . . ."'

I think she was doing her *Little Britain*/Dennis Waterman impression. I knew the only way to convince her was to start singing it. I cleared my throat . . .

> *'Making a brew with a monkey in the zoo,*
> *Being the first to hear a cuckoo,*
> *Admiring the view of an Indian Sioux,*
> *All of this, yes,*
> *All of this, yes,*
> *All of this, yes,*
> *It could be you!'*

After I'd finished singing all eight verses Charley looked at me blankly, so I sang it to her again, this time doing the little dance routine which I thought could accompany it in the opening title sequence.

'What do you think?' I asked, when at last I got to the end.

'When did you write that?'

'Last night.'

'How long did it take?'

'About ten minutes.'

She said the song was 'interesting', but that she'd envisaged a 'slightly cooler' theme tune; she said she was thinking of asking the Arctic Monkeys to record something. I argued that my song was retro-cool and reminiscent of Roy Castle singing the theme tune for *Record Breakers*. Charley said it sounded more like Black Lace.

'I really think I should do it,' I said. 'And I'm sure Annie Reichman and Michael Rimmer, the Head of Programmes at ITV, will agree with me.'

My veiled threat hung in the air.

'Let me think about it,' said Charley, but we both knew that I'd get my own way.

As I left the office she shot me a look; it could have been passion, it could have been anger, I'm not sure which.

20 MARCH

I wonder if Charley still fancies me and is harbouring a secret desire to get back together with me. I occasionally catch her looking at me and shaking her head.

I guess she's just thinking of what could have been.

21 MARCH

I thought Charley was looking a little stressed today so I decided to send her a text to cheer her up:

I'LL NVER 4GET THE VD WE SHARD 2GETHER

She didn't reply. With hindsight, maybe I should have actually written 'Valentine's Day'.

17:

Dominic Mulryan interviews Charley O'Neil

DM
Had your feelings for Simon changed?

Charley O'Neil
Well they hadn't changed exactly, but I was obviously trying to be professional about it. I still considered him my best friend, but things weren't the same and we both knew they never would be.

DM
So your relationship was the classic scenario of best friends sleeping together only for it to end up destroying their friendship?

Charley O'Neil
I never said it *destroyed* our friendship, I just said that things were different.

DM
He still seemed to be flirting with you, though?

Charley O'Neil

Yes, but he was pretty rubbish at it, wasn't he? It all seemed so transparent and forced. He obviously thought I should be impressed by the fact that he was about to be a big TV star. He couldn't understand that I'd have preferred it if he'd stayed as a nobody. I wanted him to be the person he was before he got the big break, the person who did all that stuff for me on Valentine's Day, but I think, deep down, I knew that was never going to happen again.

DM

So did you start to regret your romantic entanglement with Simon?

Charley O'Neil

Romantic entanglement? Bloody hell. I never thought of it like that. I didn't regret it, but it obviously didn't help when we had to work so closely together.

DM

You were officially the executive producer on It Could Be You! *but Reichman gave Simon that title as well. That must have been very difficult for you professionally?*

Charley O'Neil

Well, I'm not going to lie to you . . . it was very difficult, because Simon really struggled with the whole concept of producing. Of course, in all the publicity in the lead-up to the first series we called him a 'visionary' and the 'creative driving force behind the show'. The problem was that Simon started to believe all the hype; he seemed to totally forget that it was just part of the image that Bassani and Reichman were creating for him.

Simon thought that because he had the word 'executive'

in his title, he should be consulted on every aspect of the production. Some people are good at making creative decisions, but Simon wasn't. He always made his decisions based on whether it was good for him personally, and not necessarily whether it was good for the show. Obviously we pandered to him because he was the star, but I think we shouldn't have let him get away with quite as much as he did.

DM
With hindsight, what would you have done differently?

Charley O'Neil
Well, I wouldn't have let him record the bloody theme tune, that's for sure.

18:

Extracts from Simon's diary

24 MARCH

The whole production team were crammed around the CD player in Charley's office as I confidently pressed play.

This was the first time I'd heard the theme tune outside the recording studio, and I have to admit I was slightly disappointed. The high-energy Euro-disco-dance beat which I'd insisted on just sounded a little tinny and cheesy, and I couldn't help noticing that my vocals weren't as strong as I'd hoped. There were a couple of very conspicuous bum notes in there, and I'd obviously struggled to hit some of the higher ones. As the music pumped around the office, Charley and several of the production team started to look slightly worried. I explained to them that it was supposed to sound like that because I am a spontaneous, free-form jazz singer who doesn't conform to the accepted convention of singing in the same key as the rest of the musicians. They didn't look convinced. Personally, I blame the recording engineer who made me sing it over and over again. He didn't realize that, just like Frank Sinatra, the nuggets of pure gold I was producing had to be captured in one take, otherwise the magic is lost. I said this to the team and suggested that on the first show I should maybe sing the theme tune live.

For some reason they didn't think it was a very good idea.

26 MARCH

It Could Be You! is getting so much publicity and I think it's fair to say that my face is absolutely everywhere. The public must love me at the moment. Either that or be sick of the sight of me, I'm not sure which.

We're six days away from the first broadcast and I can already feel that it's going to be something special. Everybody's talking about it, and people seem genuinely excited about the prospect of a big Saturday night light entertainment show that has a real touch of class.

The Sunday papers are really pushing it: 'a return to the golden age of television' said the *News of the World*, and the *Sunday Mirror* described me as the 'Saviour of Saturday Night Television'. I know that's an expression from Bassani's press release, but it still made me feel pretty good.

I just hope I can live up to all the expectation.

27 MARCH

This morning, I appeared as a guest on GMTV, where Penny Smith introduced me as 'Britain's brightest young star'. At lunchtime I was on *Loose Women*, where Coleen Nolan said I was going to be 'very big, very soon', and this afternoon I was on *Richard & Judy*. Richard introduced me as 'the future of British light entertainment' and I corrected him by saying I was 'the future of British *television*, not just light entertainment'. They both laughed, which I found strange because I wasn't joking.

Tomorrow morning I've been invited to be a guest on *Coffee Morning with Mike and Sue*. I used to be the show-business reporter on the show, and they want me back for a 'hasn't he done well'-type spot. Sadly, the show has really gone downhill recently. The ratings have plummeted and every newspaper article says that Mike and Sue are past their best and that they're struggling to get the big guests to appear. The two of them have been at the top of the mid-morning TV tree for about twenty years, but suddenly the tabloids are saying that the show seems quite dated. Everyone in television is speculating that it's only a matter of time before it is cancelled and put out of its misery. Personally I think it would be a great shame. What about all the classic television they've given us over the last twenty years? Admittedly, most of it has been born of the fact that they really *really* hate each other. Their constant on-screen bitchiness, point scoring and one-upmanship has been the stuff of legend, and that's why, until recently, we've tuned in in our millions. Probably everyone's favourite was the time they interviewed the lion tamer, and Sue (always the brave one) agreed to put her head in the lion's mouth.

'Watch out for the bad breath,' said Mike, inevitably watching from a safe distance.

'Actually, it's not too bad for a lion,' said Sue.

'I was talking to the lion!' said Mike.

Sue shot Mike a really vicious look (a look she gave him so often that, for a short while, giving someone a dirty look became known nationally as giving someone a 'Mike and Sue').

Great television.

Does all that count for nothing? It seems to me that no matter what you do in this business and no matter how high you climb, one day you're going to be out, and when the door closes it stays closed for a very long time. It scares me how easily television will kick someone when they're down and twist the knife of betrayal and duplicity. Why is everyone suddenly so negative about Mike and Sue? Why can't people be more sympathetic towards two colleagues who are obviously going through a difficult time? Why can't the television industry be a little more supportive of two such truly great broadcasting icons?

28 MARCH

I turned down the appearance on *Coffee Morning with Mike and Sue* because the show's rubbish, nobody watches it and I don't want to be associated with their failure.

You can't be too careful in television.

29 MARCH

Three days until the show goes out live.

I'm sure somebody's made a mistake somewhere along the line and it shouldn't actually be me who's been given this opportunity.

30 MARCH

Two days to go.

I keep expecting a knock at the door and when I refuse to open it, the Talent Police will burst in and tell me it's the biggest April Fool joke in history and can Billy Fox have his career back please?

31 MARCH

One day to go.

This is all I've ever dreamt of, and everything my life has been building towards. Ever since I was a child, my every deed, my every action, my every waking thought has been injected with a glimmer of hope that one day this might happen for me, and finally, tomorrow, it's about to.

This is where my journey begins.

Or is it where it ends?

1 APRIL

I'm having an out-of-body experience and enjoying a natural high from which I don't ever want to come down. I'm floating above myself and I can see me sitting below, naked apart from a towel draped around my shoulders. I'm staring into a mirror with a great big grin on my face which I hope will never go away. As I glide blissfully around the ceiling, I'm aware that this is the Number One dressing room at LWT. There's a large red velvet settee, a bouquet of flowers and a gold star on the other side of the door, with my name in the middle of it. The Real Me leans back and looks up at the Other Me on the ceiling. We smile and give each other a big thumbs up.

'Remember this moment,' I tell myself, and I know that I always will.

I'm on a high because the first *It Could Be You!* has just finished and, even though I say so myself, it was brilliant. More importantly, *I* was brilliant. Knowing how well it went now, I can't believe how nervous I was at the beginning of the show . . .

'*Ten seconds to live on air.*'

I was standing behind the large chrome-effect sliding doors waiting for my cue. I turned up the volume on my talkback and adjusted my earpiece. *Ten seconds to live on air.* She'd said it in such a matter-of-fact way, as if broadcasting live to eight million people was the most natural thing in the world. She said it as if it would be easy and she didn't know what all the fuss was about. She said it without knowing that those ten seconds were about to be the longest ten seconds of my life.

'*Nine.*'

Now she sounded as if she was a record being played at half speed. Her words were measured and sluggish, as if she was talking in slow motion. In the background I was aware of my theme tune being played. I turned around to face the monitor so I could watch the titles going out live. I was impressed by what Charley had done with them. They looked really fresh and original and even the theme tune sounded cool. They'd done away with the slightly naff Euro-disco beat and dubbed on some sort of upbeat jazzy drum and bass remix. When the vocals kicked in I was pleasantly surprised at how good I sounded. They'd obviously managed to tweak something, because suddenly I sounded like a big black gospel singer. It's amazing what they can do these days. As I watched the titles roll I thought it looked like a great show, and at that moment I wished I was sitting at home watching it.

'*Eight.*'

I was aware that waiting for me on the other side of the sliding doors were nine cameras and the five hundred members of the public who made up the studio audience. I could hear the warm-up man saying the punchline to a joke I didn't get, and giving the audience last-minute instructions on what to do when they saw me. I detected a hint of resentment in his voice. I'd met him earlier on, backstage, and as I shook his hand I could tell by the look in his eye that he was jealous of me. Why you? he was thinking. Why have you been given this break? What have you got that's so special?

As I stood there waiting for the doors to open, I couldn't help thinking exactly the same thing.

'*Seven.*'

'Let me hear you scream,' the warm-up man shouted, and the audience duly obliged. I screamed too, but for a completely different reason. I'd been hit by the thought of eight million people sitting in their homes waiting for this show to start. Had they rushed home from their Saturday afternoon shopping to see this? Were families settling down with TV ready meals hot from the microwave? Had they Sky-Plussed it? Were they excited about it or were they saying, 'Come on then Mr Big Shot, let's see what you can do'?

'*Six.*'

Did they already know that I was a fake and a charlatan? Had somebody leaked the truth that I was out of my depth and punching above my weight? Maybe they knew that I wasn't really good enough for this sort of thing, and the real reason they were tuning in was to see me fail?

'*Five.*'

Nervous tension filled the air and the level of expectation was unbearable. I wanted the voice to stop counting and go back to ten again. I wanted her to count down from ten for eternity, but never get past five.

'*Four.*'

I started to regret the shot of vodka I'd had in my dressing room, but then immediately regretted that I hadn't had more.

'*Three.*'

I closed my eyes and desperately tried to control my breathing.

'*Two.*'

My hands were shaking and I was starting to sweat.

'*One.*'

I felt a panic attack coming on and I had an uncontrollable urge to run away.

'*Zero.*'

Then I wondered if Billy Fox would be watching this.

'*And cue the voice-over.*'

On the monitor I could see that they'd mixed from the titles to a live sweeping crane shot of the audience clapping and cheering. There was a drum roll and a big, booming, prerecorded voice with a mid-Atlantic accent announced:

'Ladies and gentlemen, no matter where you're watching this, it could be you! So please welcome the man who makes your dreams come true! It's Mr Saturday Night himself . . . Siiiiiiiiiiiiiiiiiiimon Peteeeeeeeeeeeeeeeeers!'

The audience screamed, the doors slid open, the spotlight hit me and all my nerves just completely evaporated. The performer within me took over; I instantly became a different person and the show started rolling like a huge snowball, gathering momentum as it went. If those initial ten seconds were the longest of my life, the next hour was the shortest. It disappeared in a flash, but I was in control and knew exactly what I was doing. I was totally on top of my game: if I was a footballer I'd have scored a hat trick, if I was a golfer it would have been a hole in one. I grabbed the show by the scruff of its neck and elevated it to unexpected heights. I was a television animal, stalking my prey and devouring it with salacious delight. I was sharp and focused, funny and quick-witted (yes, I fluffed a couple of the punchlines but I like to think that it all added to the live ambience). The show flowed beautifully, all the items went to plan and the whole thing was over before I knew it. As the final credits rolled there was a standing ovation from the studio audience.

Admittedly the warm-up man had told them to do it, but it still looked pretty impressive.

Even though I knew it had gone well, the initial euphoria I'd experienced in the dressing room, when it was over, had started to wear off by the time I got to the after-show party. Being an entertainer with a fragile handle-with-care ego, I found myself in sudden need of reassurance. In the green room, everybody came up to me, shook my hand and said how great the show was and that it was destined to be a big hit. That was all very nice to start with, but it wasn't very long before I wanted to hear how great *I* was. I tried subtly fishing for compliments, but it didn't really work. The members of the production team only wanted to talk about how well their particular items had gone; they would then start talking enthusiastically about ideas for future shows. That was the last thing I wanted to hear, so in the end I gave up with the restrained approach and asked them bluntly what they thought of my performance.

The general consensus was that I'd been marvellous, but strangely that didn't make me feel any better. People would tell me how wonderful I was but I didn't really believe them, so I'd ask them to tell me again. I was obviously experiencing some sort of a comedown from the high of hosting a live TV show. I didn't want the high to disappear so I tried to keep it going with free champagne and shots of vodka. This was obviously a mistake, because from that moment on I don't really remember much else about the party. I do remember the director telling me I'd done a great job (I didn't believe him), Michael Rimmer, the boss of ITV, shaking my hand and saying I was excellent (I didn't believe him) and Annie Reichman saying I was wonderful (I didn't believe her). I also remember Charley giving me a peck on the cheek and telling me that she thought I could do better.

Why is Charley the only one I believed?

19:

Dominic Mulryan interviews Charley O'Neil

DM
Did you say that to dent his ego?

Charley O'Neil
No, I just wanted to keep his feet on the ground. The truth is, Simon was brilliant on that first show. I'm not just saying that because he was a friend or someone I'd had a . . . someone I'd had a 'romantic entanglement' with, as you call it. I'm saying it as a producer with over ten years' experience of working in television. I always told him he was born to be a game show host, and that night he proved he was. The one thing in life he could do well and the one thing he could do better than almost anyone else in this country was host a game show. He came alive when he was doing it and seemed to become a different person. Of course he had his weaknesses: yes he was crap at gags; yes he sometimes stumbled over the odd word; yes he occasionally forgot the names of the contestants and on one memorable occasion, the name of the show he was hosting, but all that added to

179

his appeal and enhanced the image that Annie Reichman was trying to create for him.

DM
And what was that image?

Charley O'Neil
I guess it was an Everyman image. She wanted him to appear as a normal guy who'd walked in off the street and was just having a go at being on television. In many ways he was, but there was a lot more skill involved than that.

DM
Did you have any doubts about his ability?

Charley O'Neil
Before the first episode, I'd started to have genuine concerns over whether he could actually pull it off. I thought it might be too big for him and that he'd go to pieces, but once he was on-screen, there's no denying that he did the business. He had a real understanding of how the show worked and a natural rapport with the contestants. In the Retro Round, he knew exactly how long to leave it before giving an answer, and he instinctively knew when to throw to the break to keep the audience glued to their sets. When it came down to revealing which family was going to achieve their lifelong ambition, he was wonderful. His voice patterns were perfect and he could increase the tension by just raising one eyebrow. I know in the following months he came in for a lot of criticism, but the impact he made on that first show was incredible.

That was the night Simon Peters became a star.

20:

Extracts from Simon's diary

9 APRIL

The second show was even better and there's no denying that we have a massive hit on our hands and that everyone in the country is talking about us. *It Could Be You!* is a resounding success and the Sunday papers are full of praise for the show. Both the broadsheets and the tabloids have agreed that it's a sensation. Surprisingly, even the reviews for me were pretty good; I thought they might give me a savaging but they've actually been rather kind. I realize that they're just building me up to knock me down, but at the moment I think I can live with that. At least everyone has noticed that I've finally arrived. The *News of the World* said I was 'a star in the making', the *Sunday People* said I had 'a sparkling personality' and the *Sunday Sport* said I was 'the new Noel Edmonds', which I wasn't too sure about but took as a compliment anyway. The *Mail on Sunday* had a little bit of a dig at me, saying how I fluffed a couple of gags and messed up the intro to one of the rounds, but even they agreed that I had a 'certain appeal'.

The only really bad review was A.A. Gill in the *Sunday Times*, who said I was 'annoyingly obsequious and desperate to please, with a career which is seemingly the televisual equivalent of the Emperor's new clothes . . .'

I'd sue him if I understood what it meant.

10 APRIL

All of a sudden I'm famous.

Really famous.

I've been invited to Cilla Black's birthday party. If that doesn't mean I've made it, nothing does.

16 APRIL

Being famous means I've got millions of friends (12.2 million friends, according to this week's audience figures). It seems that I don't have to worry about being lonely any longer because the public love me, they genuinely love me and I know this because they've started to tell me so on a regular basis. Wherever I go, people call my name and declare their devotion to me.

'We love you, Simon,' they scream, from passing cars and buses.

'I love you too!' I shout back and I really mean it. I love each and every one of them and I never want the love to stop.

Everything is going so well in my life at the moment. Two months ago I was a struggling wannabe on the verge of anonymity, whereas now the whole country recognizes me, appreciates my talent and wants to be my friend. I realize I have to be careful, though; I know there's a danger that if I carry on living my life like this I could end up existing in a media bubble and losing my grip on reality. With everything happening so fast I can see the possibility of my life spiralling out of control and plummeting towards a self-indulgent void.

What I need is a rock; someone to keep me centred; a sweet girl who will help me be ordinary and make me appreciate the simple things in life. A real person who will put things into perspective for me, who will love me for what I am and who will help me keep my life as normal as possible.

17 APRIL

What I need is a celebrity girlfriend!

Surely only someone as famous as me will truly understand and appreciate how wonderful my life is at the moment. Ordinary members of the public would probably be totally overawed at just being in my presence and they wouldn't be able to cope. It just wouldn't be fair on them.

18 APRIL

I've been invited to a whole host of celebrity parties. I'm not sure whether they want me because of my scintillating company or just because of my newly acquired A-list status, but I'm getting so many invitations, it's actually becoming quite tedious. Since *It Could Be You!* started, I've received about ten a day and there's a mountain of them growing on my mantelpiece: there are invitations to charity presentations, charity football matches, charity golf days, charity lunches, charity dinners, charity balls, launches of new charities and celebrations of old ones; there are invitations to nightclubs, parties, premieres, book launches, restaurant openings, first nights and fashion shows. I've even, rather bizarrely, got a growing pile of invitations to weddings of celebrities who I've never met (I'm guessing they've signed a deal with *OK!* magazine, promised them that lots of famous faces will be attending and they're now starting to panic slightly).

This week I've already attended a few of these celebrity events, but because I haven't got a girlfriend I've turned up on my own, and I'm slightly worried that the press will start to question my sexuality.

The more I think about it, the more I realize I definitely need someone who is as famous as me, or preferably slightly *less* famous, to share the burden of going to all these parties. The trouble is, after working my way through my little black book, I realized that I just don't know that many girls, let alone celebrity girls. In fact, I only have the telephone number of one female celeb who is anywhere near as famous as I am.

Despite not being the brightest torch in the cupboard, former model Jo Heeling has been doing very well for herself lately, and has been getting an awful lot of press about a new controversial late-night Channel 4 show she's been hosting called *Sexual Heeling*, where men phone in, tell her their sexual problems, and in return she offers them advice (not necessarily medically sound advice but almost always unintentionally comedic). The qualifications she has for advising the male population on their penile problems are obviously very dubious, but she does wear very skimpy outfits while she's doing it. It's strangely compulsive viewing and the ratings for the show have been phenomenal, making Jo very hot property indeed. She's always on the covers of *FHM* and *Loaded*, and the tabloids adore her. She's perfect celebrity girlfriend material and I felt confident she'd be interested in me. Jo isn't stupid – well, not when it comes to publicity – and she knows that being one half of a celebrity couple is big news and always means twice the press coverage (not that I'd go out with her just for that, of course).

I still have her number from when we worked together on the children's TV show *A.M. Mayhem*. It was her first presenting job after she'd given up modelling and I like to think that I was very helpful to her and always made a point of giving her lots of advice.

The problem was that I hadn't actually spoken to her for about five years, and at first I couldn't pluck up the courage to call her. After a couple of hours of dithering and pacing around my flat, I finally had to watch a recording of last week's *It Could Be You!* just to convince myself that most girls would be happy to receive a phone call from me.

I punched in her number and waited for it to connect.

'Hi-yaaaaa!'

Jo's voice was unmistakable, sort of high-pitched cockney whine: Barbara Windsor on helium. *Hi-yaaaa!* was how she greeted all the callers to her show. It had become one of those annoying national catchphrases that everybody uses when they think they're being funny.

'Hi-yaaaa!' I replied.

I couldn't help myself.

'Who-zat?'

I'd forgotten how the tone of her voice had the same effect on me as someone scraping their nails down a blackboard. I thought about doing a spoof call pretending to be one of her sad-act viewers with a sex problem, but then I remembered that even though she presented one of the funniest programmes on television, Jo didn't have a sense of humour and would have probably called the police without giving me a chance to explain.

'Hi Jo, it's Simon.'

There was silence at the other end of the phone.

'Hello, Jo?'

'Who izziiiit?'

For somebody who broadcasts to the nation five nights of the week, her command of the English language was diabolical.

'It's Simon.'

This time the silence was deafening.

'It's Simon,' I repeated. 'Simon Peters.'

Once more I was plunged into a silent telephonic abyss. After what seemed an age, she spoke.

'Whoooo?'

'Peters, Simon Peters.'

'Peter Simon?'

'No, Simon Peters! P.E.T.E.R.S. . . .'

God, it was embarrassing. Surely this shouldn't happen now that I'm the host of the biggest show on television.

'I used to present *A.M. Mayhem* with you.'

'Not Slimy Simon?'

I shuddered with embarrassment at the memory of when she called me that live on air.

'Yes Jo, Simon Peters.'

'Oh hi-yaaaaa!'

'Hi-yaaaa!'

It's a knee-jerk reaction; you just have to say it.

'You've done well for yourself, aincha, Slimy?' she giggled.

'Have you seen the show?' I asked enthusiastically.

'No,' she said flatly.

That was a conversation stopper.

'Who'd'a thought it, eh? Slimy Simon becoming a major TV star?'

I decided to ignore this somewhat backhanded compliment and moved the conversation on. We did the usual chitchat about what we were up to and both exaggerated about 'exciting things in the pipeline'. Even though there are genuinely exciting things in the pipeline, I still find myself exaggerating about them. After about a minute, the conversation ground to a shuddering halt, and Jo left a pause long enough to inform me it was time to tell her the reason I was actually calling. I obviously wanted to ask her out on a date, but I stuttered and stumbled as I realized that I hadn't thought of anywhere to take her.

'I was just wondering if . . . erm . . . you know . . . er . . . well . . . erm . . .'

'Come on Slimy, spit it out! You ain't got a sexual problem, 'ave yer? Cos if you 'ave, you'll 'ave to call the show.'

Panicking, I quickly leafed through the pile of invitations on the shelf. Halfway down was the invitation to Cilla's birthday party.

'I just wondered if you'd like to come to Cilla Black's house with me?'

'What?'

'Cilla Black. She used to present *Blind Date* and *Surprise, Surprise*.'

'I know who she is but what the bleedin' 'ell would I want to go to her house for?'

'She's having a party . . . I thought . . . you know . . . erm . . . I thought you might like to be . . . erm . . . you know . . . because we're both famous now . . . erm . . . to be my date.'

Even as I said it, I realized what a bad idea it was.

'Your what?'

'My date.'

Her squeal of laughter could have been heard in Birmingham. Even though she doesn't have a sense of humour, this certainly seemed to amuse her.

'Slimy, you berk, doncha read the papers?'

I didn't like to tell her that I only read the bits that mention me.

'I'm engaged to Eddie Markham.'

'Eddie Markham?' I said, pretending not to be impressed.

Not only is Eddie Markham the Chelsea captain and an England International, he was also recently voted the Most Handsome Man in Football. Now that she mentioned it, I did recall reading something about the two of them being an item. I suppose I should have guessed. Even with all my fame and fortune, a premiership footballer is the holy grail for a girl like Jo. I just couldn't compete. I felt like pointing out that he was only going out with her because of who she was, but then I remembered that was the reason *I* was calling her.

'I'll tell you what though,' she said. 'We'll be looking for famous people to come to the wedding . . .'

I knew where this was leading. No, please don't say it Jo, I thought, please don't say it!

'I'll send you an invitation.'

She said it. And I knew there was more to come.

'You can bring a partner with you if you want to – it would be great if she was famous as well.'

The irony was almost unbearable.

'Thanks Jo, I'll check my diary.'

'See yer, Slimy,' she said and hung up.

The search continues.

22 APRIL

The fourth *It Could Be You!* went without a hitch, and I was on such a high that I decided to celebrate by going to Cilla Black's party on my own. Even though it was quite an impressive do, it wasn't quite as A-list as I'd hoped. More than anything, I was desperately disappointed that there weren't any Potential Celebrity Girlfriends there.

When I arrived I thought I'd made a dreadful mistake, as the first people I spotted were Ricardo Mancini and Max Golinski. As soon as I saw them, a cold shiver shot through my body and I had a terrible premonition that something awful was going to happen. I hadn't seen Max since I left his agency to join Annie Reichman, and I could tell by the look in his eye that, even now, it was the cause of much anger and frustration for him. He was wearing large Mike Read-style tinted glasses, a bright yellow patterned Pringle golfing jumper and beige slacks. He looked as if he was an agent from the 1980s, and in many ways he was. He just hadn't moved with the times, and when I thought of all the things that have happened for me since I left his agency, I knew I'd made the right decision.

Mancini didn't look very happy either, but having seen the show he now presents on Going Gone TV, I couldn't blame him. From across the room I heard him shouting something about the Retro Round on *It Could Be You!*, but with the music playing so loudly, I couldn't quite make out what it was. He and Max looked incensed. Everything about their body language screamed cold-blooded fury, and they stared at me as if they wanted to kill me. I didn't want to antagonize them, so I waved at them politely. As I did so, my sleeve slid down, and they couldn't help but catch a glimpse of my solid gold diamond-encrusted Rolex Oyster watch, a gift I'd bought myself after the success of the first show. Strangely enough, they didn't wave back.

I genuinely considered going home, especially when I saw that standing behind them was Billy Fox, who also kept giving me the evil eye. Several people have told me that he resents the success of *It Could Be You!*, claiming the format is very similar to *One Last Chance!* and that he holds me responsible for his career going off the rails. Personally, I blame it on his complete lack of talent. He got away with it for years, but now he's been found out and is finally paying the price for it.

I just hope it never happens to me.

I decided to stay at the party and somehow managed to avoid the Trio of Doom for the rest of the evening. The bad vibes they were giving off made me feel very uneasy; something in my psyche doesn't like people disliking me, so I did what I always do in situations like that and got very drunk, very quickly. I seem to do that a lot these days. I'd have thought my system would have become immune to alcohol, but the opposite seems to be true; I guess there's always a trace left in my bloodstream from the last time I got drunk, and I only have to have a whiff of the stuff to send me on my way again.

I seem to have three stages of drunkenness. First I get merry, then I get mischievous, then I become depressed and self-absorbed. These days, the merry and mischievous stages never last that long, but luckily, at Cilla's, I did manage to have a bit of fun.

Bobby Davro, who always seems to be at showbiz parties, came up and asked me if I was a gambling man and if I fancied livening things up a little. He said he'd give me £50 if I went up into the bedroom and managed to come out wearing a pair of Cilla's pants; he'd give me £100 if I came

190

out with a pair of Cilla's pants on my head, and £1,000 if I came out with a pair of Cilla's pants on my head with Cilla Black inside them. I shook his hand. I was obviously quite drunk because I immediately went up to Cilla and told her what the bet was, and promised to give her half the money if she'd agree to do it.

It has to be said that Cilla Black is a game old girl, and as I ran around the garden with her on my shoulders singing '*Surprise, Surprise, the unexpected hits you between the eyes!*' everyone thought it was hilarious.

Everyone it seems, except Golinski, Mancini and Fox.

23 APRIL

Why did I ever agree to run in a marathon?

Every muscle in my body cried with pain, my head was throbbing and I felt totally dehydrated. And that was just the hangover before the race even started. To be honest, I don't think it's advisable to run 26 miles and 385 yards with a hangover. I suppose I should have thought of that at Cilla's party before I started on the champagne, the vodka and the tequila shots.

I'd completely forgotten that Barnardo's had invited me to take part. They'd asked me in January before I was properly famous (when I thought I might need the publicity). With hindsight, accepting the invitation was probably my first mistake. I remember thinking at the time that I should try to get fit for it, but then I thought, how difficult can it be? (If you're keeping count, that would have been my second mistake.) After I'd agreed, I completely forgot about it until I received a call on my mobile last night reminding me to be at Greenwich Park this morning at 6.30 a.m. for the 'celebrity registration'.

I didn't get to bed until 3.30 a.m. and when the alarm went off two hours later I seriously considered calling Barnardo's and telling them I felt unwell (which would have actually been the truth, if not an understatement). But then, as it often does, my conscience got the better of me and I thought of all those poor little children and how I couldn't let them down (Barnardo's is definitely a children's charity, I checked). I climbed out of bed and headed for Greenwich.

I obviously hadn't read the invitation properly, because when I arrived I realized that Barnardo's had asked celebrities to do the run dressed up as Mr Men. They'd had all the characters especially made and the costumes were lined up inside a large marquee. I still must have been slightly drunk, because something told me that dressing up in a stupid costume and running halfway around London might be fun. I wanted to be Mr Bump but Joe Pasquale had beaten me to it (he, like me, had obviously spotted the comedic possibilities of bumping into the crowd). My next choice was Mr Happy, but he'd been grabbed by Gordon Ramsay (I think he was being ironic). I was left with Mr Tickle, which I wasn't very happy about because the arms were six feet long and dragged along the floor.

Just before the race, we all lined up and I nodded to the other celebrities taking part: Vernon Kay was Mr Bounce, Peter Duncan was Mr Topsy-Turvy and Kim from Kim and Aggie was Little Miss Lucky. I was half expecting to see Ricardo Mancini as Mr Angry, but he obviously hadn't been invited.

When the starter pistol was fired, I immediately became quite competitive. I'd heard that Gordon Ramsay was good at marathons so I deliberately tripped him up with one of my six-foot arms; it's quite a bizarre thing to hear Mr

Happy swearing like a trooper. I left him lying there and set off at a blistering pace. It seemed easy and I couldn't understand why people made such a fuss about running marathons. The other celebrities seemed to be going really slowly and I was way out in front. I was running like the wind and I had glory in my sights.

And then I hit the Wall.

This wasn't the psychological wall that marathon runners famously hit at around 19 miles. No, this was a brick wall, and it sent me flying. The only consolation was that it got bigger laughs than Pasquale doing his bumping routine. As I pulled myself back to my feet I realized three things:

1) I was absolutely knackered.
2) I was desperately in need of oxygen.
3) I'd only travelled 400 yards from the starting line.

It didn't help when it started to rain. Mr Tickle's arms quickly became soaking wet and they felt like they weighed a ton. I literally had to drag them along and I couldn't have tickled anybody if I'd tried. At the two-mile point I was so short of breath I thought I was going to die. Despite the rain, the costume was incredibly hot and all I could smell were the fumes from last night's alcohol. I had to keep reminding myself not to throw up because I thought the sight of a vomiting Mr Tickle might scare the kids in the crowd, give the charity a bad name and damage the Mr Men brand for ever (I don't think Roger Hargreaves ever did a Mr Puke, did he?).

At the three-mile point, I realized I was in trouble when I saw Jodie Marsh and that bloke in a deep-sea-diving suit overtake me. I knew this called for drastic measures. I decided the most important thing was to be seen on BBC television and to make sure that I got a namecheck from the commentators (purely to raise the profile of the charity, of course, nothing to do with personal gain). I quickly removed my costume, jumped over the crash barrier and hailed a taxi. I then took a series of short cuts to the places where I knew the cameras would be: the *Cutty Sark*, Canary Wharf, Limehouse, etc. When I got to these places I put the costume back on, rejoined the race and sprinted joyfully past the cameras, waving to the crowds as I went. Once I knew I was out of shot, I'd take the costume off again, jump back into the taxi and move on to the next camera position. The only problem I encountered was on Tower Bridge, where I had to go past the BBC reporter three times before he actually stopped me for a chat (I'm guessing he didn't recognize me with such long arms).

Doing the London Marathon in a taxi was easy, and it was only when I entered the Mall that I realized I'd probably taken too many short cuts. I looked at the clock above the finishing line and saw that, so far, it had only taken me two hours, nineteen minutes and twenty-three seconds to get there. I realize I should have hung back to make it a bit more convincing, but once again my competitive streak kicked in and I just couldn't resist it. After a sprint finish, I managed to beat a little Nigerian bloke who was running next to me, and it's the first time in the history of the London Marathon that a costume character has ever come third.

Dominic Mulryan

Following an in-depth investigation, Simon Peters was stripped of his Flora bronze medal, and when CCTV footage revealed what he'd done, the press jumped at the chance to criticize him. After two months of nothing but positive publicity, several broadsheets and tabloids ran stories condemning Peters for cheating, claiming he'd set a bad example to children.

This proved to be the first dent in Peters' public image, and for the next week there were rumours that It Could Be You! *would be cancelled. As ever, Annie Reichman responded swiftly and issued a public apology to Barnardo's, the Roger Hargreaves Mr Men estate and Deji Adu-Adenikaa, the Nigerian marathon runner who had, according to one tabloid report, been devastatingly traumatized at being beaten by Mr Tickle.*

Peters knew he had to do something to regain the public's affection. Of course, it might have been coincidence, but it was around this time that he began to throw himself into his charity work and perform random acts of kindness for people who were less fortunate than himself . . .

8 MAY

This morning, a really sweet little girl asked me for my autograph. She was very pale and thin and clutched an old baby doll close to her chest. Despite the relatively warm weather she was wearing a large duffel coat which was several sizes too big for her, and underneath that she seemed to have several layers of thick woolly jumpers. I signed my name and as I gave the piece of paper back to her, her father, who himself was wearing clothes that had obviously seen better days, told me the little girl was terminally ill. He said she suffered from a rare blood condition which means her body can't cope with cold temperatures. He also said her mother had died when she was three years old and that she'd never seen her grandparents, who lived in Australia. He asked me if I could arrange for them to fly over and visit her, or better still, for her to go and visit them.

'It would be her one last wish,' said the father, pleading with me.

There was desperation in his voice and he was squeezing

my arm tighter than he probably realized; he obviously saw me as his last chance. This sort of thing has happened to me a couple of times since *It Could Be You!* started broadcasting. Being as famous as I am now and because of the nature of the show, people think that I really can perform miracles and make their dreams come true. I glanced down at the little girl, who was looking up at me, her sunken features full of hope and optimism.

'Please,' she whispered as her large almond-shaped eyes filled with tears. 'I'll give you my dolly if you do.'

With outstretched arms, she offered me the baby doll. It looked really old and was dressed in a tatty, faded pink tutu. There were clumps of hair missing from its head and it only had one eye, but the little girl clearly loved it.

'I've had her since I was born,' she said softly. 'Her name's June.'

I swallowed hard and blinked away the tears. June was my mother's name. I knelt down to the girl's level and took her little hand in mine; it felt like I was holding a block of ice. I took a deep breath and promised that I'd do what I could to enable her to see her grandparents. I took the father's phone number and told him I'd be in touch.

When I arrived at the production office, I explained to Charley what had happened. I told her about the man and his little girl with the rare disease who'd lost her mum at an early age, and how her last wish was to see her grandparents in Australia. I told her about the tears as she pleaded with me, and the dolly with one eye who had the same name as my mother. By the time I mentioned her trembling, ice-cold little hands, tears were streaming down my face, and I asked Charley if there was anything we could do to help her.

'No,' she said emphatically. 'It's a TV show, not a bloody charity!'

Charley's my best friend, but I do think that she can be a little harsh sometimes. Maybe she's been under a lot of stress lately.

11 MAY

I can't stop thinking about the little girl and her grandparents, and feeling that I should be able to do something. What's the point of having all this fame and fortune if I can't use it to help other people?

I called Charley at the office, who told me she'd been there since six that morning getting everything ready for the last show in the series. With a heavy slice of sarcasm, she said it was a shame the other executive producer hadn't come in to help her.

'Bloody Annie Reichman,' I said. 'I'll have a word with her about—'

'I wasn't talking about Annie Reichman,' said Charley.

There was a pause and I decided to change the subject.

'I'm thinking of setting up a charity.'

Charley must have been taking a sip of tea at the time and I subsequently heard her snort and then spit it all over her desk.

'A charity?' she said, obviously finding it difficult to hide her amusement.

'I feel I want to give something back to society. I think it should be an extension of what we do on the show but without the cameras. I want to do something away from the glare of the press; I want to do it anonymously.'

'Anonymously?'

Personally, I don't think she needed to sound quite so surprised.

'Yes,' I said. 'I think if it's publicized, people will say I'm just doing it to make amends for what happened at the marathon, but it's genuinely not like that. I want to do lots of good work without anybody knowing about it. I could be the new Princess Di.'

I heard a strange muffled sound from the other end of the line.

'What sort of charity?' she said breathlessly. I got the distinct impression that at that moment she was wiping the tears from her eyes.

'I've been thinking about it,' I said. 'I'd like to give people who are really ill the chance to achieve their lifelong ambition. I'd like to give them one last wish.'

'That's a really sweet thought,' said Charley, suddenly composing herself. 'Just a minute, doesn't Billy Fox run a charity which does just that? In fact, isn't it called One Last Wish? No, just a minute . . . being the egotist that he is, I think it's actually called Billy Fox's One Last Wish. He has to get his name in there, doesn't he? So what are you going to call yours then?'

'I don't know,' I said. 'I was hoping you'd be able to help me there.'

There was a pause.

'How about something to do with dreams?'

Despite her initial scepticism, Charley was obviously now warming to the whole idea.

'Dream Academy?' I suggested.

'That sounds like a stage school for naff wannabes. How about The Dream Fountain?'

'That's good.'

'Or even better, The Fountain of Dreams.'

'That's really good,' I said. 'It conjures up an image of a fountain of wish fulfilment. A never-ending cascade of dreams in which anybody can dip their cup and take a sip.'

'Fountain of Dreams it is then,' said Charley.

There was another pause.

'Simon Peters' Fountain of Dreams,' I said, correcting her.

On the other end of the line, I heard Charley sigh.

21:

Dominic Mulryan interviews Annie Reichman

Simon Peters' Fountain of Dreams is now an established registered charity; it's already raised over eight million pounds and has helped more than five hundred people fulfil their dreams and achieve their lifelong ambitions.

The first person it helped was Poppy Johnston, the little girl with the doll who had asked Simon for his autograph. The charity arranged for Poppy and her father to fly to Australia to see her grandparents. They only intended to stay for one month, but while they were out there they noticed the climate really helped Poppy's condition, so her father decided they should stay for good. At that point, the charity was in its infancy and didn't have the funds to aid them further, so Simon himself stepped in to help. He personally paid for all their legal fees and the cost of shipping their possessions over to Australia. He also put a down payment on their rent for the first six months while the father found his feet and looked for a job.

Just for the record, Poppy is still alive today, living in the suburbs of Sydney (in a house just around the corner from her grandparents) and doing very well at school.

All of this, of course, made a very impressive story for the tabloids.

So why did Simon Peters have this impulsive urge to help others?
Was his sudden selflessness driven by genuine altruism or had the
London Marathon debacle proved to be a wake-up call for him?
Was it philanthropic self-sacrifice or did he fear his career was on a
knife-edge? Was it an incredible act of humanity or did he sense his
dream unravelling and realize how quickly it could all disappear? Did
he ultimately use the launch of a charity just to get the press off his
back and win the public's adoration once more? Whatever the reason,
it seemed to work (albeit for a short amount of time) and Simon's
Svengali, Annie Reichman, knew that he'd inadvertently found the
key that opened the door to a whole new level of stardom.

DM
Ms Reichman, did you view the charity as a career move?

Annie Reichman
Certainly. From a marketing point of view, Fountain was
a stroke of pure genius. It highlighted Simon's caring side
and elevated him above the ranks of mere celebrity. He was
still a TV presenter but suddenly he was a TV presenter
who genuinely wanted to help little sick children. Lots of
celebrities lend their names to charities to garner publicity,
but very few of them will go to the trouble of actually
setting one up. I'm sure Simon's motives for creating it
were very honourable but there's no denying it was a very
shrewd business move, and it did a lot to help his public
profile which, at that point, had certainly started to slip.

DM
The first series of It Could Be You! *had been a huge success and*
it was immediately recommissioned. Do you think at that point the
tabloids felt that Simon had it too easy and were looking for a chink
in his armour?

Annie Reichman

Undoubtedly. During his initial rise to the top they were very kind to him, but when they realized how successful he was becoming they soon started taking potshots at him in an effort to damage the brand. After the London Marathon disaster they were quite vitriolic, but with the launch of Fountain and the wonderful Poppy Johnston story it meant, for a short time at least, they couldn't write anything negative about him. I knew it wouldn't be long before they started chipping away at him again, but for the next few months they had to give him positive coverage and, of course, I fully exploited that.

DM

Did you worry that you were overexposing him?

Annie Reichman

Absolutely not.

I overexposed him, I just didn't worry about it. I usually ensure my artistes keep a low profile and actively discourage them from overexposure, but with Simon, I admit I employed a totally different strategy. He was evolving into a new kind of star and suddenly he was being mentioned in the same breath as Princess Diana and Sir Bob Geldof. That was all very well, but I wanted to keep pushing the message that he was just a normal guy who'd hit the big time and was now putting something back into society. The launch of the charity was the perfect opportunity to put him out there on the celebrity circuit.

Very often these things are all about timing, and the story obviously ticked all the right boxes. Simon's career had been moderately successful up until that point, but suddenly it exploded like a rocket. I was getting requests for him to appear on absolutely everything and I made sure we accepted them all. He was a celebrity guest on every chat show, panel show, quiz show, game show and reality show. He gave interviews to every radio station in the country and even appeared in *Trafalgar Way* and *Holby City*. Antonio Bassani planted stories about him in every single newspaper and phrases like 'Saint Simon' were bandied about. I even made sure there were calls for him to be knighted.

You may remember he also appeared on *Question Time*, giving his opinion on the changes in Entertainment Law. It was interesting because, even though he clearly didn't have a clue what he was talking about, it didn't seem to matter and the politicians sat there nodding in agreement with him.

This was the level he was now playing at.

DM
How did all this affect Simon?

Annie Reichman
It obviously meant a lot of extra pressure for him, but at first he didn't object. By his own admission he didn't have much else going on in his life, so he was able to give the media 100 per cent. He totally submerged himself in the work and in doing so created a new, heightened level of celebrity. The plan undoubtedly paid off and for those few months after the first series ended, I made sure there was no escaping Simon Peters. We both agreed we'd achieved everything we'd ever wanted for him.

Well, almost everything. I still had one more trick up my sleeve for him.

22:

Dominic Mulryan interviews Charley O'Neil

And what a trick it was.

At the beginning of the summer, Simon Peters surprised everyone by releasing the theme tune of It Could Be You! *as a single. 'It Could Be You (You! You! You!)', as it was called, was critically dismissed by those in the music industry as nothing but a novelty record. The track was voted the most annoying pop song ever in Channel 4's* 100 Most Annoying Pop Songs Ever!, *even beating 'Agadoo', 'The Birdie Song' and Bryan Adams' '(Everything I Do) I Do It For You'. The choreographed dance routine, which Simon Peters performed in the video and on several Saturday morning children's television programmes, was widely acknowledged as cringingly embarrassing. His live performance on GMTV, where he was joined by children from various nations around the world, was voted the worst moment in TV history in Channel 4's* 100 Worst Moments in TV History!

Regardless of all this, 'It Could Be You (You! You! You!)' was a massive commercial hit, selling 1.5 million records, knocking Robbie Williams off the top spot and staying at number one for five weeks.

Somewhat incredibly, Simon Peters was a pop star.

Charley O'Neil

Oh God, I'd completely forgotten about that. Out of all the things that happened in his career, I still can't believe he actually had a number one record.

DM

How did it all come about?

Charley O'Neil

In a couple of press interviews Simon mentioned that he'd sung the theme tune for *It Could Be You!* He wasn't lying because he had recorded a version of it; we just never used it on the actual show because it was so bad. I never told Simon that we'd re-recorded it because I thought it was obvious: the session singer we used was a great big black guy who sounded like Barry White, whereas Simon sounded like a strangled Joe Pasquale.

Obviously a couple of journalists got very suspicious about this, and eventually there was a big splash in one of the tabloids stating that Simon's voice had been dubbed without him knowing about it. When Simon found out, he was furious, and for a couple of days he refused to do the second series, claiming we'd made him look stupid. I told him not to be ridiculous and it was the fact that he wore sunglasses indoors that made him do that.

It could have all gone hideously wrong, but Annie Reichman is very good at turning a negative press story into a positive one. To appease Simon and to make the most out of a bad situation, she did something which, at the time, seemed quite outrageous. She suggested Simon re-record the song and put it out as a single just prior to the start of the second series. Having heard Simon sing, I thought it would be career suicide for him and worried it might damage the brand of the show, but it proved to be a stroke of genius. Reichman very quickly set up a record label called SP Records and distributed the song through that. This was a smart move because it meant that she and Simon received 100 per cent of the royalties.

DM
And the record was a surprise hit?

Charley O'Neil
Well, it certainly surprised me. They rush-released the single, and the timing of it couldn't have been better. The whole thing happened incredibly fast, and within a couple of weeks it became one of those big party hits that everybody sings at weddings and holiday parks when they're pretending they're having a good time. The song was everywhere and you couldn't escape it. It even had one of those choreographed routines which all the kids could learn and dance along with.

God, it was crap . . . I mean truly crap.

DM
Do you think Simon was genuinely popular with the British public?

Charley O'Neil
For that short period when the song was out, he seemed to be really popular. Simon did everything he could to promote the song and it generated an incredible amount of publicity. He did a whistle-stop tour of Britain and the reaction he got was amazing. When he was just a C-lister he was hardly ever recognized, and he was very rarely asked for his autograph. In fact, more often than not he'd have to go up to a member of the public, tell them who he

was and sign something for them whether they wanted it or not.

When he had the number one record it couldn't have been more different. Wherever he went, people would scream and yell and cheer and try to rip off pieces of his clothing. I actually saw it happen once. He thought he'd suffered his last wedgie at school but it seemed to become a regular occurrence again. He used to joke that he'd started wearing three pairs of underpants because the first two pairs always seemed to disappear. What did people do with Simon Peters' pants? Wear them? Hang them on the wall? Sell them on eBay? I must check to see how much they're worth these days. As long as his pants are worth more than Dale Winton's, Simon would be happy.

DM
How did Simon treat the public?

Charley O'Neil
At that time, one of his most endearing qualities was that he genuinely cared what they thought of him. He was a real people pleaser, and being a celebrity meant that he could please as many people as possible. When he met the public Simon was very good with them, and I can honestly say I never saw him refuse an autograph or be nasty to anyone – well, not members of the public anyway. Work colleagues, friends, members of his family maybe, but not the public. It never ceased to amaze me how he always had time for his fans, even those really scary ones with greasy hair and bad teeth.

Come to think of it, all of his fans had greasy hair and bad teeth.

DM

With his song at number one, Simon was a guest on a show which he'd always dreamed of appearing on?

Charley O'Neil

Yes, just when you thought he couldn't get any more exposure, I was approached by *This Is Your Life*, who told me they were planning for him to be the first subject of the brand-new series. I was quite excited about it because I knew that Simon's ultimate burning ambition was to be handed the Big Red Book; it was all he ever wanted and I know for a fact that he used to practise his look of surprise, just in case. He'd appeared as a guest on lots of other *This Is Your Life*s, but I think he felt his career wasn't of any real value until he'd actually been the subject himself. I know he was devastated when they originally cancelled the show without him having had the chance to do it. When I heard they were reviving it, I knew that Simon would be thrilled.

Apparently, when he was young he was absolutely obsessed with it.

23:

Extracts from Simon's diary

30 JUNE

I can't believe that I've finally appeared on _This Is Your Life_. To appear on _Life_ (as we call it in showbiz) means one joins the elite ranks of the light entertainment hierarchy; it is the ultimate accolade and signifies one is accepted as a member of the show-business royal family. It indicates one is acknowledged as the best and recognized as having a career worthy of celebration.

Either that or you've got something to promote.

Granted, I've got a single out at the moment and the new series of _It Could Be You!_ starts next month, but I think they would have got around to me sooner or later anyway. At least with me as the first subject, it looks like this series of _Life_ is going to be a lot more entertaining than the previous one. I'm pleased they've started having real celebrities on again and stopped featuring all those awful nobodies who flew Spitfires in the war or built nurseries in Romania. The public aren't interested in that sort of thing. I think they only want to hear about charity work when it's been done by a celebrity.

The public want to see stars whose lives have been full of glamour and excitement and ultimately they want to see famous people crying. They want to watch well-known personalities reminiscing about their years in rep and telling stories about the time they left their make-up bag at Crewe railway station. They want to see genuine celebrities who are genuinely good friends with other genuine celebrities. I remember saying this at the backstage party of Keith Chegwin's *Life* (admittedly I'd only met him once before at a Variety Club luncheon in Wolverhampton, but at least he pretended to be very pleased to see me).

I was so genuinely surprised when Michael Aspel handed me the Big Red Book that I forgot to do the 'genuinely surprised' look that I've spent the last twenty years perfecting. Real tears sprang to my eyes, which came as something of a shock because I'd thought I'd have to fake them. I don't think anyone realized how much it meant to me; this was the show I'd dreamt of appearing on since I was a kid.

When I was younger I used to spend hours in my bedroom pretending I was the subject of *This Is Your Life*. The trouble was I didn't have any real friends to come on and say nice things about me, so I'd have to play all the parts myself, including Eamonn Andrews who was the host back then. I don't think my Irish accent was very good, but if you were standing outside my bedroom you could have probably guessed who I was trying to be.

'Yes *Soimon Peters*, you thought you were here *tonoight* just to sit in *yer* bedroom and do *yer* homework . . . But no, because *tonoight Soimon Peters*, TV Legend and Game Show

210

Host Extraordinaire . . . This is your *loife*! *Da daa daaa daaaaa!*'

That's the music, by the way . . .

'*Da daa daaa daaaaa!*'

I'd then pretend to be lots of different celebrities who would come on and pay homage to me and say what a great talent I was and how I was the saviour of the British light entertainment industry. I'd do impersonations of all the stars of the day like Bruce Forsyth, Jimmy Tarbuck and Limahl from Kajagoogoo, but I'd also introduce the Dalai Lama and Mother Teresa, who'd talk about my endless charity work. The trouble was, all my impressions were rubbish.

'*Didn't he do well, good game good game, give us a twirl, Anthea.*'

That was my Mother Teresa.

I played this game many times, and looking back I remember the saddest thing was that I used to introduce my mum as the special surprise guest at the end. This was about a year after she died.

I always used to get her voice just right.

Obviously my mum was never going to appear on my real *This Is Your Life*, but I have to admit that I was slightly disappointed by the people they did get. They wheeled out an endless array of D-list nonentities; half of them I'd never met before and the other half I don't even like. I'm sure they only agreed to appear because they had something to promote and they hoped that, because I'm quickly becoming one of the biggest stars in the country, a little bit of my heat might transfer on to them.

Where were all my real friends?

OK, Charley was sitting at the back, but they didn't let her tell a story because she's not famous enough. My brother David was there, looking weird with his mad, staring, seen-

211

the-light eyes, but where was everybody else? After several years spent dreaming of being on the show, it was all a bit of an anticlimax really. Christopher Biggins came on and told a story about the time I appeared on his *Life* (the only other time I'd actually met him), and Mimi Lawson told a story about panto in Grimsby which, quite frankly, I had no recollection of whatsoever. When I questioned her about it at the after-show party, she told me it had never actually happened but because she couldn't think of anything interesting to say about me, one of the show's scriptwriters had written it for her. Charming! She then went on to tell me she was thinking of turning to God again. I introduced her to my brother and they got on like a house on fire.

I was particularly disappointed that I didn't have anyone special sitting next to me to share my big night. It would have been really good for my image to be seen sitting next to a stunning, slightly-less-famous-than-me celebrity girlfriend, who would have spent the entire programme gently squeezing my hand and gazing at me with awe and admiration. If the producers had warned me that I was going to be on the show instead of surprising me, I could have arranged to have someone there by my side. I'm sure Thornton would have done it, or better still Vorderman. Instead they stuck me next to my agent Annie Reichman, who, it has to be said, has not got a great face for television. I noticed on the monitor that the director kept cutting to a two-shot of us so I slowly edged my seat away from her, just in case the viewers thought we were an item.

The show was in danger of being just another run-of-the-mill *Life* until Aspel started telling the story of how I'd lost my mother when I was thirteen. A hush fell over the studio, and even the hardened camera crew seemed to be touched by it. It was incredibly poignant and there wasn't a dry eye in the house. My bottom lip was trembling and a large crystal tear rolled down my cheek (I left it there just long enough for them to get a close-up of it). I thought they should have ended the show on that but, of course, they always have to bring out someone special at the end. I was fully expecting it to be my father; I haven't spoken to him for three years, so it would have been an emotionally charged reunion and a perfect *This Is Your Life* moment.

Aspel launched into his spiel to introduce the surprise guest.

'So, Simon, do you recognize this voice?'

I expected my dad to say something about when I was a kid. Maybe the Vimto story or the one about the time I painted the cat.

The mystery voice started to speak.

'Well Simon, everyone is always telling me how you stole my career and one day I'm going to get my own back on you . . . Just you wait!'

The way it was delivered, it got a big laugh from the studio audience, but I couldn't help thinking it was a strange thing for my father to say.

'He's someone who inspired you as a child . . .'

I mentally prepared myself to see my dad again after all this time.

'You had nothing but respect for him . . .'

I planned to give him a big hug and prove to him there were no hard feelings.

'. . . and he influenced your career, greatly . . .'

I just hoped he wasn't going to come out and start doing ten minutes of stand-up.

'A legendary entertainer . . .'

I knew my dad had won Club Entertainer of the Year in 1972, but 'legendary' was stretching it a bit.

213

'. . . and a true icon of British show business . . .'

Blimey, I thought, Aspel's certainly laying it on with a trowel.

'This man is one of the greats!'

Just a minute, I thought, that mystery voice didn't have a Yorkshire accent.

'Ladies and gentlemen . . .'

In fact, it didn't sound anything like my father.

'Please welcome . . .'

It sounded more like . . .

'The one and only . . .'

No, it couldn't be . . .

'Billy Fox!'

The music started, the doors slid back and there he stood, doing his trademark point and wink.

I wasn't sure if it was some sort of joke. I glanced at Annie Reichman next to me and she didn't look very happy – then again, her droopy moustache always makes her look like that. She was hiding her emotions very well, but I'm sure on the inside she was seething about it. It occurred to me that Fox is also one of her clients, but I guessed the production team must have booked him direct. She grabbed my hand and squeezed it. I'm guessing she was trying to comfort me but I quickly snatched it away again, just in case they were on a two-shot of us.

Fox walked down the slope, giving me a familiar wave as he approached. I didn't really want to but I stood up and held my hand out towards him.

'Simon,' he said, shaking his head condescendingly. 'Simon, Simon, Simon . . .'

Then suddenly, without any warning and remarkably quickly for a man of his age, he grabbed my hand, pulled me violently towards him and with his free arm placed me in a headlock and started rubbing my hair really hard, the way a fifth-former might do to a first year.

'Go on, admit it,' he said. '*It Could Be You!* is a rip-off of *One Last Chance!* Go on, admit it!'

He was laughing the whole time so the studio audience laughed along with him, but the way he was rubbing my head bloody hurt. Aspel was laughing too, but you could tell he thought it had gone on too long, and he tapped Billy on the shoulder to release me. He didn't at first, so Michael had to physically restrain him.

'Just a bit of fun, Michael,' he said when he finally let me go.

He laughed, straightened his tie and then slapped my cheeks in a showbizzy way as if it had all been light-hearted teasing, but I think even the studio audience could tell that the atmosphere had changed. I was shocked and sat back down, breathing heavily and with tears of pain stinging the backs of my eyes.

Aspel tried to gloss over it and asked Fox how he'd first met me. I feared he was going to say something derogatory, but he just stood there and worked his way through a couple of weak anecdotes. He did it all through gritted teeth and although he didn't exactly say anything nasty, he did manage to make a joke about the fact that he was planning a lawsuit against me. He ruffled my hair again as he said it; I tried giving a smile but it probably came over as a sneer.

Why did they invite Billy Fox on? Surely everyone knows I hate him and he hates me? Maybe the producers thought it was just a press story and that we were actually great showbiz chums in real life, or maybe they thought it was true and realized it would be great for the ratings to have us on together. Whatever the reason, I'm sure Billy only appeared to try to improve his TV profile; his career's really gone downhill since *One Last Chance!* was cancelled. When Aspel asked him what he was up to these days, he said he spent a lot of time in his villa in Portugal trying to find himself.

I could have told him where to find himself: in the back of *The Stage* under 'Has-Beens'!

24:

Dominic Mulryan interviews Charley O'Neil

Ratings-wise, Simon Peters' This Is Your Life *was one of the most successful episodes in the history of the programme. Despite legal advice to the contrary, Simon decided not to press charges against Billy Fox and when the show was finally broadcast, the BBC had edited out the assault. It could have all been quickly forgotten, but the clip soon appeared on YouTube and the tabloids picked up on it and ran several big stories regarding Fox and Peters' animosity towards each other.*

The 'Go on, admit it' moment, as it became known, was the subject of much debate on the Internet forums, and for a short while it even became a national catchphrase. Everyone was talking about it, and it divided the country between those people who thought there was genuine tension between the two artistes, and those who believed it was all a publicity stunt dreamed up by Annie Reichman. It certainly had all the hallmarks of a Reichman special, but would she create a situation like that, knowing the sort of reaction it would provoke?

Fox's attack on Simon, whether malevolent or not, is the one thing everybody remembers about that show. However, watching a rerun of it now, and with knowledge of Simon's tragic demise, one can't help but feel a sense of sadness at his distinct lack of genuine friends.

Charley O'Neil

I'd known Simon for ten years and it didn't really hit me, until that night, that I was his only real friend. I guess his life was his career and his career was his life, and he didn't think he needed anything else. He'd dedicated his whole existence to it, and if that meant not having any genuine friends and not being able to develop lasting relationships, then that was a sacrifice he was willing to make. I think that's why he desperately wanted a celebrity girlfriend, he felt that she'd be the same as him, so the relationship wouldn't require any real depth to it . . . it's quite sad when you think about it.

DM

Why do you think the producers of This Is Your Life *invited Billy Fox to be a guest?*

Charley O'Neil

I really don't know. I guess they thought that Simon and Billy had a lot in common. Simon would have really hated that, because he said that Billy was 'old school' and that there was no place for his style of entertainment in modern television. I don't think he realized how ironic he was being, seeing as Simon was so 'old school' himself.

DM

Many people claimed that Simon had stolen Billy Fox's act.

Charley O'Neil

I don't agree with that, because I don't think Billy had an act in the first place. Having said that, there's no denying that their presenting techniques were very similar and that

Simon had obviously been influenced by Billy. Look at the hand gestures, the casual glances to camera, the dancing on the spot, the distinctive way they asked the questions. That's just the positive stuff; what about the negatives? The inability to deliver a joke, the way they'd fluff lines and mispronounce words . . . some would call it a speech impediment, others would call it an inability to master the English language. Whatever it was, there's no denying there were similarities. If you look very closely they even looked alike.

DM
So what did you think when Fox assaulted Simon?

Charley O'Neil
I was completely shocked. If you were being kind, you'd describe it as 'weird', and if you were unkind you'd call it 'car-crash TV'. I mean, he physically attacked Simon; he tried making a joke out of it but you could tell there was genuine malice there. Even when he started telling his unfunny anecdotes there was an uncomfortable tension in the air, as if there was something unsaid, something only those two knew about. I found it particularly strange because they're both old pros who would normally put on a showbiz smile but, for Simon in particular, it all seemed to go a little deeper than that. It was a surreal moment and the programme just ground to a halt. Ever the pro, Michael Aspel jumped in, handed Simon the Big Red Book and uttered the immortal line:

'Simon Peters, This Is Your Life!'

As he said it, you got the impression that as Simon looked around at Annie Reichman squeezing his hand, his brother doing the mad staring thing and Billy Fox wanting to strangle him, he was desperately wishing that it wasn't.

More than anything, I think he was disappointed that his father wasn't there.

25:

Dominic Mulryan interviews Simon's father, Tommy Peters

Tommy Peters is a tough-talking, no-nonsense, tell-it-as-it-is York-shireman. The former comedian made his living on the working-men's club circuit of the North and North-east. Tommy and Simon famously didn't get on, and Tommy had not had any contact with his son since the publication of Simon's first book, Diary of a C-List Celeb.

DM
Tommy, after your wife died it must have been difficult bringing up two sons on your own?

Tommy Peters
It was bloody difficult, I'm telling you. I mean, it's never going to be easy for anyone, especially if you're a successful working comic. And I was successful, y'know, despite what they've said in the papers about me: 'Failed comic!' I never bloody failed. I won Club Comic of the Year 1973. I was 'Tubby' Tommy Peters: a knowing wink, a cheeky smile and a meaningless catchphrase. After every punchline, I'd

say, 'Shut your cakehole!' and the audience would shout, 'You shut yours!'

It doesn't seem funny now of course, but it was very popular at the time. It really caught on in Rotherham and for a short while everyone was saying it. 'Shut your cakehole!' 'No, you shut yours!' It could have been a national catchphrase if I'd been given the chance.

I was on *The Comedians*, you know, and *The Wheeltappers and Shunters Club*. I also shot a pilot for a game show. I could have done more telly, everybody said I could, but after June died I had to look after the two lads on my own and I couldn't really concentrate on my career. I had to keep playin' the working-men's clubs just to keep a roof o'er our heads, and I had to take the boys with me to all the gigs. They'd sit in the front row with a packet of crisps, a Vimto and two straws. I don't think David used to enjoy it that much, he'd sit there with a face on him, but Simon used to love it. He'd roar with laughter even though I'm sure he didn't understand half the gags. At least I hope he didn't understand 'em, if you know what I mean, nudge nudge wink wink. Shut your cakehole!

You're supposed to join in with that bit.

DM
Do you think you were a good father to Simon?

Tommy Peters
I think it's no secret that we didn't exactly see eye to eye, especially when he went all big-time, but when he were a young lad I was a good father; a bloody good father! I remember when June was still alive, she begged me to go and watch him in a school play that he was performing in . . . a sort of nativity thing, I think it was. I had to cancel

a gig in Halifax to go and see it, which I wasn't too happy about.

Simon played the part of a sheep, and it hurts me to say this, but he was bloody awful. I said to him afterwards that he should have stolen the show as a sheep, there's ample opportunity for some great comedy business. He could have done the old woolly-jumper routine, maybe even thrown in a sheep-shagging gag; a little bit risqué for a nativity play but with a knowing wink and a cheeky smile he'd have got away with it. What did he do, though? He let it go to waste. He let the other kids get all the laughs instead. I remember the kid playin' Joseph did a great bit of business when he dropped the little Baby Jesus on his head.

Big laughs!

He then picked it up and bounced it.

Bloody hilarious!

Simon had to 'baaa' in a particular place but he couldn't even get a laugh on that. To be honest I was a bit embarrassed because it was at that moment I realized the truth: he didn't have a funny bone in his body. He was awful; bloody awful. But I'll tell you something . . . he was the only bugger who insisted on taking three curtain calls.

DM
So was Simon an extrovert as a child?

Tommy Peters
Extrovert? Oh, he was more than that, he was a right bloody show-off. I think he must have got it from his mother's side. His brother was the complete opposite, of course. Simon would be poncing about in his room pretending he was a superstar while David was in his room reading the Bible and watching *Songs of* bloody *Praise*. I had

Burt Reynolds in one bedroom and Harry bloody Secombe in the other.

And people try to blame me for being a bad father.

Believe it or not, Simon used to actually practise at being famous. He'd spend hours in front of the mirror pretending to pose for the . . . what do you call them? Those bloody photographers who killed Lady Di . . . paparazzi, that's it. He'd pout and frown and blow kisses at himself, and he'd stretch his arm out and cover the mirror with his hand as if he was blocking a camera lens, and then he'd spread his fingers wide enough so he'd still be able to see his face.

One time, I caught him in his bedroom. I'd have been happy if he was looking at bloody porn but no, he was smiling and waving and signing his name on lots of scraps of paper which he'd positioned around the room. I asked him what he was doing and he said he was arriving at a film premiere. A bloody film premiere! He must have been about fourteen at the time.

DM
I think many people were surprised that you didn't make an appearance on Simon's This Is Your Life.

Tommy Peters
Well, obviously the Beeb wanted me to do it; they wanted me to be the surprise guest who came on at the end and walked to the front, arm in arm with Simon.

'It'll make great television,' they said. 'Father and son reunited.'

'Great television costs money,' I said and told them I wanted five grand in cash.

'But he's your son.'

'And you're the BBC,' I said. 'Five grand in cash or no can do.'

They said it wasn't in the budget and ironically, considering what eventually happened, they ended up getting Billy bloody Fox. Apparently he did it for two hundred and fifty quid cash, no questions asked.

How the mighty have fallen, eh?

Billy bloody Fox!

I mean, he's just not funny, is he? He never was. He wouldn't know a punchline if it punched him in the mouth. I used to do lots of the clubs and summer seasons with him back in the early days. He died on his arse everywhere he went and was paid off more times than I've had hot dinners. He had the occasional good gig when the audience were with him but he was always a clumsy comedian, always cocking up the cues and tripping over the tag lines. He never had the rhythm. He was always a third-rate comic, and the only difference nowadays is that he's a third-rate comic who's been on the telly.

I'll give him this though, he was always full of confidence. It was as if he was totally oblivious to the fact that everybody hated him and thought his act was crap.

DM
Do you feel in some way bitter that you never had the break that Billy Fox had?

Tommy Peters
Of course I'm not bloody bitter. I could have been a game show host though, y'know, everybody says I could. As a matter o' fact, I was offered one but I turned it down. It was 1972 and I was in summer season in Skeggy. I know it was '72 because while we were there, June fell pregnant

wi' Simon. I was at the end of the pier with Rod Hull and Emu, the Paxton Brothers and Billy bloody Fox. I should have been second on the bill but my agent cocked the whole thing up and Billy Fox's name was above mine.

I wasn't best pleased, as you can imagine.

Anyway, some big-shot TV producer saw me there and asked me to go along to audition for a new game show, which they thought I'd be perfect for. At the time I was full of confidence, some might say cocky, and I thought I were goin' places.

'What you see is what you get,' I told them. 'If you think I'm perfect I shouldn't have to audition.'

I'd spent twenty-five years doing the club circuit. Twenty-five years! *That* was my audition. They pleaded with me so in the end I relented. I went along, did the audition and of course, I got the gig.

'This is it,' I thought. 'This is the Big Time.'

But there was a fly in the ointment. Humphrey Hamilton, the Head of Light Entertainment at LWT, insisted on shooting a bloody pilot show. 'What's the point?' I said. 'You've got the right host for the right show, what do we need a bloody pilot show for?'

But they insisted. We shot the pilot and two weeks later they called me up.

'We have a slight problem, Tommy,' said the producer, some posh upstart not five minutes out of bloody Oxford. 'Humphrey thinks you were a little too . . . edgy.'

'Edgy?'

'Yes, he thinks you weren't warm enough with the contestants.'

'The contestants were all bloody stupid,' I said.

'Yes, but the trick is to make them look smart,' he said. 'We want you to interact with the contestants without trying to score points off them. Like Bob Monkhouse on *The Golden Shot*.'

'I can do that,' I said. 'That's the easy bit. It's making sure I've got enough gags for the whole series, that's the real problem. This show could really eat my material up.'

'Ah . . . that's the other point. Humphrey felt you were always trying to get your jokes in.'

'But I'm a comedian, that's what I do.'

'Television isn't like the clubs, Tommy. You can't do your act the whole time.'

'But television should be like the clubs, that's what your man in the street wants.'

I gave them lots of advice and pointers on what I thought would make the show better. They took it all on board and, of course, they offered me the job . . . and they did bloody offer it to me, some people have said that they didn't but they bloody well did! It was going to be 26 half-hour episodes, which would go out prime-time 8.30 p.m. every Saturday night just after *New Faces*. The money was phenomenal.

Of course, I had to turn it down because June was three months pregnant with Simon by this point and she didn't like to be left alone. They begged and pleaded with me to do the show but I told them my family came first. They ended up giving the show to Billy Fox. Yes, *the* Billy Fox. They still used all my bloody ideas, though. The show was originally called *Wishing on a Star* but can you guess what they changed the title to?

One Last Chance!

Of course I'm not bitter about it.

26:

Dominic Mulryan interviews Billy Fox

DM
Billy, thank you for agreeing to this interview. What do you think about Tommy Peters' claims that he was the first choice for One Last Chance!*?*

Billy Fox
Yes, I think I read that in one of the tabloids. To quote my old catchphrase, 'I don't think sooooooo!' I don't know why he'd try to claim that. It's funny what some people do to try and score points and get a little bit of publicity, isn't it? Well, let me clear this up once and for all.

Most people, I'm sure, will already be aware of this story because it's in my autobiography, *The Silver Fox: A Life of Love and Laughter*, published by Bantam and available in all good bookstores and a few dodgy ones as well! Eh? Are you getting that one . . . a few dodgy ones as well! It topped the best-sellers chart for three weeks running, by the way, even outselling Bruce's book. Not bad for a boy from Stoke, eh? Anyway, as I remember it, I was in summer season in Skegness with Rod Hull and Emu. It was a nice little show, Rod was top of the bill, I was second and the Paxton Brothers were third. Very funny act, the Paxton Brothers, used to juggle live pigeons. Tommy Peters was in the show but he was way down the bill.

Anyway, Humphrey Hamilton, the Head of Light Entertainment at LWT, came to see Rod about booking him as a regular guest on some chat show or other . . . Russell Harty's, I think it was, I'm not sure. Well, the night that Humphrey H. was in, I had an absolute stormer . . . an ab-so-lute storm-er! I could do no wrong; I had 'em eating out of my hand. Anyway . . . lean in close cos this is where it gets interesting . . . there was this drunken old bird in the audience who kept heckling me. Every time I'd get to a punchline she'd shout something out, but nobody could understand a word she was saying. Not-a-word! Well, as you know, I'm at my best when I'm interacting with the public and it's all a bit spontaneous, like. I've never been much of a gag teller, but I can squeeze every last drop of comedy out of a situation that's gone a bit pear-shaped. This old bird just wouldn't shut up. Every time I said something she'd shout something back, except it wasn't a shout, it was more of a slur, so I started slurring my words and the more I slurred my words, the more she slurred hers, and the more we slurred the more the audience laughed. She was like a gift from the comedy gods and it went on like that for about fifteen minutes. Fifteen minutes! Now obviously this meant that I went over my allotted time, but the theatre management didn't mind because I was giving them comedy gold and that's what gets bums on seats.

Anyway, they made up the time by cutting down the next act . . . come to think of it, the next act was Tommy Peters; I guess he wouldn't have been too happy about it, because he'd have known Humphrey H. was in. Anyway . . . lean in closer cos it gets even better . . . I eventually got the old bird up on stage and I got the band to play 'Show Me the Way to Go Home'. We slurred our way through three verses of it! Well, by this time the audience were in hysterics and I'm sure the majority of them thought she was a plant in the audience, in fact I even threw that in as an ad-lib.

'Look at this,' I said. 'I asked for a plant and they gave me a vegetable!'

Gave me a vegetable! Woofer of a laugh. Lifted the roof off. Humphrey H. knew she wasn't a plant though, he knew it was totally genuine and he knew he'd found the host he'd been looking for.

Three months later they offered me the chance to shoot a pilot called *Wishing on a Star.* It was a rubbish title and the format didn't really work, but Humphrey H. liked working with me and he thought I had something special. I knew it was my big chance so I pitched him this idea I'd been working on which was called . . . now, lean in close cos this is where it gets really interesting . . . it was called *It Could Be You!* Did you get that? *It Could Be You!* It had the exclamation mark and everything. There are no new ideas in television, are there? Well, Humphrey didn't like the title, so I came up with *One Last Chance!* on the spot. He commissioned it there and then, and the rest, as they say, is showbiz history.

27:

Dominic Mulryan interviews Simon's brother,
David Peters

David Peters is an accountant and born-again Christian who now lives in Sheffield.

DM
David, you were obviously very young at the time, but can you shed any light on what occurred in the summer of '72?

David Peters
Actually, I think quite a lot happened in the summer of 1972.

I know my father did record a 'pilot' – as you call it – for a TV show, but I'm not sure whether it was *One Last Chance!* or not. There's always been a lot of controversy surrounding that one, and I think the mists of time have clouded everyone's memory as to exactly what happened.

My guess is that my father blew the opportunity because of his stubbornness. I can imagine him wanting to tell jokes the whole time, because that's what he did best.

When the producers said they didn't want that sort of thing, Father would have dug his heels in and told them they were wrong. Obviously you can't do that in television and the producers just went and found somebody else. My father couldn't accept that he'd made a mistake, so as the years passed and he realized he wasn't going to get another chance, he started saying that he'd turned the opportunity down because his wife was pregnant with Simon. The more he said it, the more he believed it, and he ended up blaming Simon for missing his big break. Simon was the only person he could blame.

Well, Simon and Billy Fox, of course.

DM
Did you, as a family, watch One Last Chance!*?*

David Peters
I was never a fan myself and my father certainly wasn't, but Simon never missed an episode. In fact, when he was about ten, he became totally infatuated with Billy Fox. He seemed to identify with him and recognize the fact that Fox wasn't that talented. All he appeared to do was talk to the camera, chat to the contestants and ask them questions which were written on cards. It all looked so simple.

I used to watch Simon studying the screen and I knew he was thinking, *'I could do that . . . that could be me.'* He never missed an episode. He would hang on to Fox's every word and scrutinize every move he made. Obviously, this was before we had a video, so Simon would memorize the contestants' names and then write down all the questions and answers and jokes on a piece of paper. When the show had finished, he would run to his room and re-enact it from beginning to end.

When he started working in television, I watched his shows with interest and noticed lots of little tricks that he'd obviously picked up when he was studying Billy Fox for all those years.

DM
David, your lives didn't exactly follow similar paths; how do you think you differed from Simon?

David Peters
I think the biggest difference was that Simon was completely obsessed by celebrity, whereas I never really liked the idea of worshipping false icons.

If thou walk after other gods and serve them and worship them, I testify this against you this day that ye shall perish. Deuteronomy: Chapter 8 Verse 19.

As a child I had no interest whatsoever in show business. Whenever we were taken to the theatre, Simon saw the glitz and the glamour whereas I only saw the fading facades and the peeling paint. I think I was intelligent enough to know from an early age that show business could be a very cruel and soul-destroying industry. I watched what it did to my father. I saw how the years of rejection slowly wore him down and eroded his ego like waves crashing on a windswept shore. You will keep that bit in, won't you? '*Waves crashing on a windswept shore.*' Rather good, don't you think? I write my own poetry if you'd be interested in hearing some.

DM
Maybe some other time. So what was Simon like at school?

David Peters

Following the death of our mother he started showing signs of this voracious craving to be the centre of attention the whole time. Despite his inherent shyness and his awkwardness around other people, he had to be the main focal point, and he couldn't bear it if he wasn't the person who everybody was talking about.

Usually, to gain a reputation at school, you have to be 'the one who's good at football', or 'the good-looking one who's successful with the girls', or 'the naughty one who gets in trouble with the police'. I was 'the boring one who's always picked on', especially when I first found religion. They used to call me 'God botherer', a 'happy clapper' and a 'friend of Cliff', but I didn't object because I was very proud of my faith.

For a while Simon tried to build a reputation for being 'the funny one'. I think he thought that, in some strange way, the sound of laughter would bring our mother back to life. The trouble was, of course, although he stole Dad's jokes, he was never very good at telling them and he'd always mess up the punchline. He just wasn't naturally funny and he always tried too hard to be popular. The harder he tried, the more the other kids ignored him, and the more they ignored him, the harder he tried. His constant lack of recognition caused him to become quite introverted and, ironically, the more introverted he became the more he screamed for recognition. That seemed to set the pattern for the rest of his life.

DM

So did you have any idea at that time that Simon would go on to become a TV star?

David Peters

Not at all. I never really thought he was particularly gifted, and I think he realized it too. I was always the talented one with my poetry. Simon desperately wanted to be famous, but he seemed to know from a very early age that the one thing holding him back from achieving his goal was a complete lack of talent. It didn't stop him, though; he was obsessed with the idea of being a celebrity and he watched television for hours on end, looking for the one job he could do without any real flair or talent.

That's when he set his heart on becoming a TV presenter.

28:

Dominic Mulryan interviews Annie Reichman

Simon Peters had grown up to become the TV presenter he'd always wanted to be, but even as a young child he couldn't possibly have imagined just how famous he was to become.

MipTV is the international television marketplace. Every year, TV executives from all over the world descend on Cannes and pretend to be more important than they actually are. Sunglasses, BlackBerries and Louis Vuitton briefcases are de rigueur as TV types talk shop, bitch about the competition and try to figure out a way of putting the minibar bill on their expense account.

Ultimately, it's all about business, and TV formats are the global currency. Underneath the liquid blue skies and swaying palm trees, hands are shaken and deals are struck. Cutting-edge shows and cut-throat negotiations all add to the Mip Melee, as TV executives desperately try to sniff out the next Big Brother *or* Who Wants to Be a Millionaire?

In Cannes, everyone is looking for the next big thing, and the year that Annie Reichman paid a visit, it soon became clear the next big thing was It Could Be You!

DM

How confident were you that It Could Be You! *would sell internationally?*

Annie Reichman

Extremely confident. To sell the format I'd taken a large stand on the third floor of the Hotel Palais, a prime location for anyone visiting Mip. I had two plasma screens showing *You!* on loop, and another two showing footage of the sort of hype the show had created. I took my meetings on the balcony, which had spectacular views overlooking the yachts moored in the Croisette. Hiring a stand at the Palais was an expensive exercise, and it was quite a gamble, as I only had one format to sell (most production companies have several). However, I had total confidence in the fact that *You!* was the perfect global format, ideal for selling into international territories. It was a branded, marketable product which ticked all the right boxes. From a technical point of view it had multimedia convergence and live interactivity, which at the time everyone was very keen to exploit. The show itself was packed with emotion and would appeal to the masses whatever the language; there were tears, laughter, jeopardy, wish fulfilment and aspirational sentimentality. There was even a hint of highbrow-dumb-down reality, which were the new buzzwords that year. Everybody was looking for a show with just one of these qualities. *It Could Be You!* had them all.

DM

If the press reports were to be believed, TV executives from all over the world were fighting over the rights to broadcast the show?

Annie Reichman

Absolutely. With hindsight, I should have saved the money I spent on the Palais. Everyone was so keen to buy the format, I could have sold it from the back of a lorry. The execs were queuing up to speak to me, and I quickly realized that we had a major success on our hands. Within three days I'd sold the format to twenty-seven broadcasters, including TF1 in France, Net 5 in the Netherlands, SVT in Sweden and Network Ten in Australia. RTL in Germany was a hard sell but ultimately very profitable, and I also sealed a very lucrative deal with the Asian broadcaster Star TV.

News of the show's success spread like wildfire, and very quickly *It Could Be You!* became *the* hot ticket in Cannes. The word of mouth was unprecedented, and created something of a feeding frenzy. Very often at Mip, panic sets in and execs have a real fear of missing out – nobody wants to be the television equivalent of the guy who didn't sign the Beatles. Because of this, I found myself selling a product which everyone wanted to buy. When that happens in industry, market forces dictate the cost of that product will rise in relation to its demand.

It Could Be You! was very much in demand.

DM
It was obviously very big business. How did you handle all the international sales?

Annie Reichman
I set up a distribution arm of Simon Peters Productions called NDT Distribution, and all the international sales and negotiations were channelled through that. When I returned from Cannes the madness continued, and I managed to sell the show to several broadcasters in the

newly emerging Eastern European market and even licensed the format to a broadband outlet in Bratislava called Microv. Within a short space of time we were airing in a very impressive fifty-two territories. Most of these had bought the format rights to *You!* and then made their own adaptation of it, but several of them bought the rights to broadcast the UK version of the show. This helped establish Simon as an international star, and he particularly liked the idea of being famous in a place he'd never even been to. In fact, when he found out he was famous in that country, he'd want to go there just to be recognized.

The show is still airing in many of those countries today. In Albania, where it is only one of two foreign imported shows allowed to be broadcast (the other one being *Lenny Bennett's Lucky Ladders*), Simon is known as *Njeri i Banorë*, which means 'Man of the People'. He was always very proud of that.

DM
By the end of your trip to Cannes you still hadn't sold the show to America, even though there was an awful lot of interest there?

Annie Reichman
Yes. Every major channel in America wanted the show. Fox had offered an extortionate amount of money and ABC offered a three-year deal, but that wasn't quite good enough for me. I knew *It Could Be You!* belonged on CBS or NBC. They both wanted the show, but I was playing my cards very close to my chest and holding out for the right deal.

I had a radical plan.

For the first episode of the second series I invited Chad Kowalski, the Head of International Acquisitions from NBC in LA, and Todd McLooney, the Executive Vice

President in charge of Format Development and Overseas Programme Attainments from CBS in New York. Obviously, they're sworn enemies, so it was quite a risky strategy to fly them over at the same time, but I wanted them to be aware that the other party was interested and I fully intended to play them off against each other. They both sat in the studio audience and watched the show going out live. They'd seen a tape in Cannes, but I wanted them to experience first hand the sort of hype the show was creating and how the whole country was talking about it.

The show was a great success and they both loved it; from that moment on, things started to move very quickly. Kowalski and McLooney flew back to the States on the Monday morning, and by Wednesday afternoon there was a very generous offer from CBS to purchase the American rights to make and broadcast the show. I did the one thing which any self-respecting agent would do: I called Chad at NBC and told him about the offer from CBS. This sparked a bidding war which NBC won by promising a prime-time slot and agreeing to a co-production with Simon and me as executive consultants. My long-term plan was to try to crack Simon as a TV star in the States and I tried to persuade NBC to have him as the host, but they said he was 'too normal' and 'not talented enough' for American television. America is ahead of Britain in many aspects of broadcasting, but they're not quite up to speed with the fact that having No Discernible Talent is actually a major selling point in itself.

Once the Americans came on board, the show became a very easy commodity to sell into the other territories which hadn't bitten in Cannes. On the strength of the show's global success I merged Simon Peters Productions and NDT Distribution, and with the help of Goldman, Goldman, Goldman, Goldman, Bloom and Bloom in the

City, I formed a public limited company and floated it on the stock market.

On the first day of trading, SP plc opened at a very respectable 68p per share. As *It Could Be You!* sold into more and more territories, the share price gradually strengthened and within six months was trading at an enviable 94p per share.

This success didn't go unnoticed, and it wasn't long before SP plc had come to the attention of some of the multinational conglomerates. This was at a time when many of the bigger corporations were actively investing in new multimedia production companies, and SP plc fitted the bill perfectly.

DM
You struck gold when Time Warner, the biggest fish in the media sea, expressed an interest in buying Simon Peters plc. They were keen to buy the whole company, but you didn't want to sell it outright?

Annie Reichman
Obviously, if they'd bought the company outright, they would have owned the rights to *It Could Be You!* and in my view that wasn't a viable proposition. After lengthy negotiations I suggested that Simon retained a 36 per cent share and remained as Chairman (of course, this was in name only), and I retained a 15 per cent share and become the CEO. It meant that, together, Simon and I were still the major shareholders with a 51 per cent share of the company. Time Warner agreed to this and although the deal wasn't quite as big as many of the newspapers reported, it was certainly very generous in our favour and I advised Simon that he should accept it, which of course he did. It made him very, very rich.

29:

Dominic Mulryan

Simon Peters couldn't believe his luck. In the space of one year, he'd gone from C-list nonentity to A-list superstar. Was it luck or was it planned? Was Simon Peters an exceptional artist who deserved his success, or a talentless game show host who'd landed lucky? Was he a gifted entrepreneur who created his own destiny, or a calculating and manipulative individual who would stop at nothing to achieve his ultimate goal of fame and fortune? Whatever the reason, he was, in the words of Robbie Williams, 'rich beyond his wildest dreams'.

Many people feel, with hindsight, that's where it all started to go wrong.

One year later (and just four months before Simon's tragic death), It Could Be You! *was about to start its fourth series in Britain; the show had been getting record ratings and the format had sold to an unprecedented seventy-eight territories. The Time Warner deal had gone through and Simon Peters was now a fully-fledged multimillionaire media tycoon. He was arguably one of the most famous people in the country, and according to* The Sunday Times Rich List *was also on his way to being one of the wealthiest entertainers. He was living the life of a high-profile celebrity and around him was a constant whirl* of activity, a showbiz cyclone with him at the epicentre of it. He was a bona fide, cast-iron, solid gold, diamond-studded A-lister. Simon was a genuine star and every move he made was accompanied by the constant strobe effect of paparazzi flashbulbs. He was 'in', and he promised himself he would never be 'out' again.

Simon Peters was living the dream.

30:

Extracts from Simon's diary

3 SEPT

Every morning I look in the mirror and have to remind myself that I've finally made it to where I've always wanted to be. I constantly have to reassure myself that all these material possessions are mine, because I'm convinced that one day somebody's going to come along and take them all away again. When I wake up in my six-bedroom house in Holland Park, I have to make sure I'm not dreaming. I have to pinch myself when I look out of the window and see the gleaming Java Black supercharged 4.2-litre V8 Range Rover Sport sitting next to the shining brand-new Bentley Continental GTC with its 12-cylinder, 6-litre, twin-turbocharged engine. I'm not sure what any of the technical stuff means, but I know that when I told Jeremy Clarkson about the cars I drive, he gave me a nod of approval as if to say, 'Yes, you can be in my gang.' (I have to admit I use the term 'cars I drive' very loosely, as I'm scared of taking the Bentley on the road and I only bought the Range Rover because I read that Wayne Rooney had one.)

I have so much money, I can buy anything I want. In fact, I don't even have to buy the stuff myself; a company called 2Rich2Shop buy it all and I just sign for it. They asked me what sort of things I wanted and I told them to buy me the best of everything. I have to admit that I sometimes struggle with the concept of that. I have to constantly touch the keys to the villa in Portugal, just to prove they're real. But they *are* real and they *are* mine: Everything's mine: the Damien Hirst sculpture and the Andy Warhol prints; the wardrobe full of designer suits and the cellar full of vintage Chateau Le Caillou wines; the handmade Italian sofas and the aquarium with Japanese koi carp; the top-of-the-range Torchetti kitchen and the stainless steel Maytag American fridge; the high definition 103-inch plasma-screen television and the integrated Bang and Olufsen sound system; the music room with the white Steinway Alma-Tadema grand piano and the collection of original 1952 Fender Telecaster guitars; the indoor swimming pool; the gymnasium; the hot tub; the sauna; the steam room and the wet room.

I've got it all.

I've got a Sunseeker Superhawk speedboat on order and I've even been learning how to fly a helicopter (I'm thinking of buying one, but I'm not sure which model to get). To be honest the lessons aren't going that well, but surely if Noel Edmonds can do it, I can too?

I really am the man who has everything, and the only downside is that *Through the Keyhole* has been cancelled, so the public can't fully appreciate just how wonderful my life is.

I wonder if *MTV Cribs* would be interested.

5 SEPT

I'm officially the most famous person in the country!

I've just read through all my press cuttings from last week and I was mentioned a total of 647 times. Beckham was only mentioned 538 times and Paris Hilton a paltry 221. Not that I counted, of course; when you're as rich as I am, you can pay a cuttings company to do that for you.

How did I get to be as famous as this?

I know I'd always hoped that it would happen for me, but when I analyse it, it was always more than hope, it was desire, more than desire even, it was an intrinsic knowledge that one day it *would* happen. There must be thousands . . . no, millions of people who would want to be living the life that I'm living. But it's not happening for them, it's happening for me. So when I ask myself why, the only reason I can think of is because I'm great.

I am.

I'm really great.

Luckily I've managed to keep my feet on the ground and I haven't let it go to my head.

6 SEPT

I am the Chosen One. My dream has become reality and the Goddess of Stardom has blessed me with her magical golden powers. The Great God of Fame has smiled on me and sanctified my artistic capabilities, and the Divine Spirit of Celebrity has elevated my status to celestial eminence.

Oh, and I've also been booked to appear on *Loose Women*.

11 SEPT

Bassani is certainly keeping me busy with all the publicity for the show. There's always a journalist to meet and an interview to give. I've recently discovered that there's nothing I like more than talking about myself, and these interviews give me the perfect opportunity to do just that. It's like therapy. They make me feel so alive, and I never knew I had so many interesting things to say on the subject of me. In the interviews I'm always sharp and focused and I'm obviously very enthusiastic about myself, because sometimes they can't shut me up. I catch the journalists anxiously looking at their watches, but I don't care; if they want an interview with me they'll get one, and I don't mind telling them about every single aspect of my life. I kept one journalist talking (or rather listening) for four and a half hours, and in the end he was pleading with me to let him go. He had tears in his eyes and he claimed he was missing his son's fifth birthday party. I told him he should get his priorities right, and started describing my first childhood memory of being on holiday at Butlins in Bognor Regis. When I got to the part about entering the Donkey Derby he just grabbed his tape recorder and ran away. I told Bassani that I wanted him blacklisted and that I'd never give him another interview again.

What is it with some of these journalists? Surely they should be pleased to meet me?

13 SEPT

The brass plate I've requested for my office door (with the words 'Executive Producer' engraved on it) still hasn't arrived yet. I brought this up at today's production meeting.

'Brass?' said Charley. 'Surely you deserve gold.'

I could sense the members of the production team stifling a laugh. I think Charley was being sarcastic, and if she was, I'm going to have to have a word with her about it. I'm the star of the show, I don't want the production team thinking that I'm here to be laughed at.

1.56 a.m.
Maybe she's right. Maybe gold would be better.

18 SEPT

The fourth series of *It Could Be You!* starts next week, and today I was in the *You!* studio in front of a large blue screen, shooting my bits for the opening-title sequence. Once again it was directed by Jean-Claude Beauchamp, and it's all very arty and surreal. The idea is that, using computer-generated imagery, I'll be seen walking among members of the public. When I touch one of them, that person magically gets to achieve their lifelong ambition, be it skydiving, driving a Formula One car or swimming with dolphins in the Bahamas, etc. . . .

To save me from having to go out and actually mix with the public (I think those days are behind me now), the production team have already been out and about in Britain filming hundreds of shots of ordinary people doing really ordinary things: shopping, washing up, walking the dog, etc. To highlight the drabness of these people's lives, it's all been shot in a grainy black and white, but when I touch one of them, the picture bursts into glorious Technicolor.

The titles are going to look very spiritual, and when I'm walking among the public performing the miracles, I'm wearing a brilliant white suit with my arms outstretched.

The imagery is almost Christ-like, which really appeals to me.

'Maybe I could be seen turning water into wine,' I suggested as we were waiting for the next shot to be set up.

'Maybe we could nail you to a cross,' muttered one of the electricians.

All the crew laughed out loud and a couple of them even cheered. Of course I knew they were only joking, because I'm really popular with the crew.

At least, I always used to be.

25 SEPT

In the weeks leading up to the new series being broadcast, I realize I've been a bit of a nightmare for Charley and the production team to deal with. Obviously this was stress-related, and now that I'm confident the show is as successful as the previous series (if not more so), I'm determined to make a real effort to be a lot easier to work with. I've promised myself that I'm going to calm down, enjoy the success and not get so worked up about every little thing.

From now on I'm going to be Mr Popularity.

26 SEPT

Instead of holding today's production meeting in the office, I decided to treat the team and take them to lunch at Masticate, which is *the* restaurant to be seen in (it's certainly one of the most expensive). Charley wasn't very happy about the idea and started mentioning budgets and time constraints, but I insisted, saying that it's the sort of thing big stars like me should do. Charley gave me a strange look when I said this, but I didn't care. In years to come I want people to remember me not just as a legend and broadcasting icon, but also as a really generous guy.

It would be nice if they'd say I was modest as well.

During the meal I stood up and gave a little speech, even though Charley advised me not to. I think she thought I'd had too much to drink and would embarrass myself, but I knew exactly what I was saying. I started by telling the team that the first show of the new series had done really well in the ratings (12.6 million people with a 38 per cent share) and this prompted a spontaneous round of applause. There was lots of handshaking and back-slapping, and it created a really positive energy in the room. I got so carried away I ordered twelve bottles of champagne to celebrate. As we were drinking them, I felt the team and I were finally starting to bond, so I decided the time was right to make amends and apologize for my behaviour over the last few weeks.

'I'm really sorry if I've upset anyone,' I said with genuine sincerity. I know it was genuine sincerity because it's the same genuine sincerity I use when I'm hosting a game show. 'From now on, I'm going to be more of a team player. I don't want you to think that I'm different to you just because I'm a huge celebrity.'

It got a big laugh but I'm not sure why; surely they know I *am* a huge celebrity and that I *am* different to them? Even so, I took their laughter as a compliment and carried on regardless; I figured that if they were laughing at me, it obviously meant they liked me.

'From this moment on,' I said, 'you have permission to tell me if I'm a pain in the arse.'

'You're a pain in the arse,' shouted Tristan, one of the researchers.

Suddenly a large vacuum sucked the laughter out of the room and a brittle silence fell over the proceedings; somewhere in the background a knife fell to the floor and the noise echoed around the hushed restaurant. Everyone turned to see what my reaction would be and I slowly looked at Tristan. This was the same Tristan Reece-Davis who had been so sneering and superior when I pitched my *Celebrity Peacekeepers!* idea to him at ICE Productions last year. He'd applied for a job as a senior researcher on the show; Charley had hired him without consulting me and I wasn't very happy about it.

At the lunch, he'd obviously had too much champagne and was trying to be funny. I glared at him. Charley touched my hand, and when I glanced down at her she shook her head as if to say not to make a fuss. I then looked back at Tristan, who knew he'd said the wrong thing and by this point was bright red with embarrassment and stammering his way through an apology.

An ex-public schoolboy apologizing to *me*.

I felt like the Ralph Fiennes character in *Schindler's List*, when he has the power to kill the Jewish servant but instead decides to forgive her. Just like Ralph, I forgave Tristan. I started to laugh. The tension melted away and everyone laughed along with me (or at me, I'm not sure which).

'At least he's being honest,' I said. 'I don't want people to be scared of me just because I could fire you if you're not.'

I left a comedy pause.

'Tristan, you're fired.'

More big laughs as Tristan's face went a deeper shade of scarlet. Of course I didn't really fire him, but I've marked his card and I'll certainly keep an eye on him in the future.

The lunch had gone really well and I ordered another six bottles of champagne. Unfortunately Charley said that everyone had to go back to work because we had this week's show to produce. I ended up staying in the restaurant and drinking all six bottles with the waiters.

I quite enjoy being a more relaxed boss and this afternoon I was as relaxed as a newt.

31:

Dominic Mulryan interviews Charley O'Neil

DM
By this point in his career, Simon was extremely successful. You knew him better than most; how do you think fame had changed him?

Charley O'Neil
Simon tried very hard to be one of the team but when the megalomania started to set in, one of the first things to suffer was his sense of humour.

One day, during pre-production, he came into the office and complained that the Mercedes that had picked him up was a CLK with cloth seats instead of an SLK with leather. At first I treated this sort of behaviour the way I always had, by taking the piss out of him. The next day, just for a joke, I sent a 50cc moped to pick him up, one of those they use for pizza deliveries.

Needless to say he wasn't very amused.

I can understand why his personality started to change. He couldn't quite believe that after years of struggling, he'd finally made it as the big star he'd always wanted to be. It really went to his head and his ego was constantly on the verge of imploding.

I felt responsible because I should have seen the warning signs and nipped it in the bud. I tried keeping his feet on the ground, but because I had a show to produce it was easier to indulge him and let him have his own way. The problem was, the more we gave him, the more demanding he became, especially once he realized he was becoming bigger than the show.

DM
How would you describe his state of mind at this time?

Charley O'Neil
His mood swings had started getting worse and I'd noticed he was drinking more and more. It wasn't at the Oliver Reed level and I never saw him drinking when he was working, but even so, it was a bit of a worry. I think he felt guilty about how fast everything had happened for him, and deep down he didn't believe that he genuinely deserved it. He couldn't quite believe how far he'd risen and he constantly worried that it was only a matter of time before he fell again. To counteract this, he felt he had to be even more famous, but no matter how famous he became, he was never fully content. It was as if there was a big hole in his life and he was constantly searching for something to fill it.

DM
How did that manifest itself?

Charley O'Neil
He had a nervous urgency about everything he did. Before the first show of the fourth series, he started to get really

stressed out. I knew he suffered from stage fright, but it seemed to be getting worse. He spent half the day pacing up and down in his dressing room shaking like a leaf, and the other half throwing up in the loo and insisting he couldn't go on. To get him to do the show, I had to constantly reassure him about how wonderful he was and how we couldn't do it without him. For a short while I thought we were going to have to cancel the show and get the Network Centre to put out a repeat, but five minutes before the live broadcast, the change in Simon was unbelievable. Suddenly he was the complete professional again. He was sharp and on the ball, and he emanated this self-assurance which certainly hadn't been evident thirty minutes earlier when he was crying like a baby and screaming how much he hated himself.

Once the show started, he was really on form and in total control. Admittedly he did one whole link to the wrong camera, but that's because he was looking into the Simon-cam trying to get a close-up (I told the vision mixer not to cut to it). The viewer at home would just have thought he'd made a mistake, but that didn't matter as it only served to enhance his 'charming vulnerability', which seemed to have become his trademark.

It was fascinating to watch. His unbridled confidence was matched by an equal level of insecurity, and it was as if he was almost begging the viewers to love him. I think, ultimately, that might have been the key to his success. I'm not saying the public felt sorry for him, but I think they recognized that he was trying *really* hard, and they seemed to appreciate that. I think it was the Eddie the Eagle syndrome: we Brits love a loser and Simon certainly had that quality about him.

DM

Not everyone was happy about Simon's success, though. I believe Billy Fox was particularly upset?

Charley O'Neil

Shortly after the start of the fourth series, Annie Reichman announced that she was going to stop representing Billy Fox. This came completely out of the blue, and I'm sure it would have been a bitter blow for him and ultimately quite humiliating. Billy losing his agent was very big news at the time; it made the front pages of all the tabloids and everyone saw it as the ringing of the death knell for his career.

DM

Do you think Simon made Reichman drop Fox from her books?

Charley O'Neil

Possibly. Simon had a lifelong obsession with Billy which I never fully understood. He seemed to love him and hate him in equal measure, and it was as if he spent his entire career trying to prove that he was better than him. As far as Simon was concerned, when Annie dropped Billy, it finally confirmed that he was. More than anything, it sent a signal to the world of television that Billy's career had ended and that there was a new kid on the block.

Simon was Number One. The biggest light entertainment star in the country.

DM

From reading Simon's diary it seems obvious that you contributed a considerable amount to his success. You were responsible for developing the format of It Could Be You!, *but it was Simon and Annie Reichman who received all the credit and financial benefits. What about you? Were you in any way jealous of the money Simon was making?*

Charley O'Neil

I can honestly say that I wasn't. For me it was never about the money and I was always very philosophical about it. *It Could Be You!* was a massive hit and I felt very proud of the fact that I'd played a major part in creating it, but the input I gave was relevant to the job I had. Yes, I came up with a lot of the original format, and yes, I was responsible for developing the show's content, but that's what an executive producer does. I was paid a good fee for what I did and I was very happy with it. Obviously, not everyone felt the same way as I did, and when the Time Warner deal went through, a lot of people came out of the woodwork and claimed they'd had major input into the show's development. I figured that was probably par for the course when you have a massive hit on your hands which is clearly making lots of money. I'm sure all the other worldwide hits, *Big Brother, X Factor, Who Wants to Be a Millionaire?* etc., have been through some sort of legal battle where other people have claimed that they originally thought of the idea.

DM

So who claimed they'd had input into the show's format?

Charley O'Neil

Max Golinski insisted that he'd come up with the original title and format, and Ricardo Mancini claimed the Retro Round was his idea. Rather bizarrely, Simon's brother David said that he'd helped with the original concept, and Billy Fox was adamant that the whole show was a complete rip-off of *Foxy's One Last Chance!* With the exception of

Simon's brother, they were all threatening legal action. I'm not sure how much Simon knew about these legal wranglings, because Annie Reichman was very careful to protect him from that sort of thing (it's strange, but he had a way of bringing out the maternal instinct in women). Simon was a natural worrier and if he'd known that several people were threatening lawsuits, it would have made him even more paranoid than he already was.

I think it's fair to say that at that time, there were a lot of people who weren't completely enamoured of Simon Peters.

32:

Dominic Mulryan interviews Simon's former agent,
Max Golinski

So what about the people who claimed to have had input into the
development of It Could Be You! *? Were they just charlatans chancing*
their arm and fraudsters jumping on the financial bandwagon, or did
they have a valid claim to the format rights and were they genuinely
entitled to a slice of Simon Peters' pecuniary pie? And, if they were due
a percentage of the multimillion-pound profits from the show but had
been denied it, would they have been so angered at the injustice of it all
that they committed murder?

DM
Mr Golinski, do you genuinely believe you helped develop the format
for It Could Be You!*?*

Max Golinski
Let me tell you something here and now. If it wasn't
for me, *It Could Be You!* would never have happened, it
wouldn't have sold all over the world and it wouldn't have
earned millions of pounds for the people who created it.

I am one of those creators but have I seen a penny of it? *Nishtikeit!*

When I represented Simon, I was the first person he brought the idea to and I helped him shape and develop it as if it were our newborn baby. I guided him in the right direction and encouraged him in the way a top agent should. Hand on heart, as God is my witness, may he strike me down dead or worse still turn me into a variety agent, I played a crucial part in the development of that show and all I want is to be compensated for my contribution and participation. Is that too much to ask? I spent hours working with Simon on that format, days even. I was the one who came up with the title; I remember saying to him, '*It could be you* . . . that's a great title, write it down.'

Of course it's very difficult to prove which ideas were actually mine, but that's just a loophole in the law. Reichman, the *shtik drek schlepper* that she is, and Simon, God rest his soul, may I not speak ill of the dead, obviously just tweaked the ideas slightly and claimed them as their own.

Of course, I'm not bitter about it.

DM
When Annie Reichman dropped Billy Fox, you immediately signed him to your agency?

Max Golinski
I was proud and privileged to take Billy Fox on to my books. A lot of people said to me that he was past it and that his career was finished, but I didn't see it like that at all.

'The man is a legend,' I would say to these people. 'He's the *richtiker chaifetz*, the real McCoy. Not like some of these young pretenders, mentioning no names.'

Billy Fox is a genuinely talented and funny man, and I knew that with a little bit of work and a sprinkling of the Golinski gold dust I could get his career back on track and put him where he belongs.

DM
And where is he at the moment?

Max Golinski
He's hosting *Call-a-Quiz* on Channel 895. Have you seen it? It's a sort of interactive gaming channel where the viewers phone in and play along. It's not his finest hour but when you've got a mortgage and four ex-wives to pay for, you have to take what you can get. Strangely enough, he's had lots of fan mail about it, calling him a cult. At least, I think that's what they called him; it could have been a spelling mistake.

When he first joined me, the BBC were interested in him hosting a show which was a sort of *How Do You Solve a Problem Like Maria?*, but for dogs. They were going to have a nationwide search to find the most talented dog in the country. Andrew Lloyd Webber was going to be the judge, and the most talented mutt would get to play the part of the dog in the new West End production of *Annie*. I think they were going to call it *The Dog Factory*, but I thought that made it sound like some sort of abattoir. Either that or a night-club in Essex. The whole thing sounded a little bit tacky but believe me, it was much better than a lot of the other stuff Billy was being offered. I thought it would give him the chance to get his face back on prime-time TV, where he belonged.

In the end it didn't get commissioned, which was a shame, because it would have given Billy the opportunity to have a little rapport with the owners, especially if the dogs started misbehaving. Believe me, there's nothing funnier than a dog having a crap on live television. Billy would have got ten minutes' quality material out of that. That's what he was good at: thinking on his feet when something went wrong. He'd have also earned a small fortune from all those blooper shows. A clip of a crapping dog can sell all over the world, especially if the host says something funny when the dog is actually doing it.

'Has anybody got a pooper scooper?' Billy would have said. 'Although I think we need a JCB to shift this one!'

He'd have pretended to slip in it and then got another couple of minutes of business out of trying to wipe it off his shoe. Huge laughs from the studio audience. I think the TV executives have forgotten how funny Billy could be in a situation like that. Have you seen TV executives these days? They're all about twelve years old. I've got haemorrhoids older than they are.

DM
While Billy's career started to flounder, Simon's went from strength to strength. What, as his former agent, did you think when Simon was offered a role in a film?

Max Golinski
That movie was a prophecy of doom!

Reichman should never have advised him to take it; she should have read the script, realized it was a divination of disaster and kept him doing what he did best. I always said Simon didn't have enough talent for diversification. There's an old Yiddish expression: 'If it's not made of Lycra, don't stretch it!' What was the point of him appearing in some crappy B movie when he should have been concentrating on the career that I'd created for him?

Did you see the film? Simon played the role of a TV host who was murdered when he stole the idea for a game show. You'd think he would have spotted the irony, wouldn't you?

I saw it after Simon had died. It made me cry; it gave me goosebumps; it made the hairs on the back of my neck stand up. Nothing to do with the tragedy of life imitating art, it was just because it was so bad. Admittedly there was an interesting twist at the end, but the portrayal of the central character's Jewish agent was shocking. Nobody speaks like that any more. *Nishtikeit!*

If Simon had stayed with me he would not have done that movie. If he had stayed with me he would have been happy. Poorer, yes, but happy. If he had stayed with me, he would still be alive today and we would not be sitting here having this conversation. Listen to me already, 'If if if if!' There's another expression in the old country: *az di bobe volt gehat beytism volt zi geven mayn zeyde!* It means, 'If my grandmother had balls she'd be my grandfather!' You can't live your life on 'if's.

My point is that accepting a role in that movie was a bad omen. It was kismet.

33:

2 OCT

I'm going to be a movie star!

Annie called me and said she's sent a tape of my guest appearance on *Holby City* to some American film producers. In *Holby*, I played an A-list celebrity who was in hospital with a broken arm. He was a complete diva who was very demanding, totally self-obsessed and constantly on the edge of a nervous breakdown. I've no idea why they cast me but I must have done a good job, because Annie said the film producers were keen to offer me a role in their movie. They were so impressed I didn't even have to audition.

The movie is called *Who Killed Bobby King?* It's a whodunit and I'll be playing the lead role of Bobby, an incredibly successful game show host who's murdered by someone who feels they were betrayed during his rise to the top. Bobby isn't quite as popular as he thinks, and, as the story unfolds, you realize there are more and more people with a reason to kill him. By the end of the film there's a strong possibility they all could have played a part in his death.

There's a very clever twist at the end but the storyline sounds a little far-fetched to me.

17 OCT

We start filming next week in Riga in Latvia. I was really excited when they told me this, and imagined shooting in glamorous locations in the 'Paris of the Baltics'. Apparently that's not the case; we're doing all the filming in a studio on an industrial estate, and we're only shooting it there because the producers get some sort of tax break, so it's a lot cheaper than filming in Britain or America.

I'm really looking forward to working on the film because I'm going to be starring alongside Roger De Billion, who's playing the role of the detective. De Billion is an absolute legend; completely bonkers, yes, but a legend all the same. He's a famous classically trained Shakespearian actor, but one can't help feeling that he was born out of time and should have been some sort of ancient warrior. He's a larger than life character with a barrel chest, tree trunks for arms and an instantly recognizable big, booming voice (although you could say he just shouts a lot). He also swears like a trooper and when he collected his OBE in 1998, he famously swore in front of the Queen.

He's appeared in lots of British films and always plays the same character, which is basically himself. He insists on doing his own stunts and has performed some pretty risky (publicity) stunts in real life. He walked from Land's End to John o'Groats dressed as a Viking, and made an ill-fated attempt to row single-handedly across the Atlantic. According to some stories, that's what sent him slightly mad. The lack of food and water made all the brain cells from the front of his head go to the back, and all the ones from the back go to the front.

He is, quite literally, bonkers.

23 OCT

Met Roger De Billion today at rehearsals and he told me all the things he has done in his career. He was a down-hill ski champion, rode motorbikes at the Isle of Man TT races and was a semi-professional skydiver. He even has his own helicopter, and gives stunt displays where he performs backward inverted loops while his friends are in the cockpit with him. I'm still thinking of buying a helicopter, so I'm really looking forward to getting to know him and asking him all about it.

25 OCT

This is where I belong.

Working in film is so much more exciting than working in television. I love the fact that everything has much more time and money spent on it and that it's all done on a much grander scale; I love the big heavy cameras; the big lights; the big cranes and the big trailers. I love the fact that there are lots of people who stand around and do nothing except wear baseball caps and carry walkie-talkies; they manage to do nothing with such a confident swagger that you get the impression the whole filming process would grind to a halt if they actually started doing something.

It was my first day today and I was thrown right in at the deep end with my big scene. It's the one where Bobby King is hosting the game show just before he gets killed.

The set was very impressive and I'm not sure whether it was intentional, but it looked extremely similar to the set of *It Could Be You!* There were contestants, a glamorous hostess and even a studio audience, which was a bit strange because they were all obviously Latvian extras.

When it came to my bit, I was very nervous and kept fluffing my lines or missing my mark; sometimes I did both. I did about fifteen takes and I could sense the director, the crew and the studio audience were getting very frustrated. The more frustrated they became, the worse I was and I started having a real confidence crisis. After the sixteenth take, the actress who is playing the game show hostess came over and stood very close to me.

'Don't vorry about eet,' she whispered in a deep husky Eastern European voice that sounded like dark brown chocolate been poured in my ear. 'I zink you are very good.'

I turned my head and looked into her eyes and as I did so, my heart stopped, my mouth went dry and my stomach did a double somersault with tuck and pike. She was beautiful. Absolutely beautiful. And her words filled me with self-belief.

The director instructed everyone that we were going for another take and this time, as the cameras rolled, I hit my mark, I was word-perfect and I even managed to squeeze in a little emotion. I was acting; I was actually *being* someone else. When the director shouted 'cut', the crew and audience gave me a spontaneous round of applause which I acknowledged with a modest wave, even though I wasn't sure if they were being sarcastic or not. I glanced over to the podium where the glamorous hostess with the husky voice had been standing, but she'd already disappeared back into her trailer.

When I'd finished the scene, I asked a couple of the local crew members who she was. They told me her name was Crissi Drēźhnikovă and that she was a Lithuanian supermodel. I'd never heard of her but they assured me she was very famous in Eastern Europe. I asked them for more information about her but they just laughed, shook their heads and patted me on the back. I said she was gorgeous and they agreed with me, but laughed again as they said it. I guess they thought this nerdy guy from England doesn't stand a chance with her.

Maybe they're right.

27 OCT

I think I'm in love.

When Crissi walks into the studio, she does it with such confidence. She glides in as if she's on air, fully aware that everyone is gazing in her direction. She doesn't glance at anybody and stares straight ahead because she knows the only thing in the room worth looking at is her.

I've always wanted to walk into a room like that; to radiate such confidence and to carry myself with the belief that I'm someone special. Everyone tells me I *am* special because I'm famous, but I don't always feel that way on the inside. Sometimes I feel awkward and out of place, as if I don't belong with the beautiful people. Crissi *is* the beautiful people, but when I'm next to her I don't feel threatened, in fact I feel the complete opposite; with her by my side I'm the centre of the universe, and I know that everybody is looking at me and wishing they were me.

With her, I feel special. With her, I feel I belong. Crissi is everything I've ever wanted from a woman: tall, sexy, glamorous and famous . . . although obviously not as famous as me.

She's perfect.

29 OCT

I'm going to start learning Lithuanian. I've learnt three words already and I keep practising them in front of the mirror.

'*Tave My liu, Crissi, Tave My liu!*'

It doesn't sound quite as romantic as *je t'aime*, but I'm sure she'll be impressed all the same.

30 OCT

I know I'm in love because I finally understand poetry. Love really is like a golden flame that glows inside my heart and warms my soul.

I find myself walking around Riga with a constant smile on my face, and I've noticed flowers in the hotel gardens that I've never seen before. On my iPod, I've started listening to the Carpenters, and in particular the lyrics of their love songs. In the past I've always thought they were totally soppy, but now I can identify with what Karen was trying to say. Birds really do suddenly appear when Crissi's near, and when she was born, the angels did get together and were quite successful in creating a dream come true. I think they even managed to sprinkle moondust in her hair. Although that could be dandruff – I don't think they have Head and Shoulders in Latvia.

31 OCT

I hope I'm not getting too carried away but I wonder what a traditional Lithuanian wedding is like.

34:

Dominic Mulryan interviews the legendary actor
Roger De Billion

DM
Roger, what are your memories of Simon Peters?

Roger De Billion
SP was a giant among men; I'm telling you the man was a fucking demigod. Why he pissed about doing all light entertainment shit, I will never know. Television wasn't big enough to harness the sheer magnitude of SP's talent.

Despite what the critics said, I thought he had a real flair for acting, unusual style admittedly, but he possessed a natural finesse and he embraced the text like he'd been shagging it up the arse for years. I've worked with all the great directors, love, Trev, Pete, Ken, and the one thing they look for in an actor is integrity. You have to have integrity and SP could fake that better than anyone I know.

It's a crime against humanity that SP didn't do more cinema, love. A great big dirty bloody crime!

As you know, I first met him on Ken's film version

of *Who Killed Bobby King?* Now, have to admit to being absolutely mortified when first told who was going to play the role of Bobby King. Don't really approve of 'celebrity casting', as most 'celebrities' can't act their way out of a bloody paper bag! Having said that, SP turned up and was absolutely marvellous, love. Ken had cast him as the game show host. Tricky little role to get right and Ken wanted SP to play it as himself. As himself, you see. Genius idea, fucking genius!

First day of rehearsals . . . fucking awful time for actors, first day of rehearsals. Everybody nervous and desperate to impress. I always take in a Bakewell tart and a crate of champagne to break the ice. Anyway, SP came to me and said, 'Sir Rodge.' That's what he used to call me, 'Sir Rodge'. He said, 'Sir Rodge, I want to learn from the master. Teach me, Sir Rodge, teach me to act!' I said I can't teach you to fucking act, man, acting is a gift from Melpomene, the Greek god of tragedy, you can either do it or you can't.

And he could do it.

Little shit acted me off the fucking screen, love.

Admittedly it took him several takes to get used to the filming process, but he nailed it; absolutely bloody nailed it! He was like some great method actor and he totally immersed himself in that role. Even after we'd finished filming for the day he still stayed in character. It was as if he *was* Bobby King. It was as if he really *was* that sad game show host!

I found that very attractive.

DM
During the making of the film, did you notice that Simon had feelings for Crissi Drĕžhnikovă?

271

Roger De Billion

Notice it? Notice it? You couldn't bloody miss it, love. Absolutely besotted with her! All he did was talk about her . . . Crissi this, Crissi that, Crissi Crissi Crissi . . .

No, tell a lie; occasionally asked about helicopters. Desperate to buy one, apparently. Suggested a Robinson R22 for him. Perfect for the first-timer. Offered a ride in mine but proposal declined. Think he didn't quite trust me, love, in more ways than one!

During the shooting of the film, SP was by Crissi's side every minute of the day. They became absolutely inseparable, some might say fucking insufferable. Soon as we'd finished a take, they'd be there together with their childish giggles, playful nudges and private little jokes. He'd make all the running and she'd just toy with him, the way a large vicious cat might play with a mouse.

Totally head over heels in love with her, he was. Personally, didn't get the impression she felt the same way about him. Been an actor a long time, love, can tell when people are faking it. She wasn't that good an actress in the first place and couldn't fool me with her shy-little-girly act.

If one is being totally honest with you, I wasn't that fond of her. Got distinct impression she was ruthlessly ambitious and desperate to further her career in Britain. But there was also something else, something one couldn't quite put one's finger on.

For me, the relationship just didn't ring true, so I have to admit to being slightly surprised when SP announced that Crissi was going to move to London to be with him. Thought it was strange, because a little birdie told me she'd never been able to visit Britain before because of some sort of visa problem.

At the time, everyone said how sweet it was that they'd met and fallen in love on a film set, and how romantic that he was whisking her back to England.

I remember thinking that she was just using the poor little bastard.

35:

Dominic Mulryan interviews Lithuanian supermodel Crissi Drėžhnikovǎ

Crissi Drėžhnikovǎ, or simply Crissi, as she's known throughout Eastern Europe, was indeed a supermodel with a somewhat mysterious past. Although she's arguably Lithuania's most famous export, very little is known about her background. According to her official website, she was born in the small northern town of Joniškis, just 14 km from the Latvian border, but other than that, the facts are somewhat murky. She first became a model at the relatively late age of twenty-three, and with her slender six-foot frame and her sultry good looks, she was destined for a successful career on the Lithuanian catwalk. After clawing her way to the top of the Baltic modelling industry, Crissi turned her attention to acting, and following a short run in the popular Estonian soap opera Mees ja Nais *(Man and Woman), she eventually landed the role of the beautiful game show hostess turned murder suspect in Simon's film* Who Killed Bobby King? *In the Baltics, Crissi was something of a superstar, albeit a mysterious one.*

So, had Simon finally met the celebrity girlfriend of his dreams? Or, in falling for Crissi, had he opened a whole can of Eastern European worms?

DM

When you came to Britain, were you surprised at just how famous Simon was?

Crissi

Simon had told me he was a big star in Britain, but I thought he was just saying zat. If I'm honest with you, I'd never heard of him and I couldn't believe how someone like him could be so famous. He seemed so innocent and naïve and when I first saw him I thought he was a little . . . how you say . . . geeky. You British don't seem to mind zat, though.

When I arrive in zis country and Simon met me from ze plane, I was very surprised at ze reaction he got. Even at ze airport, people would ask for his autograph and take photographs on their mobile phones. I think he was hoping I'd be impressed by how many people knew him but I couldn't help noticing zat it was a strange kind of fame; a fame I'd never encountered before. It was as if ze people didn't have any respect for him; they'd shout his name and point and laugh at him as if he was a . . . what's the word? . . . A *kvailys* . . . a joke . . . a figure of fun. Simon was totally oblivious to this and smiled and waved at everyone.

There were also lots of paparazzi waiting to get a shot of us, but I'm not sure how they knew we'd be there. Simon told them we didn't want any publicity and put his sunglasses on and his hands in front of our faces. Strangely though, he seemed to know all the photographers by name and we had to walk past them three times just to make sure zey got what zey wanted.

DM

Did you like the fact that Simon was famous?

Crissi

A lot of people used to think that I was only interested in Simon's celebrity lifestyle. I'm sure even he used to think zat. He was always trying to impress me but he was forgetting I was famous in my own country and zat I'd seen it all before.

He was always showing me videotapes of his TV shows but if I'm honest I didn't like his presenting style. I found him . . . how you say . . . ? Irritating. He reminded me of a children's television presenter in Latvia called Timmi Malletski. I was truthful with him; I told him that his performance was over ze top and that he tried too hard and was always trying to be too funny. I don't get the British sense of humour but some of his jokes were . . . what's ze word you English use . . . ? Shit.

But away from ze cameras he was a different person. Behind closed doors he was quiet and soft and gentle, shy almost; he was calm and tender and you just wanted to mother him. He was like a lost soul and all he needed in his life was a little bit of guidance. What first attracted me to him was ze fact that he had this incredible spiritual aware-ness, an almost mystical presence and an unusual ethereal quality.

Plus ze fact he was hung like a Lithuanian donkey.

DM
So you had an active love life?

Crissi
Simon Peters was ze most passionate human being I'd ever met.

He possessed an animalistic intensity which I'd never encountered in a man or a woman before. He had zis ability

276

to make me feel 'all woman', which is very important to me. Everybody talks about how untalented he was, but his biggest talent was in ze bedroom. He was very gifted in zat department; zat is where he was a genius.

We would make love for hours and hours and hours. And then when we finished making love we would start again for hours and hours and hours . . . Sometimes it would get a little . . . what's the word . . . ? Stinky.

Sorry, I mean kinky, not stinky.

Although to be honest, occasionally it got a little stinky too.

36:

Dominic Mulryan interviews Charley O'Neil

Simon's relationship with Crissi was big news, and wherever they went they were hounded by a pack of paparazzi. All the publicity was certainly good news for the makers of Who Killed Bobby King?, *which was mentioned in every press article as the movie on which the couple met. Sadly, Simon would not live long enough to see the final cut of the film, and because of the subsequent controversy surrounding its plotline it has never been given a cinema release in the UK, which caused it to become something of a cult classic. The irony of the movie's subject matter was not lost on the police, who studied the film very closely during their investigation of Simon's mysterious death.*

When Simon returned from filming in Latvia, he seemed to have it all: a movie-star lifestyle, a beautiful house and a stunning celebrity girlfriend. But how much influence did Crissi Drēžhnikovă have over the latter part of Simon's life? Was she (as many people often claimed) just a cold and calculating harlot who was using Simon to further her own ambitions? If this was the case, Simon remained oblivious to the animosity and was clearly deeply infatuated with his Lithuanian lover.

DM

Charley, were you jealous when Simon returned from Latvia with Crissi in tow?

Charley O'Neil

Of course I wasn't jealous but I did worry about him. Even though our friendship wasn't as strong as it once was, I still cared for him greatly and didn't want to see him hurt.

Like a lot of people, I thought Crissi was only with Simon because of who he was. Then again, I guess that's why he was with her. The only thing they seemed to have in common was an incredible shallowness and an unhealthy obsession with the cult of celebrity. Call me old-fashioned but, for me, that's not a good basis for a relationship.

I always think of Crissi as Simon's Yoko Ono. I can't imagine what they were like together, but I got the impression that, right from the beginning, she was trying to change him.

On a professional level, what worried me was that everything else seemed to take a back seat, including *It Could Be You!* Once he got together with Crissi his interest in the programme started to wane and the show started to suffer. He'd finally got the celebrity girlfriend he'd always wanted and nothing else seemed to matter except her.

DM

Was Crissi using him?

Charley O'Neil

I think the answer to that is pretty obvious.

DM

According to Crissi's recollections, she was actually a great help to Simon, often acting as a mentor, a counsellor and a therapist, especially when it came to the subject of his mother.

Charley O'Neil

His mother's death was one thing I could never talk to Simon about. My mother's still alive, and I think it's hard for anyone who hasn't gone through it to really comprehend how terrible it is to lose a parent, especially at an early age. They say the grieving period is a couple of years, but Simon was still grieving twenty years later. And it certainly showed; it was always as if there was something missing in his life. He craved love and affection but he didn't let anyone get too close, because if they got too close they could hurt him, the way he'd been hurt when his mother died. I think the death of his mother was still an incredibly big thing in his life. Even after all that time he was still hurting on the inside, but I don't think he'd ever really talked about it. He'd never had anyone special to share his emotions with and he desperately needed someone he could trust, someone he could open up to and someone who could help him through it.

DM

To quote your programme title, surely that could have been you?

Charley O'Neil

I guess it could have been, but it was never to be. I certainly wouldn't have thought Crissi was that person. I think it was obvious to everyone who saw them together that, one day, she'd end up hurting him more than anyone.

DM

It sounds as though you didn't have an awful lot of respect for Crissi?

Charley O'Neil

I wasn't happy with how much influence she had over Simon's life. Everything she did was geared towards generating publicity for herself.

Soon after they returned, an article appeared in the *News of the World* about how Simon had never got over his mother's death, and how he didn't think his father Tommy had been there for him when he was younger. The angle of the story was that Crissi was a great comfort to him, and there was even a long-lens, paparazzi-style photograph of the two of them, with her looking as if she was consoling him. I think Simon would have preferred to keep the death of his mother private, but he was extremely vulnerable on the subject and was always looking for guidance. I think Crissi persuaded him to do the article to show her off in a good light.

DM

In the article, Simon was quite critical of Tommy.

Charley O'Neil

I believe one of the reasons Simon sold the story was because he still had a score to settle with Tommy. He wanted the world to know that he felt his dad had failed him by not being there for him when it mattered. As it said in the newspaper, Simon was in the hospital with his mother on the night she died.

Simon never forgave Tommy for the fact that he wasn't.

37:

Extract from Simon's diary

10 NOV

Doing the interview with Crissi for the *News of the World* was like therapy, and once I started talking, I just couldn't stop. Lots of stuff came tumbling out, and I said some things that maybe I shouldn't have. I didn't intend to say anything about my father, but the journalist asked me why he wasn't there at my mother's side when she died.

The answer was that he had a gig that night. He couldn't let them down, he said. 'They'd already sold the tickets,' he said. 'They might never use me again,' he said.

Maybe, just maybe, I'd forgive him if it had been Caesar's Palace in Las Vegas. Maybe, just maybe, I'd understand if it had been the London Palladium, but the truth is that it was a dingy working-men's club on the outskirts of Middlesbrough. I know he went on stage and did lots of 'Take my wife . . . please take my wife!' type jokes. He would have done them because they were part of his act, and he wasn't going to change it just because his wife was lying in a hospital bed with only a few hours to live.

My mother had been seriously ill for some time, but her spirit was unbelievably strong. She fought the cancer every inch of the way and was determined not to be beaten by it. She put up a really good fight and went the full fifteen rounds, but eventually it ate through her body until she was so thin she was almost unrecognizable. She spent four months in hospital and no matter what combination of drugs they gave her, they couldn't stop her withering away like a summer rose in autumn.

On the night she died, I lay next to her on the hospital bed. Surrounded by machines and tubes and wires, I told her that one day I'd make her proud. She held my hand and gently squeezed it; she took a long, deep breath and with a voice which was hoarse and brittle with pain, she whispered:

'I'm already proud . . .'

She took another deep breath.

'. . . and your father would be proud too.'

That was the last thing she said. '. . . *and your father would be proud too.*'

Ten minutes later she passed away, and that's when the world I knew ended.

My mother had been the glue that held our family together, and when she was gone we fell apart like a cheap Airfix model. We were a ship without a captain, cast adrift and knowing we'd never be rescued. Suddenly there was no one there when I came home from school, no one to help me with my homework, no one to tell me what to do, no one to go to the shops for, no one to cook my meals.

No one to tell me they loved me.

My brother David cried for a whole month. I think he

must have been crying for both of us, because for me, the tears wouldn't flow. I knew that if I started crying I'd never stop. I knew that crying would be an acceptance of the fact that she was gone, and I wasn't ready for that.

I don't think I've ever accepted it.

I don't remember my dad ever letting his emotions show, either. Maybe he felt the same way as I did, or maybe he felt guilty about not being there. Whatever the reason, we both bottled it up and haven't spoken about it since. I think we both fear that if we did, the floodgates would open and there'd be a severe danger of us drowning in a torrent of raw emotion.

I think each of us had dealt with the loss in our own individual way. My father threw himself into his work, I became very ambitious and David found comfort in the Big Two.

That's God and Jesus, by the way, not Ant and Dec.

38:

Dominic Mulryan interviews Tommy Peters

DM
What did you think of the article in the News of the World?

Tommy Peters
Why did he have to go and rake all that up again after twenty years? It made me out to be a right little shit. I told them my side of the story, but did they print it? Did they buggery. As I tried to explain, I couldn't be there because I was working; somebody had to make sure there was a roof over our heads and food in the fridge.

Y'see, you don't get compassionate leave when you're a comedian. No matter what's happening at home, no matter what's happening in your personal life, no matter what's happening on the inside, you have to go and stand in that spotlight and be funny. The punters aren't interested in your personal problems; if they wanted tragedy they'd go and watch bloody Shakespeare. They don't want to see me stand in front of them and say:

'Sorry I can't be funny tonight, ladies and gentlemen, but my wife's hooked up to a subcutaneous syringe.'

If I did, they'd be waiting for the punchline. The punchline in this case was that she died and I wasn't there to say goodbye to her. To be honest, that wouldn't have got much of a laugh. And that was my job: to make people laugh. And I did make them laugh. I made a lot of people laugh.

DM
Does it upset you that you never made it as a top comedian?

Tommy Peters
People seem to think that it bothers me that I was never famous, that I never *made it*. What is *making it* anyway? If making it as a comic means reducing every audience you ever played in front of to tears of hysterical laughter, then I did make it. I made it big. I can honestly say I never 'died' once, and everybody who saw me said I should have been on the telly more often than I was. And I should have been, I really should.

The one and only time I was on *The Comedians*, they made me go on first when the audience weren't warmed up properly. I shouldn't have gone on first, everyone knows bloody Stan Boardman should have gone on first. They also edited out all my best gags; they took out all my woofers, the sure-fire gags that got the big laughs, and I noticed they left all of Frank Carson's in. They made it look as if I wasn't as good as I actually was, d'you understand?

Y'see, I was what they call in the business a comic's comic. Other comedians used to come into the club where I was playing just to watch my act, famous comedians an' all: Les Dawson, Colin Crompton, Bernard Manning . . . Bernard always said I was the best there was, which was high praise indeed from that miserable ol' bastard. He always said I had talent. Natural talent.

DM
Were you resentful of the fact that you weren't as successful as Simon?

Tommy Peters
How do you measure success?

If you measure it in pounds, shillings and pence, then of course he was more successful than me, but if you're talking about raw talent, Simon didn't even come close. I know it might sound harsh but I'm just trying to be honest here. As far as I'm concerned, he didn't have a funny bone in his body.

Y'see, I was born funny; it's in my bones and I couldn't help but make people laugh. Right from an early age I was telling jokes, doing impressions and pulling funny faces, and I knew it made me popular. I was the class clown, the one at the back who was always mucking about. It all came very naturally to me: I instinctively understood how comedy worked. I understood the mechanics of it; I understood the little intricacies that make a joke fire or misfire. There's very little difference between a gag that dies on its arse and a gag that makes people piss their pants. It could be just a word or a pause or a look. One comic can murder a joke, while another can make it the funniest thing in the world.

There's an old gag where I say, 'Ask me what the secret of good comedy is.' And when you start asking me, I interrupt and say, 'Timing!'

It's a good gag, but it's not strictly true. Of course you need timing, but just because you can time an egg, it doesn't make you a great chef, does it? What you really need is rhythm. All the great comedians have rhythm. It's all in the delivery:

The situation, the punchline, BANG!

The set-up, the tag, BANG!

The story, the joke, BANG!

That was the trouble with Simon. He never had rhythm . . . or timing . . . or gags.

To be honest, he just wasn't very funny.

39:

Dominic Mulryan

The fact that Simon wasn't 'naturally funny' (or, more to the point, the fact that he wasn't as funny as Tommy) obviously concerned him a great deal. Towards the end of his life he developed an irrational fear of telling jokes on live television, and very often, when performing scripted material, he would not get the timing quite right and would stumble over the punchline. It became something of a trademark, and while it was endearing to some, it didn't go unnoticed in the world of entertainment. Frank Skinner once famously remarked that Simon Peters had the comic timing of a water buffalo.

This irrational fear is very evident in Simon's diaries. The following entries were written towards the end of the fourth series of It Could Be You! *Despite Simon's negative state of mind, the show was still at the top of the ratings and pulling in a weekly audience of twelve million viewers.*

29 NOV

Just finished tonight's episode of *You!*

It went OK, I suppose. The surprise 'live hit' we did on the busker in Newcastle (a member of our team dropping

£20,000 cash in his hat) was one of the best we've ever done, and the spoof sketch with me dressed as Elton John and then Elton coming on dressed as me was genuinely very original. The studio audience were in absolute hysterics, which I've come to learn from experience means the sketch was at least mildly amusing.

The trouble is, since Crissi told me she doesn't find me very funny, I've started to realize that she's right and that I don't know what good comedy is. I find it more and more difficult to judge what's amusing and what's not.

The scriptwriters come into a production meeting with a couple of ideas for gags and sketches. They read them out and the team start howling with laughter; I laugh along too, but the truth is, more often than not I just don't get it. Then, on another occasion I'll say something which I find hilarious; I'll have tears rolling down my cheeks, but as I look around the meeting I realize I'm the only one who's laughing. People join in but I know they only do this because I'm the boss, and they think I might sack them if they don't.

By the way, the story in this week's *Sunday Mirror* about me sacking a production assistant for putting sweeteners in my coffee instead of sugar just isn't true. It's a pack of lies and I want to set the record straight here and now:

It was tea, not coffee!

That's a joke, by the way.

It was *tea*, not coffee! *Ba-dum tish!*

Short and to the point. It has a set-up, a punchline and it even has rhythm. It's a classic reversal. You think it's going to go one way but it takes you the other. *Tea*, not coffee! That's funny, isn't it? Isn't it? Maybe it's not. I just don't seem to know any more.

Perhaps I never did.

30 NOV

I'm onstage in a trendy London comedy club called the Funny Bone. The spotlight is blinding me, but I can just about make out the faces of the people in the front row of the audience. They sit there staring at me, and I know what they're thinking:

'*Go on then Mr Big-Shot TV Star, make us laugh . . . let's see how funny you really are.*'

I pick up the microphone.

Feedback.

A cough from somewhere in the audience.

Was it a cough or somebody saying *Fuck off*? I'm not sure.

Suddenly I'm lost and I don't know what to say. The beginnings of a thousand different jokes go hurtling through my mind, swiftly followed by a thousand different punchlines, none of them fitting together. Panic sets in and I'm the comedian's equivalent of word-blind: I'm joke-blind, I've got gag dyslexia, I'm in the middle of a joke blizzard and I can't see any way out. The jokes fall from my mouth in no particular order, the set-up from one gag randomly stitched together with the punchline from another.

'*My dog's got no nose. Jamaica? No I always walk like this!*'

An eerie quiet falls over the audience.

'*Take my wife. Dr Who? No I'm chewing a toffee!*'

They can smell my fear.

'*Knock knock. Rabbit droppings? April Fool, it was dead already!*'

They know I don't belong here, they know I'm an impostor. They start to boo and hiss and jeer and heckle.

'*Waiter waiter. A sunburnt nun? Four elephants in a Mini!*'

They tease and taunt and mock and scoff.

'A man walks into a bar. Peanuts? No, Kermit the Frog in a blender!'

They sneer and scorn and shout and spit.

'I went to the doctor. How does it smell? I said I'm not having that end, you've had that end in your mouth!'

Silence.

And then, from somewhere in the darkness, a beautiful sound rings out. Can it be true? Listen. There it is again.

Laughter.

It's music to my ears as its sweet, melodious timbre drapes itself around my shattered ego and gently massages my broken confidence.

'Everything's OK,' whispers the laughter seductively. *'They like you. You are funny.'*

Suddenly the security blanket is snatched away from me as I realize the laughter has a sharp, sarcastic, hollow tone to it. They're not laughing with me, they're laughing at me. They're mocking and taunting me with their disdain. Their howling ridicule gains momentum and sweeps through the room like a Mexican wave. They're in hysterics, but I can't stop them. I'm drenched in sweat and I can't breathe. I'm dying a slow horrendous death: death by fear, death by humiliation, death by unfunny jokes.

From behind the curtain, the now familiar pair of black-leather-gloved hands slowly reach out and grab me around the neck. At first I think it's a gag, a new version of the old music hall hook, this club's way of getting rid of the acts they don't like. It soon becomes clear that it's not a joke. The hands clasp my neck even more firmly and start to squeeze. Still the audience laugh, oblivious to my pain. As the hands tighten their grip, I drop to my knees and find it difficult to breathe. The audience roll around on the floor, laughing feverishly, pointing at me and begging for an encore. More, they want more. The gloved hands squeeze tighter still and I start to choke. My eyes are wide open, streaming with tears and pleading for help, but no one comes to my assistance. I gulp for air but there's none to be had, and I know I've breathed my last. The hands release their grip and as I fall to the floor in slow motion, I see my assailant removing his gloves and grabbing the microphone.

He is the host and compère of the club.

He is also my father.

The last thing I hear before I wake up is my dad saying, *'He turned out to be a bit of a disappointment, didn't he? He wasn't funny at all.'*

5 DEC

I seem to be getting worse.

Whenever they persuade me to do a joke on *You!*, I have a real fear of messing it up. When I'm reading the autocue and I know the punchline is approaching, I start to panic. I can see the big letters thundering towards me like a freight train coming out of a tunnel, and I know there's no way to stop them. When they finally arrive on the screen and I have to read them out, I have no control over what I'm saying; I stammer and stutter and just like in my dream, the words seem to fly out aimlessly and erratically. I then have to apologize, correct myself and repeat the punchline by which time, of course, the moment has gone.

Last night I saw Alistair McGowan doing an impression of me on his new TV show. He just stood there saying strange random words which made no sense whatsoever. It was a running gag and every time they cut back to him, his ramblings became more and more obscure.

'Can you cuckoo ping-pong believe that I've Pepto-Bismol monkey tree managed to get to the shoeshine shoeshine shoeshine top of the entertainment industry just the one bag of coal please clunk click every trip when I can't even string a sentence together.'

Big laughs from the studio audience.

Ronnie Ancona was standing next to him, pretending to be Crissi. When she spoke, it was in a really deep bloke's voice, which I didn't think was very funny at all. It certainly upset Crissi, who spent the whole night in the toilet crying.

I'm really worried about the fact that I keep messing the gags up, but Charley says it's endearing and that it's good to give them something to do an impression of, otherwise I'd be bland and boring like that old fart Billy Fox. Even now, Charley knows how to say exactly the right thing.

I've analysed it and I think I have a phobia of punchlines. Gagaphobia or jesterphobia, or more likely jocusphobia (*jocus* is Latin for jest . . . you see, I've even looked it up).

*Note to self. New game show called *Jocusphobia*: a nationwide search to find the worst comedian in Britain.

The problem is, I'd probably win it.

40:

Dominic Mulryan interviews Charley O'Neil

DM
At this point in his career, Simon seemed to be struggling to handle the pressure.

Charley O'Neil
I think Simon was overexposed and that was a dangerous thing; his lack of talent was beginning to show through. It was becoming clear that he wasn't cut out to perform week in week out at the highest level, and the cracks were starting to appear. I was worried about him and I thought he desperately needed a break. I knew he'd been planning to go to his villa in Portugal, but the Network Centre wanted him to host a live New Year's Eve special which was to be a spin-off of *It Could Be You!* called *It Could Be Your Neighbour.* To me, it sounded like a terrible idea. I tried to explain to the Network Centre that Simon needed protecting and that he was only as good as the show he was hosting. I warned them that if they didn't get the format right, they could

have a real turkey on their hands. I also knew that Simon wasn't very keen on doing the show because, in his words, 'it didn't have an exclamation mark in the title'.

Simon had been a very lucky man and he knew that. As with a lot of these things, it had all been a matter of timing, and he'd been the right face in the right place at the right time. Six months earlier or six months later and it could have been a totally different story. Maybe the television industry would have decided that light entertainment was dead again; maybe *It Could Be You!* would never have been commissioned; maybe Annie Reichman would never have taken Simon on to her books and maybe he'd have been just another out-of-work game show host. If all that had happened, maybe Simon would still be alive today.

Who knows?

As it was, Simon was living on the edge and his nerves seemed to be getting worse. I tried to help him but he was so wrapped up in Crissi that he wouldn't listen to anyone else.

DM
If Simon was living on the edge, the Sun *newspaper was about to publish a story that would tip him over it.*

Charley O'Neil
Yes, that came as a massive blow to him. I knew they were going to print it, but there was nothing I could do to stop it.

Annie Reichman had called and asked me to go and see her at her office. I thought she was going to try to persuade me to be the executive producer on *It Could Be Your Neighbour*, which was something I really didn't want to do.

When I walked in, she looked very serious. Annie always

looked serious, but I could sense this was different. She sat me down and said she had something important to tell me. She said the so-called journalist, Peter 'The Ferret' Finch, had been to see her, and that he was going to run a story about Simon.

Finch was known as 'The Ferret' because once he got his teeth into something he wouldn't let go until he'd gnawed through to the bone (he also actually looked like a ferret). This guy was the scum of the earth, and he'd been making up stories about Simon for the previous six months. I detested the man because he gave the distinct impression he genuinely enjoyed ruining people's lives. I was surprised that he'd gone to see Annie in person, because he'd usually just run a story without bothering to check that it was true.

I told Annie that I wasn't worried because The Ferret ran a story about Simon pretty much every day of the week.

'This one's different,' she said, and I could tell by the look in her one good eye that she meant it.

When she told me what it was, I sat there dumbstruck, not fully taking it in. As she related the story to me, I could only think of one thing:

This was going to change Simon's life for ever.

41:

18 DEC

I spent all day staring at the headline. It didn't matter how many times I said it or where I placed the intonation, it just sounded like random words thrown together, which I couldn't fully comprehend:

SIMON PETERS IS BILLY FOX'S SON!

Six words, twenty-five letters, one apostrophe and an exclamation mark:

SIMON PETERS IS BILLY FOX'S SON!

Two names, a noun and a verb are all it takes to destroy my life.

SIMON PETERS IS BILLY FOX'S SON!

If it is destroying my life, why do I feel so calm about it and where did this sense of serenity come from? I'm obviously happy with the billing; I would have been particularly distraught if it had said *'Billy Fox is Simon Peters' Dad!'*, but surely I shouldn't even be thinking about that?

Am I in a state of shock?

I know it's only a matter of time before the dark clouds of depression start rolling in from the horizon, but at the moment I feel totally in control as if it isn't actually happening to me. I feel as though I'm floating in the air and looking down on another Simon Peters, who has just discovered his whole world is not what he thought it was.

Or has he?

I can't believe the headline but at the same time it doesn't surprise me either, and I know this isn't one of those outrageous stories that The Ferret has made up; I know I'm not going to be calling my lawyers and suing the *Sun* for libel; I know those six words say it all, and that they're probably the most honest thing the tabloids have ever written about me.

I know it is the truth.

I think subconsciously I've known it all along, and this headline is the missing piece of the jigsaw that I never thought I'd find.

SIMON PETERS IS BILLY FOX'S SON!

All my life, people have said that I resemble him and that I've got a lot of similarities in my presenting style.

Well, now I know why.

When I analyse it, I've always had a strange affinity with Billy Fox. Ever since I was a kid, I've been drawn to him and felt a strange concoction of paradoxical emotions towards him. I felt admiration; envy; devotion; distrust; loyalty; resentment; friendship; bitterness; love and anger. I hero-worshipped him but at the same time I hated him as well; he was everything I ever wanted to be but I never wanted to end up anything like him. I felt all the mixed-up, muddled-up feelings a son might feel for his absent father, but I never acknowledged them or understood their significance.

I think I never wanted to admit to myself that he could be my dad, because admitting it would mean my mother had had some sort of an affair with him, and even now that's something I just can't accept. It obviously happened at the beginning of the summer season in 1972 but why would my mother do it? Was she so unhappy in her marriage that she saw Billy Fox as a way out? Did he charm her with his game show smile and witty one-liners? Did she fall head over heels in love with him? Did she see something in him that she didn't see in Tommy? Did she think there was a chance for a better future with a guy on the way up, as opposed to a third-rate comic going nowhere?

Or was it just a one-night stand? Was the passion of the moment so overwhelming they just couldn't help themselves? Was it a quickie in the dressing room while Tommy was onstage doing his opening spot? Did they hastily get dressed afterwards and promise never to say a word?

Or did he force himself on her? Did he threaten to tell Tommy they were having an affair if she didn't let him do as he pleased? Did she beg him to stop? Did she fight and scratch and claw at him but he was just too powerful for her?

When it was over, did my mother cry for hours and hours? Did she think she'd done a terrible thing? Did she blame herself? Did she regret it for the rest of her life and swear to herself she'd take the secret to her grave?

Was it guilt that ate away at her, and not cancer?

'. . . *and your father would be proud too.*'

Was she talking about Billy Fox on her deathbed?

'. . . and your father *would* be proud too.'

Proud if he knew I existed?

It's strange, but I don't have any desire to see Billy Fox. I think if I saw him now, my feelings would be exactly the same as they've always been: admiration; envy; devotion; distrust; loyalty; resentment; allegiance; bitterness; love; hatred . . .

What does Tommy think of all this? He must be absolutely devastated. He had a terrible temper when I was growing up and a really short fuse.

Actually, I know just what he'd say.

He'd say, 'I always knew there was a reason he wasn't funny.'

23 DEC

I have two fathers but I'm loved and wanted by neither.

My brother told me that Tommy is furious about the story and doesn't want to speak to me about it. I know we haven't exactly seen eye to eye over the years, but at least I've always called him Dad; I don't think I'll ever be able to call Billy Fox that, especially because he so obviously doesn't want anything to do with me.

I feel lost, like an orphan who hasn't got a father at all.

What is a father, anyway?

Surely a father is someone you can look up to and respect; someone to motivate and stimulate, to encourage and to inspire; someone whose opinion you value and someone who will always be there for you. As Mark Twain once said, 'A father is someone to go fishing with.'

Tommy never took me fishing and I've got a feeling Billy Fox never will, either.

I'm becoming slightly obsessed by the fact that he's my father now. But what does that mean, 'my father *now*'? Surely he's been my father all along, biologically if not emotionally.

I think about him all the time, but I don't seem to be able to formulate any genuine feelings for him. Is all this supposed to make me into a different person? Am I supposed to *think* differently? To *act* differently? How do the public expect me to behave? Do they think I've changed? Do *I* think I've changed? I don't know what I'm supposed to feel, so I don't feel anything at all. My heart and mind have been anaesthetized by the whole thing, and it's left me with a large emotional void where a thin veil of security used to be.

At least I've got Crissi to help me through the shock of it all. She fills the yearning chasm in my life and I've surrendered my heart to her completely. She's all I've got. She is my rock, my soulmate, my lover, my nurse and my analyst. She means everything to me and I know we're destined to always be together. Nothing can destroy the love we share; nothing can come between us.

24 DEC

SIMON PETERS' GIRL USED TO BE A MAN

Oh God!

42:

Dominic Mulryan interviews Charley O'Neil

Charley O'Neil

On Christmas Eve, Peter 'The Ferret' Finch revealed in the *Sun* that Crissi used to be called Christophe. She is a post-operative transsexual who had the full operation in 2001 before managing to launch a successful modelling career.

While the Billy Fox story came as a complete shock to everyone, I think Simon was the only person in the country who was in any way surprised by this one. Yes, Crissi was slim and stunningly good-looking, but there was obviously something very different about her. They say love is blind; well in Simon's case it must have been blind, deaf, dumb and stupid not to notice her huge hands, her deep voice and an Adam's apple the size of a golf ball.

When Crissi first arrived in the country there were lots of whispers and rumours, but nobody actually said anything in the press. You can imagine that when the story finally broke, they had a field day with it. Even though Crissi loved publicity, she obviously couldn't stand the tabloids' devastating intrusion into her past life. She packed her bags and went to Heathrow to catch the first plane back to Lithuania. Simon followed her to the airport, and in front of the assembled paparazzi (who followed them everywhere) they had a blazing row. Crissi blamed Simon for leaking the story. She said he'd made her a laughing stock and ruined her life, but he was claiming it was the other way around. Apparently Crissi was hysterical, and as she was escorted through to departures, she was screaming at Simon that she wished he was dead.

The timing of the story couldn't have been worse, as Simon was in the middle of pre-production for *It Could Be Your Neighbour*. The whole thing totally destroyed his confidence and he never really recovered from it.

DM

The Crissi Drēžhnikovă story was the straw that broke the camel's back and after twelve months of incredible success, Simon Peters' world had finally started to crumble and his life unravelled like a cheap woollen jumper. The fame he'd so desperately craved didn't bring him the happiness he desired, and to compensate for it he'd started to drink more heavily and became reliant on prescription drugs.

Seemingly, Simon became increasingly difficult to work with. One moment he'd be happy, the next he'd be wallowing in the depths of depression. He would be generous and giving with one hand but cruel and mean-spirited with the other. He'd be the nicest person in show business, but within the blink of an eye he'd be acting like a spoilt child, never letting up until he got his own way.

The celebrity lifestyle he'd been leading came at a price, and it seemed that Peters was finally paying the bill.

43:

Extract from Simon's diary

26 DEC

I spent most of Christmas Day with Jack Daniels, but he can be slightly depressing company. Mr Prozac popped along in the evening but even he couldn't cheer me up, so the whole day passed in a blur and apart from those two, I had nobody to share it with.

Nobody.

It Could Be Your Neighbour broadcasts live to the nation in five days and even though today is Boxing Day I phoned every member of the team and told them they had to come into the office for a production meeting. Obviously they weren't very happy about it. Charley said it could wait until tomorrow but I insisted.

Don't they understand? The pressure to keep up the standard I've set myself with *It Could Be You!* is immense, and the panic has already started to set in. I think the big problem is that, ultimately, I know that I'm destined to fail. It's inevitable. Fear has gripped me by the throat, claustrophobia is pressing at my chest and paranoia is never more than a whisper away.

In the office I knew the team were speaking about me behind my back; I heard them laughing and giggling and sniggering but when I turned around they stopped.

In the meeting, Tristan Reece-Davis, the senior researcher, showed me some videotapes of the families who were going to be appearing on the show. Suddenly and without warning, my mood changed violently and the room grew very hot, very quickly. I'm not sure where the emotion came from, but it boiled to the surface and exploded in a fit of rage.

'These families are too fucking good!' I shouted at him. 'What I need are stupid people. Stupid people make classic television and classic television wins awards. I want grannies with no teeth and fat men who wobble when they laugh; I want mums who can't dance properly and granddads who do awful Elvis impressions. I want ugly stupid people who I can laugh at and take the piss out of and score points off and make them feel bad about themselves and prove that I'M FUCKING BETTER THAN THEY ARE!'

I was screaming at him by this point and slamming my fist on the table to emphasize every word.

There was a stunned silence in the room.

As soon as the words left my mouth, the red mist started to lift and I knew I'd gone too far. Charlie said they'd look for four new families, but I could tell the team weren't very happy about having to find them at such short notice, especially over the Christmas period. I knew they'd spend the rest of the day bitching about me.

As they left the room, Charley looked at me with a mixture of anger and pity. She shook her head.

'And merry Christmas to you too,' she said flatly.

I took a deep breath and tried to calm myself.

'What has happened to Simon Peters?' I cried.

'Simon Peters?' she said. 'Wasn't he the bloke who was eaten by his own ego?'

She wasn't being funny or sarcastic. For once, Charley meant it.

44:

Dominic Mulryan interviews Charley O'Neil

Charley O'Neil

Simon changed drastically over that Christmas period, and he made it more and more difficult for me to be friends with him. He'd always suffered from terrible insecurities, but the fame and success had magnified them tenfold, and it was the classic scenario of an artiste who just couldn't cope with it all. His life was falling apart and one of the symptoms was his extreme mood swings. He'd always been subject to them, but they suddenly seemed to get a lot worse and that made it very difficult for me to work with him, especially when I was trying to make an upbeat inspirational game show. I'd agreed to executive-produce *It Could Be Your Neighbour*, but I'd done it against my better judgement. I just didn't really believe in it as a format, and I thought it had disaster written all over it.

DM
Did all this put a strain on your relationship?

Charley O'Neil

During that pre-production week, there was a definite tension between us; I guess it had been building up for some time. We started arguing and snapping at each other over the slightest thing. His constant navel gazing and self-indulgent psychoanalysing got too much for me, and it reached the point where I just couldn't stand it any more.

It all came to a head when he suddenly fired Tristan, the senior researcher. Simon had caught him doing an impression of his 'I'M FUCKING BETTER THAN THEY ARE' speech, which was actually remarkably accurate and very, very funny. I didn't agree with Simon's decision and I didn't like the fact that he'd humiliated Tristan by firing him in front of the whole team. Simon and I had a quarrel about it, which quickly escalated into a personal slanging match. It all got very heated; he constantly reminded me that he was the boss and I constantly reminded him that he was a self-obsessed, talentless prick. The argument was so bad that neither of us wanted to back down, and it soon became clear that one of us would have to leave the show.

I think you can probably guess who it was.

I cleared my desk, walked out of the office and booked myself two weeks holiday in the Algarve.

45:

Extracts from Simon's diary

28 DEC

I've been voted the third most hated man on television.
THIRD!

Surely I should be first; at least it would mean that people are talking about me, but THIRD? It's so inconsequential.

The poll is in the Christmas edition of *TV2GO!* magazine. Mickey Spillers the TV chef came second, and Billy Fox came first. BILLY FOX! I know it's not a genuine poll and it's just a load of journalists sitting around the office wondering who they can slag off, but even so, surely I should have beaten Billy Fox? He now works on *Call-a-Quiz* on Channel 895, and everyone knows that isn't proper television (although since getting all the publicity about being my father, he's even disappeared from that).

I genuinely believe that the journalists wrote his name because they knew I'd read it and that it would wind me up.

3.32 a.m.

What is happening to me? Why do I want to beat Billy Fox even in an *unpopularity* contest?

29 DEC

Two days until *It Could Be Your Neighbour*, and the press seem to have launched a hate campaign against me.

I feel like King Neptune holding back the tide of public opinion as the waves of criticism come crashing on to my shore. The current is strong and I can feel myself being swept away and sucked into a vortex of hatred and condemnation. I'm lost in the choppy seas of the vast showbiz ocean, and my ship has been blown too far off the planned route to be able to charter a course back to calmer waters.

'Career overboard,' they scream.

I've tried swimming to the safety of my self-esteem, but it's been punctured too many times, and now lies deflated like an old rubber ring. I constantly try to reassure myself with the memory of being voted *TV Chat*'s Personality of the Year 2004, but even that is a lead weight round my neck. (It literally was a lead weight you wear round your neck; quite a crappy award when you think about it.) I'm drowning in a sea of vitriol and the caustic comments burn through my confidence like acid through glass.

In show business, no one can hear you scream.

30 DEC

I feel a fraud.

One day until *It Could Be Your Neighbour*, and I don't think I should even be here. How did I climb as high as

311

this? How did I get to the top when I was only ever really good enough to get to the middle? How did I ascend to this position without somebody discovering the truth and pressing the alarm button? Why didn't the showbiz police notice me early on, put me in a blue coat and escort me back to Pontins where I belong?

Everything's getting too much for me and I don't think I can cope for much longer. Since Charley and Tristan left the production, everybody keeps asking me questions that I don't know the answers to. I feel trapped and I just want to escape and hide in a corner, but I know I can't do that because there's too much responsibility resting on my shoulders. The ITV network are expecting me to work a New Year's Eve miracle and I have to deliver the ratings, otherwise it could be the end.

The end of everything.

Maybe that wouldn't be such a bad thing, because I don't think I can stand any more of the pressure that goes along with being a major A-list celebrity. I never wanted it to be like this, anyway. Yes, I always wanted to be famous, but I only ever wanted a *little bit* of fame. I just wanted to be asked for my autograph occasionally, because I thought that scribbling my name on a piece of paper would prove that my name actually meant something; that *I* meant something. I think the main reason I sought stardom was because I wanted everyone I went to school with to be sitting at home, pointing at the television and telling their kids, 'I used to go to school with him.' I wanted them to be jealous of me. I wanted them to acknowledge my existence and realize they'd been wrong about me.

With hindsight, maybe they were right all along.

I never wanted the whole nation to know everything about me, because deep down there isn't that much to know, and what there is to know isn't that interesting. I'm not even a real person any more; instead I'm just a slab of meat who everybody wants a piece of. The shareholders, the investors, the bankers, the television executives, the producers, the directors, the researchers, the runners, the fans, the journalists, my agent . . .

My agent.

Annie Reichman is worse than everyone else put together. She keeps pushing me to do more shows, more interviews and more publicity for *It Could Be Your Neighbour*, even though I've told her that I've got nothing left to give. We had a meeting today to talk about the future, which was slightly ironic because the future for me is just a large black void. I tried explaining this to Annie, but I broke down in front of her and started to cry. I wanted her to mother me and tell me it would all be all right but instead she said something very disconcerting.

She said, 'You do realize you'd be worth more money if you were dead.'

She had a strange look in her eye (the good one) when she said it. I hope she was joking.

2.54 a.m.
Annie Reichman never jokes. Annie Reichman hasn't even got a sense of humour.

46:

Dominic Mulryan interviews Annie Reichman

Annie Reichman
It was merely an off-the-cuff remark.

Simon was obviously going through a difficult time, and I was trying to console him by pointing out that he was one of those few truly successful artistes who can earn even more money for their estate once they're dead.

Record sales, DVD sales, book sales, etc. can multiply several times over if an artiste dies, especially if they die in tragic circumstances. When the pop star Troy Coral died of a drugs overdose, his album immediately sold an additional one million copies. When the cult comedian Peter Davey died in a car crash, sales of his DVD increased by 210 per cent. I represented both those artistes and witnessed how lucrative death can be.

Having said that, it's not something I recommend to my clients as a career move.

DM

Were you aware that, by this point, Simon had an awful lot of enemies, many of whom might actually wish to see him dead?

Annie Reichman

Well, let's put it this way: I realized he wasn't going to win any popularity contests.

47:

David Mulryan interviews David Peters

DM

From speaking to you, you seem to have taken a very keen interest in Simon's career.

David Peters

He was my brother.

DM

You mean your half-brother.

David Peters

Yes . . . my half-brother.

DM

Is it true you watched every one of his shows religiously?

David Peters

I certainly wouldn't say 'religiously', but I felt duty bound to support him.

DM

In his diary, on 9th February, he recounts a conversation where you said to him:

'I'd like to see an uplifting, feel-good show where people are given the chance to achieve their lifelong ambition . . . it should be heartening and enriching; spiritual, almost. Everyone has the opportunity to appear, everyone thinks it could be them . . .' *This obviously bears a striking resemblance to the show that eventually became* It Could Be You! *Were you aware of your input?*

David Peters

When I saw the show I couldn't help noticing that it had been . . . shall we say . . . inspired by what I'd said to Simon.

DM

Simon claimed the idea as his own and eventually made an awful lot of money from the worldwide sales of the show. How did you feel about that?

David Peters

As I say, he was my brother . . . sorry, my half-brother; I was very pleased for him.

DM

You didn't feel that you were entitled to any of that money?

David Peters

I'm not interested in money but I felt that he could have at least, perhaps, acknowledged my contribution.

DM

Do you think you got on well?

David Peters

As well as can be expected.

DM

You seem to have been very different. Some might describe you as being as different as Cain and Abel.

David Peters

I see the point you're trying to make, Mr Mulryan, and I think it's hardly fair.

DM

Remind me, was Cain the older brother or the younger?

David Peters

He was the elder.

DM

And didn't he kill his younger brother because he was envious of him?

David Peters

You remember your Bible studies well.

DM

David, were you envious of Simon's success?

David Peters

Absolutely not. Do not envy a sinner, thou dost not know what disaster awaits him.

DM
Sorry?

David Peters
Old Testament.

DM
Do you think Simon was a sinner?

David Peters
We are all sinners, Mr Mulryan. I've just noticed that people in show business sin more than most.

DM
So does that mean Simon deserved the 'disaster' that befell him?

David Peters
I don't think he deserved it, but I've come to terms with the fact that it was obviously God's will.

48:

Dominic Mulryan interviews Billy Fox

Billy Fox
All that negative publicity about me being his father ruined my career. Bloody ruined it.

After forty years as one of the country's most popular and well-loved entertainers, suddenly I was the bad guy who'd abandoned Simon Peters as a child. It was as though they'd forgotten everything else I'd ever done, and that was all I'd be remembered for. Nobody talked about the classic moments of television I'd created, or the years of laughter I'd provided. Nobody mentioned that I'd hosted the longest-running game show in the history of British television, or the fact that I was the only performer to ever win twelve consecutive Variety Club Awards. Twelve! It was as if all that wasn't important and everyone had suddenly decided that I was *persona non grata*. Nobody wanted to know me; I was a social pariah and professionally I was out in the cold; a washed-up old has-been with nowhere to go. They even fired me from the crappy job on *Call-a-Quiz*; how humiliating is that?

Simon Peters had stolen my life, he'd stolen my career, he'd stolen the format to my TV show and on top of that, he was accusing me of forcing myself on his mother. How much more damage could he do? That whole scenario created a feeding frenzy and the bloody tabloids were hounding me every single day.

I used to love talking to the press when they were interested in hearing how wonderful I was, but suddenly they wanted to paint a different picture. I couldn't stand it any longer and I had to get out. I issued a press statement saying I was retiring from the business and going to live in my villa in Portugal. The truth was I didn't even own a bloody villa; I'd had to sell that when the work dried up. I actually stayed in a one-bedroom third-floor apartment overlooking a building site. The paint was peeling and the air conditioning didn't work properly. I sat in that room for weeks, sad and lonely and knowing that I'd lost it all because of one person.

Show business had been my life, do you understand? Something in my psyche needed the adoration of the British public; I needed their love the way that most people need the love of a family. Without that blanket I felt myself withering away, and it wasn't long before I turned to the bottle for comfort. It was a very dark time for me, and the only pleasure I got was from the knowledge that *It Could Be Your Neighbour* was going to fail dismally, and that Simon Peters was about to experience a career backlash himself.

DM
Did you hate Simon Peters?

Billy Fox
That's a very strong word. If I did feel that way about him,
I certainly wasn't the only one.

49:

Dominic Mulryan interviews Max Golinski

Max Golinski

There's an old Yiddish expression, 'Be kind to the people on the way up, because they'll be the ones who will be shitting on you on the way down!'

Simon had followed a treacherous path to the peak of Fame Mountain and when he got to the top, he realized the view was not quite as spectacular as he thought it was going to be. As he clung on by his fingertips and looked down from his precarious precipice, all he could see was a long line of people who he had upset on his way up there. He had walked over so many friends, he should have been wearing hiking boots. He did so much trampling he should have been a member of the Ramblers Association.

Nobody had sympathy for Simon's predicament. There is only one thing people don't like more than a person who is successful, and that is a person who is successful and just moans about it the whole time. 'Oh woe is me, I have forty million pounds in the bank. I just can't cope!'

Do you realize that I should have been earning 15 per cent

of that forty million pounds? Do you know how much that is? Well put it this way, I would have been the Six Million Dollar Man, but without the bionic arm. It should have all been so different, and what Simon didn't realize was that I could have helped him. Everything he was unhappy with in his life, the success, the fame, the money . . . none of that would have happened if I'd still been his agent.

A lot of people thought he deserved to be suffering. Let's not forget that he was a thief who had taken all that money under false pretences. He had stolen, yes, stolen the idea for *It Could be You!* from myself and my clients, Billy Fox and Ricardo Mancini. Ricardo Mancini! Now there's a boy who should have been a star. Good-looking and talented, the complete package. He should have been the multimillionaire media tycoon. He should have been the chosen one.

It Could Be You!? *Oi a shkandal!* It Should Have Been Him!

50:

Dominic Mulryan interviews Ricardo Mancini

DM
Ricardo, were you jealous of Simon's success?

Ricardo Mancini
I wasn't exactly jealous but I strongly believed that he didn't deserve it, particularly because he stole my Retro Quiz format and made an absolute fortune out of it. It was definitely my idea; there's no denying it. I remember mentioning it to him at a showbiz party; I told him I had this idea for an elimination quiz, which tapped into the national obsession for nostalgia. I knew it was a winner. It was going to be my ticket back to the big time; it was going to prove that I was more than just a shopping-channel presenter and that I could still cut it on prime-time.

When I first saw *It Could Be You!* I couldn't believe he'd done it. I became slightly obsessed by it, and for a long time it was all I thought about. I used to tape all the shows and watch them over and over again and try to work out why Simon Peters had been so successful and not me. It used to eat away at me, especially when I knew that I was more talented than him. Have you ever been in a situation like that? Have you ever watched somebody do something that you know you could do so much better? It's quite a soul-destroying experience. The only thing that kept me going was when he started getting all that negative press on the lead-up to *It Could Be Your Neighbour.* I knew that by that point, his time at the top was coming to an end.

I think he knew it too.

51:

31 DEC

8.04 p.m. Dressing room #1. LWT Studios.
So this is what happens when the bubble finally bursts . . .

I can't believe it. What went wrong? Why was the show such a disaster? It had all the ingredients to be a hit but there was something missing: that magic, that sparkle, that little bit of glitter which made *It Could Be You!* so special was somehow absent from *It Could Be Your Neighbour* (I knew it should have had an exclamation mark). The whole thing just didn't click; the pace was slow, the studio audience were unresponsive and the gags, which seemed like sure-fire woofers in rehearsal, died a slow and agonizing death.

It should have been great. With the exception of Charley, Tristan and a couple of researchers who I'd sacked, it was the same production team that worked on *It Could Be You!* It was the same writers, same set designer, same director, same producers, same host . . .

Same host?

327

Maybe it wasn't the same host? Maybe I've changed? Maybe I've lost it? You often hear of top athletes losing their form, golfers who suddenly can't putt, cricketers who suddenly can't bowl, footballers who suddenly can't score (usually when they pull on an England shirt). What if I suddenly can't host a light entertainment show?

It was painful to perform and must have been even more painful to watch. We began broadcasting live to the nation at 7.00 p.m., and it wasn't long before I could feel my confidence starting to drain away. As I stood there reading the opening link from the autocue, I had a moment of blinding clarity and it suddenly hit me:

'This is crap,' I thought.

I've presented crap shows before; some would say I've built a very successful career presenting nothing but crap shows. That's as maybe, but the golden rule is not to let the audience at home know that you know it's crap. The moment that happens you're in trouble. Tonight, I couldn't hide it. The viewing public would have seen the realization in my eyes, and everything about my body language would have screamed out to them, *'This is crap.'*

I sensed them switching off in their millions. In my head, the sound of canned laughter was replaced by the noise of people reaching for their remote controls, and every word I spoke seemed to be accompanied by the click of an off button.

Surely a true star would have carried the show; Dale would have made it work, and Bruce, and Ant and Dec, and Cheggers (all right, maybe not Cheggers). But I didn't. I failed. Everything's been so going so well for so long, I'd almost forgotten what the pain of failure felt like. Suddenly my career has gone into a nosedive and I feel as though I'm playing a great big game of Celebrity Snakes and

Ladders. I've been to the top of the ladder but now I've rolled a double six, and I'm sliding all the way back down to the bottom. Once I get there I'll have to start calling the bingo at a holiday park or, worse still, go back to daytime television.

Maybe there's some sort of puncture-repair kit for burst bubbles? If there is, I probably don't deserve it.

I know I shouldn't drink before a show, but I had to have a couple of vodkas because the Valium I'm taking to stop the panic attacks makes me feel really sluggish and the Prozac I'm taking to counteract this gives me the shakes. Vodka does just enough to take the edge off.

As I write this I'm looking at my tongue in the dressing-room mirror. There's a thin layer of yellow fur lying there like a squashed caterpillar, and if this were a cartoon there'd be green fumes emanating from it. God, I look rough. I'm sweating; my eyes are bloodshot and even through the thick TV make-up I can see that my skin is red and blotchy. The doctor said that it's stress and that I need a break. I'm supposed to be going to Portugal tonight on the 10.30 flight to spend New Year's Day in my villa, but I have an uneasy feeling about it. I have a sense of impending tragedy and my whole life seems to be spinning out of control. I'm in a juggernaut thundering towards my final destination, but the brakes have failed and I have no way of stopping it.

Where did it all go wrong?

Is it because people hate me? I used to think people hated me because they didn't know me, but now I realize that the people who *do* know me, hate me even more. Everybody I've ever worked with seems to detest me, and every relationship I've ever had has ended in tears. Crissi; Charley; Tommy; Billy, Max and even my brother David; nobody cares for me and all I feel is a constant sense of loathing from everyone I meet. I've no friends, I have lawsuits against me and I can name several people who would rather see me dead.

Surely they should like me?

Surely the whole idea of me being famous was that it made me popular? Surely stardom should have made me loved?

The more famous I became, the less secure I felt.

I always thought it would be the other way around; I thought fame would turn me into some sort of invincible superhero whose feelings can't be hurt, but it's actually made me more sensitive and insecure than ever. I thought stardom would diminish all my personal problems but instead it seems to intensify them. I thought that being an A-list celebrity would make my whole life wonderful, a non-stop whirl of parties, champagne and caviar. In a way it is like that, but the parties are crap, the champagne's flat and I never liked caviar to begin with. What is caviar, anyway? Fish sperm or something, isn't it?

Talking of fish sperm: why don't the press just leave me alone?

I guess I was always aware that they disliked me and didn't think I deserved the success I was enjoying (they'd be very happy to discover I wasn't enjoying it at all). They knew I wasn't talented enough to be where I was, but they had to bow to public opinion and report what they saw, and what they saw was a television phenomenon, a genuine star created by the people, for the people. Of course, they weren't going to let me get away with it for long. Slowly, they chipped away at the image that I'd created: a snide comment here, a derogatory piece there, all the time just waiting for me to fall but at the same time building me up even more, because they knew the higher I climbed, the greater that fall would be. They bitched and carped and criticized and generally took the piss out of me, until eventually it seeped into the public consciousness that maybe I wasn't all I was cracked up to be. Every time a journalist wrote something nasty about me, a little bit of the old me disappeared and I knew I'd never be able to get him back again; it's a shame, because I was quite fond of the old me, but I don't like the person I've turned into. The more they write it, the more I believe it; the more I believe it, the more the public seem to lose interest and begin to see through the thin veneer of my talent.

To succeed in show business you need talent, ambition and drive. I always had the ambition and drive, but it's only now I'm realizing that I possess very little talent. I must have been so arrogant not to have noticed. There are thousands, probably millions of people out there who are more talented than me: people who can sing, people who can dance, people who can play a musical instrument. *People who are funny*. They're all so much more gifted than me, but they don't have the big house in Holland Park, the Bentley and the private helicopter (I've finally bought a Robinson R22 and it's been delivered to the villa in Portugal, ready for me to try out tomorrow).

As I've slowly begun to acknowledge my complete lack of ability, my confidence has evaporated and I've started to live in constant fear of somebody knocking on my door and telling me there's been a terrible mistake and that the lifestyle I've become accustomed to was never meant for me in the first place. They'd tell me I don't deserve all the material possessions and that they were actually meant for someone with genuine talent, some handsome guy straight out of drama school who can make a guaranteed contribution to the world of entertainment. Little by little, bit by bit, piece by piece, they'd strip me of everything I've got, leaving me naked and exposed for the world to see the inept charlatan that I really am.

Maybe that wouldn't be such a bad thing.

Where did all that burning ambition come from, anyway? That desire? that desperation? That hunger for fame? Why was I cursed with that indomitable thirst for recognition? Did I get it from my father, whoever he may be? Was it nature or nurture? From Billy or from Tommy? Just my luck that it was probably from both of them. Why couldn't I have had at least one father who was a bricklayer or a coal miner? All I crave now is normality and anonymity. I want to go outside my front door without having to check if photographers are hiding in the bushes; I want to walk down the street without people pointing and staring; I want to go to a supermarket and buy a tin of mushy peas without the checkout girl laughing and giggling; I want to go back to the old days before *It Could Be You!*, before the hit single, before the film, the awards, the success, the fame, the money, the big house, the flash cars and all that other stuff which seems to make people angry and jealous of me. I want to go back to when the press couldn't even spell my name right, when it was *Simon Peterson* or *Peter Simonson*, or even better, *unknown presenter*; I want to be a struggling C-lister again. No, more than that, I want to be a nobody. No, even more than that (and I never thought I'd say this), I want to be a member of the public.

I don't want to do this any more. I don't think I *can* do it. Maybe I never could.

Is this how it all ends?

52:

Dominic Mulryan

The day after this entry, New Year's Day, Britain lost its biggest TV star when his helicopter crashed into the Atlantic off the coast of Portugal.

So what happened on that ill-fated afternoon?

Of course, there's a strong possibility that it could have been a genuine accident. Maybe there was a technical fault with the helicopter or maybe it was pilot error. Maybe Simon, who was obviously not very experienced, should never have been at the controls, especially if he was under the influence of alcohol or drugs. All of these explanations seem very plausible, but let's not forget that the police evidence hinted at the fact that the control linkage to the helicopter's rotor arm had been 'deliberately weakened by hand'.

Could it be that it was weakened by Simon Peters' own hand?

He was obviously emotionally unstable at the time, and many of the entries in his diary hinted at the fact that he'd contemplated suicide. But if that were the case, would he really have gone to the trouble of weakening the linkage to the rotor arm, and how would he have known that this would inflict sufficient damage to cause the helicopter to malfunction? Surely if he was going to commit suicide he'd have taken the more obvious rock 'n' roll route of a drugs overdose. And would he really have gone all the way to Portugal to do this?

So if not an accident or suicide, was it murder?

There's certainly no shortage of suspects. Simon had obviously made himself extremely unpopular among his colleagues and peers, but who would have hated him enough to want to see him dead?

Tommy Peters obviously felt very ashamed of the fact that Simon was not his biological son and, in a bizarre twist of logic, he seemed to blame Simon for it. He clearly hated the fact that the story had been splashed all over the newspapers, and was resentful of Simon for being so successful in an industry where he himself had accomplished so little.

Hell hath no fury like a woman scorned? Did Charley O'Neil hold a deep-seated grudge against Simon for dumping her, and did she feel betrayed when he claimed all the accolades and financial rewards for It Could Be You! when she'd done all the work? Having suffered the pain of unrequited love, did she feel humiliated when the love of Simon's life turned out to be a man? Charley was in Portugal at the time of the crash.

Was public humiliation the motive for murder? When the tabloids revealed the truth about Crissi Drěžhnikovă, she felt she'd been made a laughing stock and was hounded out of the country. She obviously blamed Simon for this. While researching this book, I've discovered that in her home country of Lithuania, Crissi was just as famous for her violent temper as she was for modelling, and in her previous life as a man, she'd actually served time in prison for Grievous Bodily Harm.

Was Ricardo Mancini so jealous of Simon's success that he felt the need to kill him? He felt, quite rightly, that Simon had stolen the idea for his Retro Quiz and in doing so, ruined Mancini's chance of a return to prime-time television. Recent evidence has come to light that Mancini was also in Portugal when Simon's helicopter went down. He was supposedly on a golfing holiday and what's more, he was there with his agent, Max Golinski.

If Golinski committed the murder, then surely it was a financially motivated one. He was upset that Simon had left his agency just months before making forty million pounds, and he felt he hadn't been properly rewarded for his years of hard work developing Simon's early career. He was also in the process of suing Simon, claiming that he had helped him to create the format for It Could Be You!

Golinski was an incredibly bitter man, but he wasn't the only one.

Could Billy Fox, Simon's natural father, have murdered him? Was he so angered by the press revelations that he focused that rage on his illegitimate son? He's admitted to being in Portugal at the time of the crash, and he certainly had the motives. He felt that Simon had been instrumental in his career downfall, and just like Golinski and Mancini, he thought Simon had stolen the format to his show. Even though he'd started legal proceedings against him, deep down he must have been aware that it was notoriously difficult to win a case of that kind, and he must have realized he was destined to fail.

Interestingly, Fox was also represented by Golinski.

Billy Fox, Ricardo Mancini and Max Golinski were all in Portugal at the time of Simon's death. Could the three of them have planned the murder together?

What about the other people who could have been responsible? What about the public and the people Simon worked with? His agent Annie Reichman thought he would be worth more money if he were dead; his brother (or half-brother) David was a religious zealot who felt Simon had brought shame to the family name, and let's not forget Tristan

Reece-Davis, the senior researcher from It Could Be Your Neighbour, *who was fired by Simon in humiliating circumstances.*

It seems that everyone had a motive to murder.

During the writing of this book, new evidence has fallen into my hands which sheds light on the mystery surrounding Simon Peters' death. Following painstaking research and fearless investigative journalism, I can now reveal the answer that the world of entertainment has been searching for.

Who killed Simon Peters? The answer is clear.

It appears that nobody did.

53:

Simon Peters

I've always been obsessed with the idea that Elvis Presley faked his own death. I really like the notion that, having been the biggest star in the world, he's currently walking around Memphis as a nobody and just living his life doing really normal things. Whenever I think of Elvis still being alive, I have an image in my head of him doing his weekly shop in his local K-Mart, wearing large gold-rimmed sunglasses and a white, diamond-encrusted, Las Vegas jumpsuit; he does the gardening in his famous fifties gold lamé jacket and the washing up in his '68 comeback-special black leather catsuit.

Imagine how good he'd be at karaoke.

The beauty of it is that everybody would just ignore him, thinking he's some sort of dodgy lookalike, and anyway 'it can't be the real Elvis because he's been dead for thirty years'.

I wanted to be like Elvis.

It all got too much for me and I just couldn't take it any more. After *It Could Be Your Neighbour*, I was booked on to a late-night flight to Portugal where I was going to spend New Year's Day celebrating the success of the show, but I just didn't want to go. I sat in my dressing room staring at myself in the mirror, and knowing that I'd lost all respect for the person who was staring back at me. I didn't recognize him any more, but I knew that whoever he was, I didn't like him and didn't want anything to do with him. I sat there for what must have been an hour, lost in a maze of self-loathing. It was New Year's Eve and I had no friends and no family to speak to.

I'd never felt so low in my life.

Why wasn't I happy to be in the Number One dressing room at LWT? It had everything a major celebrity could need: a red velvet couch, a plasma-screen TV and even a small kitchenette. In the corner there was a cooker and as I looked at it, I slowly fell into a surreal, trancelike state; I walked over to it, knelt down, opened the oven door and put my head inside. It was a perfect fit and was strangely comfortable. I felt totally calm and relaxed, as if putting my head in an oven was the most natural thing in the world. Using my right hand, I felt for the controls. I found the knob, pushed it down, turned it to the right and waited.

About thirty seconds later it started to get very hot. That's when I realized it was an electric oven.

I laughed.

I laughed out loud and then suddenly I had an epiphany. I felt slightly light-headed, small black dots danced before my eyes and I thought I'd seen the light. I had, but it was just the oven-door light. I still had my head inside the cooker.

I removed my head and sat on the floor, happy to be alive. The experience made me realize that I had to do something radical to change my life, because the life I was leading obviously wasn't worth living. I had to give up drink and prescription drugs, but, more importantly, I had to quit the one thing I was addicted to more than anything:

Celebrity.

It had been my religion. I'd worshipped at the altar of stardom but I knew I had to renounce my faith, and to do that, it would take drastic action. I realized I had to act quickly and started to formulate an audacious plan.

I called the actor Roger De Billion, who I'd worked with on *Who Killed Bobby King?* I knew he'd enjoy a challenge; he'd started his career as a stuntman and was completely barking mad, just what I needed if my plan were to work. I explained my idea to him and he spent the next five minutes screaming with hysterical laughter.

'It's just like the old days,' he boomed. 'Pete O'Toole and Dickie Burton would have fucking loved it, love. Fucking loved it!'

Once he'd stopped laughing and telling me about other similar escapades he'd done with Oliver Reed, he enthusiastically agreed to do it. I asked him if he minded being away for New Year's Day, but he said he was a Mithraist who didn't adhere to the Gregorian calendar, and was actually still celebrating the ancient pagan festival of *Natalis Solis Invicti*. I didn't have a clue what he was talking about, so before he could change his mind I arranged for a taxi to pick him up, booked him on the same flight as me and met him at Heathrow airport. It was a close thing but we just made the flight.

As I sat next to Roger on the plane and he started telling me all about the time that he and Sir Anthony Hopkins had tried to invade Poland, I knew I was in for a very long journey. We eventually went over the plan again in greater detail and made sure we hadn't missed anything. Roger is a very experienced helicopter pilot, and it was he who (rather mischievously) suggested weakening the control linkage of the rotor arm 'to give the bastards something to talk about'.

The next morning we emerged from my villa and after shaking hands and wishing each other Happy New Year, Roger climbed into the helicopter and twenty minutes later crashed it into the sea.

It was as simple as that.

Apparently he'd done a similar stunt in the action film *Blades of Destiny*, and it was all to do with timing when to jump out. When I picked him up in my brand-new Sunseeker Superhawk speedboat, he had a great big smile on his face and asked if we could club together to buy another helicopter just so he could do it all over again.

I dropped Roger off at a secluded beach, swore him to secrecy and gave him the keys to the villa and the speedboat as a way of saying thank you. I didn't tell him where I was going and he didn't want to know. He shook my hand again, gave me a big bear hug and wished me good luck. He called me a 'lucky fucker' for getting out of the rat race, but I think he meant it as a term of endearment. I then got into the car which Roger had hired in his name (the plan was for me to abandon it when I got close to my destination, and then he'd wait for two days before reporting it stolen).

I drove across the Spanish border at Valenço do Minho, where I knew there wouldn't be passport control, and I then spent the rest of the day driving up through Spain and into the Pyrenees. I kept driving, deeper and deeper into the mountains. It was New Year's Day and although the roads were sometimes treacherously narrow and winding, at least they were quiet.

I eventually arrived in a small Basque village called Lesaka. The whitewashed, stone-built houses with their long sloping rooftops gave it character, but I figured it wasn't distinctive enough to attract many British tourists. I booked into a tatty-looking hotel and was very relieved when the somewhat dour landlady didn't speak English (as my own private little joke I checked in under the name of Shergar Lucan and she didn't even bat an eyelid).

The next morning I drove the car ten miles further into the mountains, parked it on the side of the road, ripped out the stereo to give the illusion it was car theft, left the doors open and then walked all the way back to Lesaka, dumping the stereo on the way. I stayed in the hotel room for three days and then, after several rather difficult and prolonged conversations with the locals, where my only means of communication was sign language, pointing, and slow-shouted English, I managed to rent a small semi-derelict farm just outside the tiny hamlet of Etaxalor.

That became my home for the next six months.

I lived a very simple life. There was no television and I didn't even have a mirror to look at myself. Every day I would walk three miles to the local *denda* for my bread, and on the way back stand and watch the *pelota*, a strange mixture of squash and tennis, which all the locals seemed to play. I went about my business in total anonymity and managed to avoid the few British tourists who did venture that far into the mountains. I loved the fact that nobody knew who I was, and that the locals only thought of me as a mad eccentric Englishman. I felt totally free of the shackles of expectation and I even started to like myself again.

One evening, as I was strolling back from the village, I noticed a flickering orange light in the downstairs window of a small farmhouse. At first I didn't think anything of it and continued walking. After a few paces something made me stop, and as I turned and looked again, I saw a small group of people outside the farmhouse running around in what seemed like a state of panic. I shielded my eyes from the setting sun, and as I looked more closely I realized that the orange light was in fact the flames of an out-of-control fire.

That's when I heard the children crying.

I guess you never know how you're going to react in a situation like that. If you'd have asked me six months previously, I'd have said that I'd have run away, because that's the sort of coward I was. But I didn't run away. I found myself sprinting towards the house. I vaulted the gate, ran past the people who had congregated outside and burst in through the doors. Thick black smoke immediately engulfed me and I started to choke. I turned to leave, but once again I heard the children's cries and now they were turning into screams. I grabbed two tea towels and fought my way through the smoke towards the sink. I turned on the tap, soaked the towels and wrapped one of them around my head. I then ran up the burning stairs, taking them three at a time. At the top of the stairs I was blinded by the smoke. I could just make out two rooms to my left and one to my right. I opened the door to my right, but the room was empty. I went back on to the landing and kicked open the door of the bedroom opposite. Inside were two children, a little girl who was about three, and a small baby who couldn't have been more than six months old. I grabbed the baby and wrapped the wet towel around his body. I took the second towel from my head and wrapped it around the little girl. I picked her up with my spare hand and swung her around on to my back. The smoke was stinging my eyes, and with every breath I took I could feel my lungs burning.

I went out on to the landing but the stairs were now engulfed in flames and there was no way down. I heard shouting outside. I went back into the bedroom and over to the window. The group of people I'd passed on my way in were in the garden holding out a blanket. They were shouting and indicating that I should drop the baby. I leant out of the window as far as I could, but he would still have to drop about fifteen feet. They were shouting at me. The smoke was filling my lungs and I was beginning to feel light-headed. I released the baby and he fell silently into the blanket. I heard an explosion from inside the house and part of the building started to collapse. Below me, the four men and three women were holding out the blanket again and screaming at me. I knew it was my only chance. With the small girl in my arms, I jumped into the darkness.

I woke up in the local doctors. A kindly-looking old lady with silver hair told me in broken English that the baby and the little girl were both fine and healthy. I had suffered from smoke inhalation and minor burns, but other than that I was OK.

Once I'd totally recovered and started to go out again in the village, I noticed that the locals would point at me and smile. Men would come up to me and shake my hand, and mothers would come up and kiss me on both cheeks.

'*Eskerrat ema*,' they would say. Thank you, apparently.

'*Heroi, Txapeldun*,' others would shout. Hero.

They worshipped me as a hero, and somewhat ironically I became a celebrity in their village. They even asked me to officially open their winter fiesta, but I didn't mind because I was famous for a reason, a real reason; I wasn't just famous because I wanted to be.

All this made me start contemplating everything I'd done in my life. During the long winter evenings I sat in front of a spitting log fire, thinking about all the people I'd left behind. I knew that if I was ever to be totally happy I had to right a few wrongs, build a few bridges and start the lonely walk along the road to redemption.

I knew I wasn't quite ready to sit and talk with Billy Fox, but I began to think that I'd like to make amends with Tommy. He'd brought me up as a child, and it must have been very difficult for a widowed man to do that, especially someone trying to carve out a career in show business. I also wanted to somehow arrange a financial settlement for my brother David, Ricardo Mancini and Max Golinski for their input into *It Could Be You!*

More than anything, I had an overwhelming desire to contact Charley. I didn't know how I'd do it or how she'd react, but I knew I owed her the biggest apology ever. I'd buy her a thousand bouquets of flowers and a million boxes of chocolates just to say I was sorry. It wouldn't be enough, but I wanted her to be aware that I'd started to get a little bit of perspective back into my life, and that I was finally becoming the person that she always knew I could be. I wanted to somehow tell her that I was a changing man and that I was intending to start a completely new life and move to a place she'd once mentioned, a place far away where I'm completely unknown. I wanted to ask her to come with me, and tell her that I knew we could be happy together.

Who knows, I thought, maybe we could have those grandchildren after all.

I wanted to do all those things, but I didn't know how to go about doing any of them. How do you tell people that you're not actually dead?

The answer seemed to find me.

One day, after six months of living in Etaxalor, I noticed that a tourist had left a copy of the *Sun* newspaper in a local café. In it, I read that an investigative journalist was writing a book about what had happened on the lead-up to my 'death', and that he'd gained access to my diaries. I knew it was my opportunity to get back in touch with my old life.

I called Annie Reichman and told her I was still alive. Strangely, she didn't seem at all surprised to hear from me and took it totally in her stride.

'Genius,' she said. 'Absolute genius. We'll make a fortune out of this.'

After living such an uncomplicated life for six months, her blatant capitalism took me completely by surprise. I told her I didn't want a fortune. I told her I wanted to stay in hiding but that I was ready to tell my side of the story. She told me to call back in two days and when I did so, she'd arranged for Dominic Mulryan to be in her office. I spoke to him at length and agreed to write something for his book. I guess the result is what you're reading now.

I told Annie that my only proviso was that the tabloids didn't get hold of the story until the book was published, just to give me enough time to move on. Annie said she'd keep it out of the press, but in the two days after I'd first called her she certainly hadn't wasted any time in trying to kick-start my career again.

She told me she'd had secret talks with a film production company about making my story into a movie. Apparently they want it to be a comedy drama shot in a documentary style. They'd interview all the people involved, so there'd be lots of talking heads intercut with TV footage of me, and then the twist at the end that I faked my own death.

Even more interesting than that, Annie had talked to the top executives at ITV and pitched them my old idea of *Celebrity Peacemakers!* She felt the time was right for a show like that, and apparently the execs loved it. In a conference call she also pitched it to CBS in America, who were very keen to make it as a co-production with ITV and turn it into the biggest and most expensive game show ever. The idea is that it would be simultaneously broadcast all over the world, giving it a potential audience of six billion people. They loved the idea of the end game being at the United Nations, and the fact that every person in the world would have the opportunity to enter. They wanted to add an extra twist by giving away a billion pounds and creating the first ever game show billionaire. Annie told me that when she pitched the idea to the Americans they started talking about possible hosts, and Todd McLooney said that they needed someone with worldwide appeal.

'They have to be normal but accessible,' he said, 'just like that dead guy Simon Peters used to be!'

She didn't tell them I was still alive, but suggested to me that it could be my comeback.

My comeback.

It would make me one of the biggest stars in the world, and would mean that I wouldn't be able to go anywhere on the planet without being recognized.

Me. Simon Peters. A worldwide megastar.

'Is it *Celebrity Peacemakers* with an exclamation mark?' I asked.

'Of course,' Annie said.

I told her I'd think about it.

THE END

DIARY OF A C-LIST CELEB
by Paul Hendy

Languishing a good few rungs below Keith Chegwin and
Su Pollard on the showbiz ladder but above that scouse
bloke who won the first series of 'Big Brother', Simon
Peters feels he's doomed to a career in the celebrity limbo of
daytime TV game shows and home shopping channels. His
invitations to all the right parties are forever going missing
(he blames the postman – jealous, you see) and he invariably
sleeps with all the wrong people; his agent has trouble
remembering his name and even his stalker is more famous
than he is. And just when things couldn't get any worse (and
let's be honest, who's ever won a BAFTA playing panto in
Grimsby) the plug is pulled on his TV show and stardom
beckons his worst, most-loathed enemy . . .

But, however riddled with insecurities he may be, Simon knows
he's got what it takes to make it and he's not going to let a silly
little thing like a complete lack of talent get in the way.

Giving fame a long overdue (but not too hard) slap in the face,
Diary of C-List Celeb is a wickedly funny, deliciously observed
novel of burning ambition and unrequited love, celebrity
punch-ups and serial bad dressing, by a new literary
talent who knows this world all too well.

'It's bloody genius, very funny and leg-crossingly embarrassing'
Davina McCall

'Very funny . . . and spookily close to the truth!'
Ant and Dec

'I don't know what Simon Peters is worried about,
at least he's got panto'
John Leslie

9780553816259

ONE BIG DAMN PUZZLER
by John Harding

'THIS MASTERLY TRAGICOMEDY, AMBITIOUS IN
SCOPE AND EXECUTED WITH WIT
AND EXUBERANCE'
Daily Mail

On a remote South Pacific island, the struggles of an elderly
tribesman to translate *Hamlet* into local pidgin English are
interrupted by the arrival of an unexpected visitor. William
Hardt is an obsessive young American lawyer who has come to
help. From that moment on, nothing will ever be the same –
for what (and who) William finds on the island will challenge
both his and our notions about love, life and even death.

Achingly funny and profoundly moving, *One Big Damn
Puzzler* confirms John Harding as one of contemporary
fiction's most entertaining and observant
chroniclers of the human condition.

'A LOOPING, PLAYFUL FLIGHT OF FANCY . . .
GAUGIN-GAUDY, AND AS RICH AND SPICY AS A
GOOD DISH OF YAM STEW'
Daily Telegraph

'LAUGH-OUT-LOUD FUNNY, AMBITIOUS,
CAREFULLY CONSTRUCTED, ADDICTIVE, THIS
NOVEL IS ONE BIG DAMN FINE ACHIEVEMENT'
Glasgow Herald

'BLACKLY COMIC . . . INTENSELY LITERARY . . . AN
ALLUSIVE *TOUR DE FORCE* . . . A THOROUGHLY
ENTERTAINING READ'
The Times

'A RAMBUNCTIOUS NOVEL FILLED WITH
MEMORABLE CHARACTERS AND GENEROUS
HELPINGS OF WIT AND COMPASSION . . . YOU'LL
BE HOOKED TO THE VERY END'
Good Book Guide

9780552999809

THIS AGE WE'RE LIVING IN
by David Wilson

Only two big facts are known for certain: you are on a large spinning rock hurtling through space at about 67,000 miles an hour, and one day your body is going to die. Will a new pair of shoes <u>really</u> help?

Worth's 12th law of shopping

George Worth is a grumpy lifestyle columnist who works in a woman's world. He hates fashion, mobile phones, computers and Young People. At night he goes home to a borrowed Labrador and feelings of guilt about his dead wife.

Justin Smith is a Young Person. A bright newcomer, he's always on his mobile to his girlfriend, surfing the Net and keeping abreast of the latest trends.

Then comes the day when Justin's girlfriend throws him out and he finds himself having to share a flat with George. As the women around them watch and wonder both men start to work out what really matters among the obsessions and distractions of modern life.

Laugh-out-loud funny, moving and revealing, this is a novel that confronts the big question: Can shopping solve everything? Why are boxers better than Y-fronts? Are lifestyle writers secretly in the same mess as everyone else? And if life is a journey, who the hell changed all the signposts?

9780552773782

THE KILLER'S GUIDE TO ICELAND
by Zane Radcliffe

*'Callum looked out over Reykjavík, its colourful dolls' houses
snuggled together, their rooftops so sharp and precise against a
blue-screen sky. He loved this daft capital, this gale blown
toy town with whalebones under its flagstones . . .'*

But Callum Pope cannot escape the horrors of his past.

He has fled his native Glasgow to make a fresh start in
Iceland with Bírna Sveinsdóttir, the pretty glaciologist
who is slowly thawing his heart.

He has moved in with Bírna, her indomitable mother
(who happens to believe in fairies) and her eleven-
year-old daughter – who refuses to believe in Callum.
He tries hard to adjust to this new life among three
generations of singular females, however, the dark
secret Callum is hiding is about to raise its malign
head, threatening not only to destroy his relationship
but also the life of a young girl . . .

Perceptive, expansive and chilling, *The Killer's
Guide to Iceland* is a novel about love, loss and persistent
light, from the award-winning author of *London Irish*

9780552772174